THE SHELL KEEPER
Published by Robin P. Nolet
Copyright © 2011, 2016 by Robin P. Nolet

ISBN-13: 9781974635290

This is a work of fiction. Names, characters, places and incidents are either the product of the author's imagination or are used fictitiously, and any resemblance to actual persons, living or dead, business establishments, events or locales is entirely coincidental.

Printed in the USA.
Cover design by Julie Beckett

Interior Format

THE *Shell* KEEPER

Robin P. Nolet

*For my family, who believe in me
and put up with me. I am grateful
and truly blessed!*

*"Patience, patience, patience is what the
sea teaches. Patience and faith. One should
lie empty, open, choiceless as a beach,
waiting to for a gift from the sea."*

Gift From The Sea
Anne Morrow Lindbergh

One

Out of the welter of life, a few people are selected for us by the accident of temporary confinement in the same circle. We never would have chosen these neighbors; life chose them for us. But thrown together on this island of living, we stretch to understand each other, and are invigorated by the stretching.
~Anne Morrow Lindbergh

"DO YOU FEEL TENSE?" ASKED the male voice on the tape.

"Yes," Del said, resisting the sob that clutched at her chest, threatening to overwhelm her again with tears. Her attorney had been so nice, considering. Del could imagine meeting her for lunch. It was reality that was hard to imagine. When had meeting with her divorce attorney become reality?

"Tension is the antithesis of relaxation," the tape continued. "To completely release the tension and achieve a fully relaxed state you must first tense every muscle, beginning with the muscles in your head and neck. Have you tensed them?"

"Mm-mmm." Del nodded, her face scrunched up tight.

"Good," Dr. Spiegelman said, soothingly. "Now add the shoulders, working the tension down your arms and into your hands. Don't release the tension in your neck and head!"

"Mm–mm," Del mumbled and shook her head as she clenched the steering wheel tighter.

The intersection wasn't busy. Good thing, Del thought, she was too stiff to look both ways.

"Now work the tension down through your chest..."

TRAFFIC AT GWEN'S BAKERY HAD stalled to the usual late-morning lull. The air was scented with the spicy sweetness of cinnamon apple pies that cooled on racks in the kitchen. Gwen sat at the front counter, behind the register, wading through a sea of numbers on a spreadsheet. It was a quiet bit of time in the day and she used it to try, once more, to tweak her bottom line into submission. Her husband, Andy, thought the trucker's union was going to call a strike. Gwen's bakery did well enough, but could they get by without Andy's income? And for how long?

An errant strand of brown hair freed itself again from her ponytail and she pushed it once more behind her ear. One more thing she had to get under control. She ought to get her hair cut, she thought. Her friends had *styles*, not just cuts. But, when you're mixing cake batter or rolling dough the only style that counted was in your skill. Maybe someday, when she had more time, she would get a style. She would manicure what was left of her fingernails after endless dish washings, and lose those extra pounds that kept her in a size twelve instead of a ten. Maybe. First, though, there was that damn bottom-line.

The scratch of a chair against the aging wood floor broke her concentration. She looked up to see if her remaining customers had finished their coffee and pastry.

"I don't care what he thinks of the offer," the man said, buttoning his double-breasted suit coat as he stood. The professionally attired woman still sat. "And frankly," he continued, "I don't give a fuck what you think either. It's not your offer, it's mine. Tell his agent that's my final number. He can take it or he can wait another year and half for a better one." He snapped his briefcase shut, grabbed his cell from the table, and strode to the door. "Call me," he added and pulled the front door shut behind him, jarring the miniature wind chimes that hung from the knob.

Gwen pulled her sweater tighter against the crisp autumn chill of the Colorado mountain air that blew in. She looked back at the spreadsheet, preserving her customer's privacy, but even at a glance she could tell by the grim set of the woman's otherwise attractive features that rage and frustration were brewing beneath the surface.

"Asshole," the woman said under her breath. Noticing Gwen's glance, she said to her, "A first class one, too, not one of those beginners." She gathered papers from the table. "No, he's been honing his asshole skills for years now. Lucky me, I'm the target du jour."

Their eyes met. Gwen hadn't recognized the man, but this woman had been in before and, though they'd never actually introduced themselves, Gwen was a good businesswoman. She tried for a sympathetic expression but couldn't help feeling confused.

The woman stood and pulled a black suit jacket on over her white silk blouse. It fit so well, Gwen knew it had to be designer. She flipped her shoulder length black hair free from the collar, smoothed the wrinkles from the matching skirt and shoved her files into a large, black leather satchel.

"It's like he friggin' expects me to genuflect when he comes and goes!" She ripped the satchel's zipper shut.

"Well...," Gwen said, unsure what to say next.

"I'm sorry." She nodded at Gwen, softening her tone and patting her chest with her hand. "Normally, I keep this stuff in check, but sometimes..." She sighed heavily.

"Your boss?"

"No, worse, he's a client."

"Oh?" Gwen had occasionally seen her meeting people for coffee, pastry, and business. But, as with so many others, she'd never given much thought to the details.

"I'm a real estate agent. He's one of my buyers."

"That's worse?" Gwen closed her ledger, giving up on the numbers for the moment, and went to clear the leftover dishes from the table.

"Oh, yeah. Employees and employers know who's who and what the rules are."

"Usually," Gwen said, glancing at the clock. Her employee, Cammi, was running late; no surprise there. Gwen set the dirty china on the counter and grabbed a wet cloth to wipe down the table.

"Right. But in my business, people forget the rules. Oh sure, plenty of them are okay, some are even nice. I'm part of their team."

"This guy didn't seem like a team player," said Gwen, rinsing cups and dishes in the sink.

"No, he falls into the master and slave category. And I don't even mean in the kinky sense, which wouldn't be all that bad, judging from the way he fills out a suit."

"You mean, after that..."

"Oh, no, I only mean it's too bad he's such a friggin' bastard." She set her briefcase by the counter and eyed the remaining pastries in the case. "Which he is, jerk thinks just because I'm his agent he can order me around, threaten me even."

"Why do you put up with it?"

"To begin with, I've got a contract with him. I'm legally bound to look after his best interests. Of course, I could tear up the contract and tell him to take a hike."

"Why don't you?"

"Probably should. But it's gonna be a big paycheck when it's all done."

Gwen glanced at her ledger. Not long ago she might have been tempted to feel judgmental about such a statement. Now, she had her own set of worries. "I can understand that." She rinsed the last cup, set it to dry and slowly, thoughtfully, wiped down the stainless steel counter.

The woman watched her for a moment, then crossed her arms and leaned her chest against the counter.

"I'm Claire," she said, and reached an arm over the case, holding out her hand.

"I'm Gwen." Gwen took the offered hand. "Very nice to meet you."

"You're incredibly kind to say so, considering all the shit I've vented your way the last few minutes." Claire wondered if she'd hit some raw nerve.

"We all have our share."

"True. Listen," Claire added, "I don't want you to think I'm all about the money. People usually are decent, but sometimes you put in so much for one sale, well, I guess you take whatever comes to make it work. It's like I've paid my dues. I deserve the payoff, so I'll hang on no matter what."

"Like a pit bull."

Claire smiled. "Sometimes. This idiot keeps coming up with new and inventive ways to make me earn every cent, and pay for it at the same time."

"Still worth it?"

"Hmmm," she nodded. "And think how much fun it will be, when the deal's over, to make a little Kyle doll-that's the asshole's name, Kyle-and murmur voodoo curses while sticking it with pins and burning it in effigy." She smiled, savoring the thought even more than she enjoyed Gwen's reaction.

Gwen clutched her towel somewhat defensively as she considered Claire's plan.

"Just kidding," Claire said with a half-smile.

"Sort of."

"Sort of," she agreed. "Maybe, instead, I'll tell every woman in town what a prick he is. Word will get around, I'll see to it."

"Claire, I've only just met you, officially, but I see it's wise to stay on your good side."

"Don't worry. Your pastries are so delectable; I'm the one who wants to stay on *your* good side."

"Oh?"

"I don't want to get kicked out. Sometimes I take something home-you might have noticed-it's like pastry therapy after a long, shitty day with Kyle-clones. So, I suppose I'd better keep my venting to myself."

"I'll tell you a little secret about *my* job." Gwen's voice dropped, as if someone might overhear, though the bakery was empty. "People come in for a slice of cake, a piece of pie, whatever. They have coffee. One minute they're talking about how delicious it all is and the next minute I'm hearing about the diet they're going on, or their father who has Alzheimer's, or their son who needs tutoring. It's therapy, all right."

"Really? I bet you hear more than that." Claire grinned.

"Sure, but I keep it to myself. I'm like a bartender; I know everybody's secrets."

"You better not tell, or you'll end up with no business."

"Yep."

"Seems like a strange place to talk about a diet, though."

"It's guilt. People can't resist goodies-thank goodness for

me they don't-but something about telling me they're *planning* a diet, well...it's a mental eraser for the calories."

"Now that you mention it," said Claire, considering the contents of the case, "I need to start a diet, too, what with the holidays coming up."

"Well, Claire, might I suggest a pre-diet send-off of chocolate mousse cake?" Gwen pushed aside the back door of the case, awaiting Claire's decision.

"You seem so nice for such a devious person!" She laughed.

"I'm really not deceptive; it's all in the case for the world to see. Cake?" Gwen smiled, her hand on the plate.

"The best deception is right out front. And no, no cake." Claire teased the moment, knowing from the look on Gwen's face that she'd expected otherwise.

"None?"

"Nope. Coconut cream tarts look good, though."

"Ahhh," Gwen said, "now I know your weakness."

"Make it two. I'm starting a diet soon, you know."

"God knows *I'm* always starting a diet soon."

"I think I'll get a coffee for the road, too." Claire glanced at the street beyond the shop. Dust swirled in the air; leaves flew and fell in each new puff of wind. "I think we've hit the high for today; looks cold out there."

"Indian summer is my favorite time of year, but even I can't believe it's staying so nice this late into October," Gwen said, passing a Styrofoam cup to Claire.

"I think the *summer* part is blowing away fast." Claire stood at a rustic black baker's rack stocked with tea bags, pump thermoses of brewed coffee, and all the necessary condiments.

The bakery's whitewashed walls held photos of people Claire had seen in the shop and around town, paired with watercolors of seashells. Claire found the shop's seashore theme a pleasant break in this landlocked mountain town

where ambience usually meant rustic wooden interiors rem-
iniscent of either barns or ski chalets-sometimes both. Even
the nearby reservoir couldn't equal how alive the sea made
her feel. She wondered if Gwen felt the same.

"Weatherman said we might get our first snow of the year
tonight," said Gwen. "You want to join the pool?"

"Pool?"

"Pick a date on that calendar," Gwen said, pointing to a
calendar hanging on the wall beside the bakery case. It's a
dollar for each pick. If the first measurable two inches, not
just one, piles up on the edge of that big planter outside at
the foot of the porch steps, you win all the money in the
kitty."

"If the deal with the asshole falls through, would it be
enough to keep me inebriated for an entire day?"

"Maybe even a weekend. I get good turnout. See?" She
pointed to the calendar. There weren't many choices left.

"What the hell."

"Be right back-need a smaller box for the tarts."

"Okay." Claire contemplated the calendar. In the silence
she could hear the hum of the refrigerated case and the whis-
tle of every gust outside. She picked three dates and wrote
her name in each square.

"Feel lucky?" Gwen asked, carrying a box.

"You can call it luck if you like, but somebody has to win.
I'll take three." She dug three dollar bills from her purse.
"Just upping my odds."

The screech of tires against pavement stopped them both.
They turned toward the street and the sickening sound of
crunching steel and shattering glass.

Two

"OH, SHIT!"
"I'll call 911–see what happened." Gwen dropped the boxes on the counter and reached for her phone.

Claire turned the doorknob and a gust of wind blew the door free from her hand, slamming it against the arm of a sofa that sat at the front of the store. The wind chimes jangled wildly as she reached to close the door behind her while pulling her jacket shut with her other hand. Her hair whipped against Claire's face, forcing her to release the door again to push it from her eyes. Again the door flew open and chimes clattered.

"I've got it, just go!" Gwen yelled over the wind.

The bakery was in a small stone house that sat at the top of a juncture of three roads. From its porch, the lower road cut a view through the pines to the Blue River reservoir below, surrounded on all sides by the Rocky Mountains. The corners of each juncture were marked with huge stone flower pots. Over four feet tall, they were twice the size of the planter at the foot of the steps leading to Gwen's Bakery and Cafe.

Across the street, a minivan had plowed into a pot. Shards of cement, clumps of soil, and the remains of a lovely autumn display of orange pansies and vinca vines littered the hood and the ground below.

A small, holiday scarecrow that had been planted amongst

the flora was splayed across the windshield and a gentle plume of steam drifted from beneath the hood.

In the aftermath of the collision there was an odd stillness accompanied by the wind, the steam's soft hiss, and a gentle sobbing from within the vehicle.

"Car hit the planter across the street," Claire yelled in to Gwen. "I think someone's hurt–I'll check it out!"

"Someone's coming!" Gwen yelled back, cupping her hand over the receiver. "Tell them someone's coming!"

Still clutching her jacket, Claire held her hair from her eyes and walked quickly, heels clicking against the pavement. She sidestepped the debris that had been the flower pot.

The minivan's windows were darkly tinted, making it hard to see inside, but Claire could see someone slumped over the steering wheel. The sobbing continued from within.

Claire tapped her manicured fingernail on the window. "Are you okay?" No response. "Hey!" She tapped louder and pulled at the locked door. "You okay?" The sobbing stopped and the figure sat up. "Unlock your door!" Claire shouted.

*W*HAT WAS THAT? DEL THOUGHT, stifling her tears. She sat up and gasped when she saw the scarecrow staring in at her through the windshield.

"Unlock your door!" someone yelled.

Her ears rang. The air seemed dusty and her lap was filled with a deflated air bag. "Oh, my God...," she mumbled as she looked beyond the windshield at the mess she had created. She had always so admired those flower pots. Del focused again on the air bag, the contents of her purse scattered all over the van's floor;

Dr. Spiegelman's soothing words still coming from the tape she'd been listening to.

"...and continue breathing deeply while you release all cares, first from your toes, then the arch of your foot and up into your ankle–slowly, don't rush it. Now, release–"

"Hey! Can you hear me? Open the door!"

Del jumped as the voice yelled at her and, looking out the driver's side window, she saw a woman's face looking back. "Oh, my God, what have I done now?" she whispered to herself, and little sobs returned, one, then another, and another.

"Stop! Don't start that again. Open. The. Door!" the woman ordered.

Del obeyed. She swallowed a sob before it leaked out and reached for the handle. As the door swung open the woman looked in. Their eyes met and, for a moment, Del felt the same way she'd felt when she'd met her therapist, Dr. Spiegelman, for the first time: like she was being assessed.

"Okay, let's turn off the car," said the woman, her tone softening. She reached inside and turned the key.

The comforting sound of the tape was gone, replaced by a howling wind that blew in through the door. Del's hair, a lengthy mass of frizzy, aging blonde had come free of its barrettes and flew with abandon around her face and shoulders. She brushed it back to little effect.

"Are you all right? Can you move?" the woman asked.

"Yeth, I thik I'm-oh! Ma lipth! Ma tong-theya numb!" Del touched her lips gingerly. "Am I bleething?" Blood was so messy. She'd have to pay to have her silk blouse cleaned again. And her gabardine slacks!

"No, you look fine, just fine," the woman said, wrapping a warm arm around her shivering shoulders. "It's the dust from the airbag-it'll numb your lips for a little while, but they'll be better soon. Can you walk?"

"Umm...I thik tho," said Del. Then, suddenly fearing the worst, "Ith anyone hurt? Did I hurt anyone?!"

"No. You killed the flower pot, is all. 'Course, pretty soon they'd have pulled out all the flowers and that stupid scarecrow and stuffed it with one of those God-awful gold Christmas trees." She referred to the seasonal displays the town put in the flowerpots every year in place of summer's flowers. After the scarecrows came little Christmas trees, and finally, town maintenance gave in to the cold, bare dirt until it was once again time to plant flowers in the spring. "As far as I'm concerned you did the town a favor-one less scarecrow."

"I like tha thcarecrowth," Del protested, meekly.

The woman looked at Del and nodded slowly. "Of course you do, sweetie. Now, you've got to get out of the cold; you're shaking pretty bad."

Del tried to agree but realized that her teeth were now chattering so much she could barely speak. She stepped one foot out the door. "Oh, my p-purth!"

"I'll come back for it. Let's get you inside. Come on."

Del did as she was told.

GWEN SET A CUP OF hot tea in front of Del, who wrapped her hands around it. The heat from the cup seemed to ease her shivers.

"I'm Gwen. Here." She handed her a damp washcloth. "You might want to put this on your chin."

"Huh?" She looked puzzled as she lightly touched her chin with the cloth, then, eyes wide, "it stingth!"

"Looks like you skinned it on the airbag. It's not bleeding, just red."

"I didn't even notith," she said.

"This is Claire," Gwen said, nodding at Claire as she walked back into the bakery holding a small blanket.

"Had this in my car, thought it might help," said Claire, wrapping the blanket around Del's shoulders. "And I got this out of your car," she added, setting Del's purse on the table in front of her. "I think I got everything. Your stuff was all the hell over the place, so you'd better check it out."

"Oh, thank you! Thank you th-tho much." She set the washcloth down and pulled her purse onto her lap. "Ummm...I'm Adele. Well, Del. Thath's what my f-friends-" she sighed heavily, shaking off another shiver, "call me."

"Sounds like the numbness is wearing off," Claire said.

"Hmm-mm," Del agreed. She looked into her purse. What had she wanted, she wondered and shook her head. Why couldn't she keep her thoughts straight?

Gwen rubbed a hand up and down along Del's arm, in an effort to comfort her. A faint siren drifted in and out with the wind. "Sounds like they're coming at last; help can take a while to arrive in the mountains."

"You look pretty good," said Claire. "How do you feel?"

"O-okay...I think."

"So what happened? Some jerk cut you off?"

"Oh, no..." She sighed again and stared into her purse.

"So, you...lost control?" Gwen asked.

"Hmmm, sorta," she said, with a nod.

"Sorta, how?" Claire asked, looking from Del, to Del's bag and then, eyebrows raised in a silent question, to Gwen.

"You sure you're all right?" Gwen moved her hand to Del's back and rubbed softly between her shoulder blades.

"Yes, I mean no, I mean, oh, what have I done now...," The sobbing returned.

"There, there," said Gwen, patting her back. In the distance the sirens grew louder, and Gwen thought it was just as well. Maybe Del had a concussion.

"What do you mean?" Claire asked.

"It's just," Del said, "here I was, trying to take control, and I end up losing it!"

"Take control? Was there someone in the car with you?"

"Dr. Spiegleman."

"There's a doctor out there?" Claire asked. "Where'd he go? He should help you!" She started toward the door.

"No!" said Del, reaching out a hand to stop her. "It's his tape. He's my therapist, and he gave me this relaxation tape he made, to help me, ummm...focus."

"You were listening to a relaxation tape while you were *driving*?" Claire looked at Gwen and mouthed, *Nuts*?

Gwen frowned and shook her head. "So you...fell asleep?"

"No, it's just for releasing tension. You're supposed to tense up every muscle in your body, then, starting with your foot-your toes, actually-you release the tension. But, when I tensed up my toes-my foot, I, I..."

"You floored it," said Claire.

"Accidentally! I was so surprised. Next thing I knew," she looked at Claire, "you were tapping at my window."

"Don't get me wrong, Del," Gwen said soothingly, "but I don't think that's the sort of thing to do while driving."

"You think?" Claire said to Gwen, sitting back in her chair, her arms crossed.

"I-I know..." Del's tears flowed afresh.

Gwen placed a box of tissues in front of Del. Del used three, then, wadding them up, shoved them into her purse.

"I've got trash. Over there." Gwen pointed to a wastebasket beside the wrought iron bakery rack.

"It doesn't matter," Del sighed.

Gwen looked at Claire; Claire shrugged. Gwen rested her hand on Del's and asked, "What's up?"

Del was surprised by the concern she saw in Gwen's eyes.

"What do you mean?" she asked.

"Why do you need relaxation tapes?" Gwen asked softly.

"Well...I've been..." She looked into her purse. Del hadn't told anyone, really, and she didn't know Gwen. Then again, she reasoned silently, maybe telling a stranger would make it easier to tell others. Eventually, she would have to tell everyone. Now that the kids knew, others would know too.

"My husband is divorcing me." She glanced up to see what sort of impression she'd made. Neither of them seemed too shocked, but Del felt shocked at herself. She couldn't shake feeling shocked.

Claire leaned toward her. "So, were you...fooling around?"

"No!" she said, clutching her purse defensively.

"Sorry, didn't mean to offend you. It's only, well..."

"I think what Claire means," Gwen said, trying to calm her, "is that it-the way you put it, that is-is that it sounded like he's divorcing you for a reason."

"It's not me," Del said, defensively. "It's *him*. He's the one who decided he couldn't be married anymore. I didn't *do* anything. I don't have a choice."

"Everyone's got a choice, sweetie," Claire said.

"That's what Dr. Spiegleman said, but he's wrong! I don't have choices-and it's all happening so-" She gulped new sobs.

Del couldn't bring herself to mention that she was on her way home from her first meeting with her attorney. She'd filled out the necessary paperwork for the amicable termination of fourteen years of marriage, resulting in two lovely children and-not that the state of Colorado cared-one cheating bastard.

The wailing sirens grew louder and Del felt panicked, as if an alarm had been triggered for her life.

"I don't know what I'm supposed to do," Del said.

"They're just gonna want to know what happened," Claire

assured her.

"No, not about them."

"About what, then?"

"About...everything!"   She pulled a fresh wad of tissue from the box and buried her face in it.

Outside, a fire truck and police car pulled up by the van.

"You just sit here and rest," Gwen said.   "I'll go get them." She stood.

"Don't volunteer any details; just tell them she's here," Claire said to Gwen.   "And you didn't see anything-you didn't, after all."

Gwen looked at Claire, a little puzzled, but nodded all the same and left.

"Listen, Del, sweetie-you listening?"   Claire touched Del's arm.   "Yes..."   She pulled her face out of the tissue.

"Listen to me," Claire ordered.   "I know it was an accident. I know you didn't mean to push so hard on the accelerator. You were only trying to relax, right?"

Del nodded.

"Right.   But that could get complicated, make it look like you weren't driving safely, in your own stressed out way."

"But-"

"Just listen."   Claire held up her hands.   "And do what I say."

Del nodded again.

As Claire spoke, she saw Gwen approach an attractive, female police officer who was talking with the firemen while they walked around the wrecked minivan.

Gwen talked with her, but not too much.   *Good girl*, she thought.   Claire liked people who caught on fast.   Del was catching on fast, too.   Claire thought this might work. Del seemed much calmer, now that she had a plan.   Claire thought she'd be fine, if she could only stay calm and tell her story.   Then she could go home and listen to that damn relaxation tape in a more appropriate environment. Like her bed; with a large glass of wine.

The details covered, Claire nodded toward the window. "Gwen's bringing one of the officers in now; one of the firemen, too. Maybe he's a paramedic."

Del followed her glance out the window. "Oh, no," she whispered frantically.

"What?" Claire looked at Del and then back out the window. "What's wrong?"

"It's her!"

"Her who?"

"The officer."

"You know her?"

"She's my husband's-*girlfriend*."

Three

GWEN AND CLAIRE STOOD BY the counter, trying to maintain a distance that would give Del, the paramedic, and the officer some privacy while still allowing them to follow their conversation. Gwen busied herself tidying up dishes and serving the occasional customers who trickled in during the slow, late morning hours.

Out front, a tow truck pulled up beside Del's van while a couple of firemen moved some of the larger chunks of the shattered flower pot from the street. Gwen knew it wouldn't be long before Art Adams, head of Blue River maintenance, would have the pot replaced. She made a mental note to make Art's favorite: hazelnut biscotti.

Claire rifled through paperwork in her briefcase, placed a call on her cell, and generally wondered why she stayed. She didn't know Del, after all. She didn't even know Gwen, really. Still, it didn't feel right to leave. It would be like leaving a puppy by the side of the road. She could stay a little while longer, she reasoned. Her next appointment wasn't for a couple of hours, and she was used to working on the run.

The young paramedic was finishing up, and the *Girlfriend*, as Claire had come to think of the female officer, waited patiently for her turn to talk with Del. She had already collected Del's license, etc., and was writing up the details.

"I'll give you a few minutes with her, Officer," the paramedic said finally , "but then I want to take her over to St.

Francis hospital and let them run a couple of tests. Might have a concussion. Don't want to take any chances. You feel up to a few questions?" he asked Del. "You could wait."

"No, I'm okay," Del said meekly.

"You can have these back now," the officer said, holding out Del's license, registration, and insurance. Del leaned forward to take them and her purse spilled onto the floor, its contents scattered again.

Claire went to help, but the *Girlfriend* had already set the license and papers on the table and, along with the para-medic, was helping Del retrieve her possessions. Claire picked up the purse and sat it on the table beside the license, which caught her eye. The Del in the picture barely resem-bled the Del she'd only just met.

The woman at her feet looked almost like she'd dressed in the dark. Her gray gabardine slacks were a good start, even the lime green silk blouse would have been fine, but she'd topped it off with a bulky knit cardigan with an orange and red jack-o-lantern design that offended the eye from neck to waist. Her hair was a long, unruly mass in a non-descript shade that, if necessary, could be called blonde and her nails looked more gnawed than manicured.

Del's picture on the license looked pulled together. Her hair was shorter, brighter, and styled. Her clothes-what could be seen of them, looked stylish. Claire looked at the date of birth and ran the math in her head. It put Del ten years younger than Claire would have guessed. She looked like she'd been through-the-wringer *twice.*

"That's about everything," the *Girlfriend* was saying as Del sat back in her chair, retrieved the purse and quickly shoved her belongings back in.

Claire noticed Del was trying to avoid eye contact with the officer, but the female officer was very patient and, Claire thought, downright kind.

She leaned over the counter and whispered to Gwen, "If that's his girlfriend, I don't think she realizes this is his wife."

"Probably doesn't know he *has* a wife," she whispered back.

"Okay, you're all set," the paramedic stood and packed up his gear. "As soon as you're done here, give me a holler and we'll take her over." Then he added to Del, "Do you have someone who can drive over to Green Valley to pick you up from the hospital?"

"I won't be there long, will I? I need to be home before my kids get back from school." Del's voice trembled.

"Probably not long, but you might want to call someone to pick you up. A neighbor? Your husband?"

"Maybe..."

Claire saw Del glance at the officer, who seemed to take only the expected amount of interest in such a conversation.

"No way she knows," Gwen whispered.

"Either that, or she's really cool under pressure."

Claire watched the paramedic leave, noting the healthy, well-cared-for physique. If she hadn't had the puppy to watch over, she thought, she would have

definitely done something about him. How old, she wondered–late twenties, maybe early thirties. Claire didn't like to dip too close to the cradle. Maybe twenty-nine, she thought, that would only be ten years younger. She tried to draw the line at ten...or so.

Gwen noticed Claire's expression and followed her glance. "Nice kid," she said.

"*Very* nice."

"Tell me what happened, Mrs. Rufino," the officer said, jotting a little note on a pad.

"Well, umm," Del glanced at Claire, "I was coming up Pine Glenn Drive and I was, well, almost at the intersection–"

"Were there any other cars around?"

Gwen saw Claire mouth the word *no* at the same time Del said, "No."

"So you were the only car on the road?"

"Yes."

"Okay, then what?"

"Ummm, like I said, I was just about to the intersection when a deer, you know, ran in front of the car."

"A deer?"

"Ah-huh. It was so fast. You know how deer are?"

"Sure," said the officer with a nod.

Gwen looked at Claire, who smiled back. "Everyone knows how deer are," Claire said.

"Well, I was just so startled, you know?" Del continued. "One second I was driving along and the next, there was this deer. Of course, I didn't want to hit it, I didn't think about it, I guess I swerved and the next

thing I knew, well, she-" Del turned and pointed toward Claire, "was tapping on my window, asking if I was all right."

"That's correct?" the officer asked Claire.

"Yes."

"Did you see the accident? The deer?"

"No, we were in here when we heard the crash. That's when I ran out."

"You see it?" the officer asked Gwen.

"No, I called you folks."

"Neither of you saw it actually occur?"

"No," they answered in unison.

"So," she turned her focus back to Del, "a deer ran in front of the car, you swerved to avoid hitting it and hit the flowerpot instead."

"Yes."

"Okay. I think that's all I need for now. I'll write up the accident report, give you a copy for insurance, and round up the paramedic. You sit tight, okay?"

"Okay." Del smiled weakly.

"By the way," the officer said, "are you Micky Rufino's wife?"

Del's mouth dropped open and her eyes grew wide. She stared at the woman, unable to speak.

"The attorney?" the officer said.

"Sweetie, you okay?" Claire walked over to Del. "Sorry, maybe she does have a concussion," she said, trying to cover for Del's obvious anxiety.

"Could be," the officer agreed.

"Yes!" Del suddenly said firmly.

"You have a concussion?" Claire asked.

"No, well maybe, but yes, Micky Rufino is my husband."

"Oh," the officer said. "I just wondered. Don't know anyone else named Rufino in the area. I run into him now and then in court. Just met with him last week, actually, about a juvenile case. Trying to get the kid some help. Your husband's representing him. He's a good attorney."

At that Del was speechless.

The officer stared at her and then said, "Maybe you do have a concussion, Mrs. Rufino, how you feeling?"

A little squeak came from Del, but nothing more.

"I'll get the paramedic," she said, and left.

"That was awkward," said Gwen, coming around the counter.

"You sure that's his girlfriend?" Claire asked.

"I saw them together..."

"I don't know, sweetie, unless that was in the biblical sense, hard to pin that one down. What were they doing?"

"Having lunch-he touched her hand across the table. I saw that!"

"Well," Gwen looked at Claire, then back to Del, "I'm not sure that hand-touching would be considered adultery. And sometimes lunch is just lunch. I see a lot of men and women who meet here for lunch, and there aren't many I'd accuse of anything more."

"She's right; maybe it wasn't what you thought."

"Maybe...but he was friendly."

"Is he normally not friendly? I mean, what sort of a guy is he?"

"Oh, everyone likes him," Del said. Then, realizing she was defending him, added, "of course, they don't *know* him. Not like I do." And her attention fell, again into the depths of her purse. She dug out a cell phone and said, "Excuse me; I need to call my neighbor."

"Sure." Gwen joined Claire back at the counter. "A deer?"

"Everyone knows deer have a pesky way of running in front of cars around here," Claire said, slowly packing up her briefcase.

"True."

"A deer is plain and simple. A relaxation tape leaves unanswered questions. It's messy."

"True."

"She's got enough mess already."

"Very true."

Four

Del
Thursday

WORST DAY OF MY LIFE! What a wreck! And *she* was there! I've never been so *uncomfortable* in my life!!! I can only imagine how he will laugh about me tonight when she tells him. She acted so innocent-but I know the truth! (I think.)

My poor van is in the shop. Fred at Stateside Insurance took a look at it and he thinks it can be fixed-thank *God*! But it will be at least a week. He's getting me a rental-they will deliver it in the morning-but a compact! Afraid to ask what all this will cost.

What am I going to do? This is all Dr. S.'s fault-I'm never going to see him again!!!

(p.s. two gals at bakery were so nice. Gifts?)

Claire
10-19

9am: Meet Adam (what an asshole) Brock at bakery.

2pm: Close Mountain View Ln. /get paid! Take closing gift.

7pm: Listing appt. 13425 Pikes Peak Dr. /Terri and Bob McMillan (2 sons Brad and Kyle, dog Amber)

To-Do:

Counteroffer for Adam (A.) Brock

Mountain View file-to close, and process. Get Paid!

Prepare for listing appt. with McMillans.

Get Listing. Create file to submit tomorrow.

Research properties for Lamberts-if time.

Notes:

A.B. was his usual self-what a waste. Phoned in verbal counter (basically said "eat shit" to their counter-but of course, more diplomatically than my client did). Still under deadline, waiting for response.

Closed Mtn. View, deposited commission check. Nice people. They loved their gift. To-Do: Add them to Xmas gift basket list.

Got McMillan listing. This one will be a pain, sellers are overpricing. I'll give it a month; see if they come to their senses.

Met owner of coffee shop (Gwen). Seems nice. Also met gal who crashed her vehicle out front (Adele-Del-Ruffino). Basket case. But a nice kid. Divorcing. Possible listing?

To-Do: Pull legal on Rufino property, just in case. Altogether it screwed up my schedule, but...

Gwen
Thurs.

Met a couple of interesting people today. Claire has been in before. She seems tough, but I think there's more there. Del crashed her car out front into one of those pots at the intersection.

I remember when Art down at town maintenance complained they had to get a special fork-lift to put those in place on the corners. Poor Art. (Try to remember to make hazelnut biscotti when it is replaced. Art's favorite.) Del is sweet, but her plate is full. Hope things work out for her.

Cammi was late for work again. No fresh powder yet to delay her, so it must be a guy. I'd fire her, but she's good, when she's there. I know she needs the salary to make ends meet while she's in college. And I like her.

Our ends are meeting, just barely. Andy still doesn't know if the trucker's union is going to strike. Why do they always do this when the holidays are coming up?

One more month until Jeff is home from college for winter break. Can't wait!

Five

THE HOUSE WAS QUIET; COMPLETELY, totally, eerily silent. No, Del thought, she did hear *something*. Like an undercurrent to the silence; the hum of life. Maybe it was the refrigerator, or the furnace, or the water sitting in the pipes, waiting for her to turn on the tap. Who knew? Del didn't.

All she knew was she had never really heard it before. She should have been comforted by it, she thought. But it only made her as lonely as she'd ever been in her life.

This was the first night the kids had spent at Micky's house. Well, she thought, townhome, really. Not really a house. Not really the solid home that she had. For now. But the kids had been excited about going down there. His complex had a pool, and a hot tub. The pool was closed for the winter, but the hot tub wasn't. They'd both taken swimsuits. And they'd taken Sandy, their dog, too.

Del missed her kids, but she realized she missed Sandy even more. *Was she nuts*? she wondered. She knew the kids loved that little straw colored miniature poodle. Okay, so Micky probably loved the dog too. She'd agreed Sandy should go where the kids went, but it really didn't sink in, until tonight, how alone she'd be without them all.

Even when the kids went to bed there had always been Sandy. Even when Micky *worked late*, there had always been Sandy.

Since Micky had officially moved out three weeks ago,

Sandy had still been there, nestled up against some part of her every night, all night long, and there to lick her face in the morning, even before the kids were up.

Yes, now she was truly, completely alone.

In the second that she felt the tears begin she knew that she had to fight them back. Giving in to tears always felt like she was losing. And crying made her head hurt, and her eyes red and puffy. She'd heard crying could be cathartic but for her, it only made her feel worse.

It wasn't always easy to fight the tears. When she'd crashed her van outside Gwen's Bakery it had all been so totally over-whelming. She'd fought and failed against the tears all day; in front of strangers, even in front of that woman.

Had she made a fool of herself? Was that officer really involved with Micky? It was like the crack in their marriage had let the trust leak out. Once it was gone, it was hard not to feel distrust all the time. Had she been suspicious of a perfectly innocent person? Had she been rude?

That night, after the kids were in bed and she was alone in the house, she had thought to herself, *if I can't cry now when can I cry?* So, she'd grabbed a throw pillow from the couch, and sat there, sobbing into it until she had to stop and pull the pillow away to catch her breath.

Then she'd washed her face with cold water and gone to bed, where she cried into another pillow until she was so exhausted she slept at last.

In the morning her face was red and puffy and her head ached. Enough, she'd thought to herself. Enough tears. If they don't help I don't want them.

Now, and for the first time, really, since the whole divorce thing had started, she thought about what she should do next. Not just next -right now, but next- for the rest of her life. She couldn't sit on the couch and cry. She spotted the bowl of Halloween candy on the counter, leftover from the night before. No, she'd had enough of that.

She raised her hand to her mouth and nibbled at the nail on her index finger. Her hand brushed against the scab on her chin where the airbag had skinned her. She could almost cover it completely with foundation, but it still felt like fine sandpaper. She rubbed her finger along it and the rough edge of a nail caught the corner of the scab.

"Ouch!" She looked at her chewed fingernails; an old habit in times of stress that had returned. A couple of her fingers had raw spots where she'd chewed the nail too far. *Too much!* she thought.

Del clasped her hands tightly together. "Enough," she said to herself. She had to stop chewing her nails and take control of her life. She needed something to do that would give her a reason to get up in the morning. She needed a job.

If it wasn't a *calling* or a *career*, that was okay. For now, it would be enough. For now, she only needed a reason, beyond her kids, to *be*.

And some money wouldn't hurt either, at least until the final settlement was determined.

Micky was paying her a sufficient amount each month to more than get by. It seemed only practical to make some money she could put away, into her own little nest egg.

For the first time in her life she thought about creating security for herself, by herself. The feeling was unnerving, but the idea felt good.

That was it, then. In the morning she'd start her job search. Del didn't really know how she'd do that, but simply having the plan was enough. She heard the humming silence again and realized she hadn't heard it for several minutes. She'd been too *busy*.

Well, if being busy took away the hum, she thought, maybe now was a good time to do the laundry. She'd never done the laundry at night before. That was a daytime job.

She liked to be free in the evening to spend time with the kids. Before.

Del took her basket from the laundry room and went, at night, to gather dirty clothes from her children's rooms.

Cara was ten and her room still looked like a little girl's room with its pink and white ballet theme. There were still stuffed animals and Barbie dolls but Cara had also started cutting pictures of cheerleaders out of magazines and taping them to her mirror.

Her best friend's older sister was a cheerleader at the high school. Now the younger girls were fascinated by the glamorous life they assumed cheerleaders must lead. Not to mention the uniforms.

When Cara and her friend discovered that cheerleaders sometimes wore their uniforms to school–all day–before games, it was the final factor that convinced them that they must also be cheerleaders. And so, they began schooling themselves in all things cheerleader.

Micky thought it was cute. Del did too, up to a point. There was a part of her that worried about a ten-year-old who was already fantasizing about high school. She worried about Cara's dreams not coming true. So she accepted the cheerleader phase without encouraging it too much. Phases, she knew, usually passed.

That's what she'd thought about Micky when he first talked to her about separating. How long had that been? Seven months? Eight? They had talked about it and decided that anything this important should involve a professional, so they sought out a therapist. Dr. Spiegleman.

Del was thirty-six; Micky thirty-eight. Del thought Micky was having an early mid-life crisis. He did work hard, she reasoned. Maybe he needed a vacation. But really, even then she knew the truth.

They had met at the local college and married while he

was in law school in Denver. Micky's family had money so
she'd never really had to work, but she took a part-time job
anyway, at the library, just to stay busy. Del had majored in
English, so a library seemed a natural place to be.

Then Nate was born, then Micky graduated from law
school, then Cara was born, then Micky made junior partner. They bought the beautiful home overlooking Blue
River Reservoir and considered themselves fortunate.

Micky's firm decided they needed him at the Denver office.
It was just over an hour's drive, in good weather, down to
Denver. Del worried about the times when he drove home
in bad weather late at night.

They decided it would be a good idea to get a little place,
the townhome, for him to stay in when he worked late or
when the weather was bad. It seemed a smart move, and
probably a good investment. But he worked late more and
more. Even in good weather.

Soon, it wasn't unusual for him to spend the whole week
in Denver and only come home on the weekends. Then
only on Sundays. That was when they finally talked and Dr.
Spiegleman came into the picture.

The doctor listened to their story, and considered Del's
mid-life crisis theory. He thought it was very perceptive
of her, but he thought other things, too, that Del wasn't so
sure about. Still, Micky seemed to put a lot of store in the
doctor's advice, so they kept going and they kept trying all
the exercises the doctor gave them to improve their com-
munication.

It seemed to Del, however, that she was the one doing all
the work on their relationship. And still, Micky was working as hard as ever. Shouldn't he be spending more time at
home? What about time for the two of them?

They weren't talking enough, the doctor said. They
weren't sharing their true feelings and listening to the oth-

er's feelings. The doctor wanted them to spend more time having constructive arguments, so they did. But instead of not talking enough they were simply arguing more.

Del didn't feel that therapy was helping, but Micky thought Dr. Spiegleman was the best; one of the senior partners had been through couple's therapy with him. Del agreed that was a good sign, until she found out that the senior partner was divorced.

Del picked through the clothes Cara had scattered across her bed while packing to go to her father's. Most of them were clean, so Del hung them up.

Cara had taken her Halloween costume with her, so her father could see it. She'd been a cheerleader, of course. Well, Del thought to herself, at least the kids had been home for Halloween. And they'd be home for Christmas, too. She and Micky had already agreed. But they'd be with him for Thanksgiving. Was it even worth buying a turkey this year? she wondered.

She threw a few dirty pieces in the basket, and emptied a few more from a hamper in the corner.

Nate had borrowed an old pair of his father's khakis, a worn blazer and a tie he tied loosely over a worn Beatles t-shirt. He'd messed up his hair and smudged some of Del's eyeliner on his face and called himself a Hobo. Most of that costume had gone to Micky's too, but the t-shirt lay on the floor beside a small pile of empty candy wrappers.

Several dirty athletic socks were bunched in a cubby beneath Nate's desk, forcing Del to crawl underneath and dig them out. She could imagine her twelve-year-old sitting at the computer in the evenings and, night after night, push-ing the socks off his feet and into the growing pile. Kids, she thought, never looked beyond the moment.

Back in the laundry room she loaded darks first, checking pockets as she went. She'd learned the hard way not to let

Cara's tube of sparkling lip gloss or Nate's yellow highlighter slip by. She never knew what she might find, and of course, there were the things she never wanted to find.

Like the hotel receipt from Micky's three-day trip to the convention in San Diego she'd found a few months ago. These things came up now and then, nothing unusual. Del had glanced at the receipt, thinking she would leave it on his dresser so he could file it away. Junior suite for one. Room service for two? Twice? That was the first time it occurred to her that the problems in her marriage could be real problems. Of course, it was probably a meal with a business associate. Probably working late, as usual.

But she'd found other things: an earring that wasn't hers, lipstick on a Kleenex. What a cliché, she'd thought, when she found the Kleenex. But it was a very real Kleenex and very red lipstick. Not her shade at all. After a while it was hard to reason these things away, but harder still to confront the truth.

She dug a matchbook out of Nate's pants pocket, along with one bent cigarette. Del stood there, holding them in her hand.

She frowned and wondered if she ought to be concerned. Kids will experiment, she knew. If she made a big deal about it, could turn into a major deal, just to spite her. Maybe it was part of acting out; a reaction to his parents' pending divorce. Dr. Spiegleman had advised them to expect such behavior.

Actually, the kids hadn't seemed that surprised when she broke the news. Micky, of course, was in Denver. She did it alone, but in a way that was better. She was there on the first day of kindergarten, there for the first dentist appointment, there for every first, good or bad. It felt right to be there for them, alone, for this. Still, she'd ached to save them from the worry and confusion she'd seen so clearly on their young faces. She could face the truth, if she must, but it broke her heart to make her children do the same.

She set the cigarette and matchbook aside and continued sorting, glancing now and then in their direction, wondering if she should just throw them out. Why look for confrontation? Didn't they all have enough to deal with? Wait and see if it happens again. She threw them in the trash and the phone rang.

"Rufino residence," Del said. She could smell the tobacco on her hand. A memory swept over her of the first fight she and Micky had had. Del smoked, now and then, when she and Micky had first met. He wanted her to stop.

"Del? You there?" said a voice on the other end.

"Hello? Sorry, just some static on my end. Guess my phone needs to sit in the charger for a while." Del covered for her lapse. "Angela?" she asked, recognizing the voice.

"Hi, Del. Sorry to call you so late, but I've just been swamped with prep for the Ladies League holiday luncheon. You know how that goes."

Del knew. She'd been an active member of the Blue River Ladies League for several years. The luncheon was the annual holiday event designed to simultaneously reward volunteers and raise funds for the league's charity.

"Yes, I certainly do."

"Del, I know you asked for a reprieve this year from your usual duties, but we are coming down to the line on this one and, well, Carolyn could use a little help."

Del's exact words to Angela had been: *"I'll have to beg off this year from the holiday luncheon. My mother hasn't been well and you know how that goes. I expect I'll be needed now and then and of course, there's no way of knowing when. I couldn't leave you empty-handed at a moment's notice, so..."* _

Del's mother, who lived across town, was fine. She hadn't told her about Micky yet and the kids had agreed to let her do the telling, but she'd avoided it so far.

Mother hadn't liked Micky since the day Del brought him home to meet her family. Her father had died the year before she'd met Micky. Del was the youngest of five, and the only girl. Her brothers had been friendly enough. Still, even they never truly warmed to him.

Del's mother was a task for another day. Tonight, she had to continue the ruse that allowed her to beg-off from her responsibilities for the time being; to avoid the truth a little longer.

Illness of a family member was the most acceptable excuse for recusing oneself from charitable responsibilities. A marriage falling apart and the end of all one's hopes and dreams for the future wasn't necessarily *not* a reason, it just wasn't one to bring up if one could help it.

Del had recommended Carolyn. They had co-chaired in the past and Del thought she was up to going it alone.

"Well, I don't know."

"I'm so sorry to ask this of you, Del. What with your mother's condition and all. But if you could take only a couple of hours to help Carolyn out, I know it would get her on track."

"Sure," Del said, after a moment's pause. "I suppose I could help out-a little. After all, I am available, unless something comes up, of course."

"Oh, of course, we totally understand, Del. If your mother needs you, you simply must leave. But, in the meantime, if you could just lend a teensy hand to Carolyn, to get her focused, well, that would be fabulous."

"I'll call her in the morning."

Angela gushed her thanks and signed off. She needed to get her kids to bed, she knew Del understood, she said.

Del stood, watching water flow into the washer, her finger tips pressed to her mouth as she contemplated calling Carolyn. Whatever job she found–and she *was* going to find a job–she would still have time to advise Carolyn.

It wasn't, after all, so much a matter of having the time that had caused her to beg off from her usual Ladies League position. It was the thought of spending her time with all those women who felt the freedom to busy themselves for the good of others because their own good was assured.

Those women didn't complain of unhappy marriages. They were busy planning cruises for their tenth anniversaries or family vacations to Hawaii.

Listening to all that happiness was more than she could bear. But she did miss her volunteer work. They would have to know eventually. Everyone would have to know. Wouldn't that be better? Wouldn't it be a relief to do whatever she wanted without worrying what others thought?

She smelled the tobacco again and remembered how she'd given up smoking because Micky thought it was bad. Well, of course she knew it was bad, but he had taken away her right to make that decision. He'd taken away her marriage, her kids, her dog, and her bad habits.

Del picked up the cigarette and put it in her mouth. It hung a little to the left, but it would do. She struck the match just as the water flow stopped and the agitation began. She blew out the match, setting it and the cigarette down.

Del finished loading the washer, and then she realized she didn't want her laundry to smell like cigarette smoke. She didn't want her house to, either.

There was only one solution. She poured herself a glass of white zinfandel. Micky thought it was an immature wine for an immature palette. Del liked the taste, so she'd bought a large bottle that afternoon.

She put on a coat and wrapped a scarf around her neck, took the glass and Nate's cigarette and matches and went to the back yard. She sat on the wooden swing set, lit her cigarette, inhaled, coughed, drank some wine, and inhaled again. Just like a twelve-year-old to have a menthol cigarette.

Del looked at the clear night sky, so dark in the mountains that the stars of the Milky Way were like a path of diamonds laid out for her to follow.

The breeze picked up and she wrapped her scarf around her head. The wine glass was cold, but its contents warmed her. She inhaled slowly, blew out slowly and swung slowly back and forth.

Out here there was no humming. She heard the breeze rippling through the last remaining aspen leaves. She heard her wind chimes tinkling, a neighbor's dog barking, and the rhythmic creaking of the chains as she swung, heel to toe and back again. She smelled the cold air, full of pine scent.

Del looked at the vast night sky and wondered where that path of stars would lead her. Shouldn't something so infinite intimidate her? she wondered. Instead, she had a little glimpse of the promise that an open path and an unknown future had given to so many before her. Deep inside, a stream that had been dry for a long time began to trickle.

Six

"ELLEN WAS TIRED OF HEARING how good your hazelnut biscotti are, Gwen. I had to promise next time I stopped in I'd get a dozen to share."

Art Adams had finally brought his crew to replace Del's broken flowerpot, and, as Gwen had planned, Art's favorite biscotti were ready for him to purchase.

"I knew you'd replace that pot sooner or later."

"Oh, definitely sooner," he said, digging in the pockets of his freshly pressed khaki's for his wallet. As the manager of town maintenance, Art took his position very seriously. His thinning brown hair was neatly trimmed. An all-business white shirt and striped tie were covered by a royal blue pull-over that didn't completely obscure the beginnings of a belly. Clearly, he enjoyed Gwen's pastries by day and a few beers at night. Still, the cuffs of his khakis were often caked with mud and, beneath it all, not Italian loafers, but serviceable work boots. Art could be depended upon to get a job done.

"You know the mayor," he said, "he has to have the work done in time for the Christmas trees. Couldn't have a corner in town without a pot sporting a tree, could we?"

"It does look nice." Gwen smiled.

"Looks nice to the tourists, you mean. Got the machines running most nights, spitting out snow up on the ski slopes. All they need are a few decent snowfalls from Mother Nature and it won't be long before we're open for the season."

"Weather report says snow tonight."

"Hope not, my money's on a couple days next week," Art said, pointing to Gwen's first-snowfall pool calendar. "I know snow's good for business, but I was enjoying having the place to ourselves for a few weeks between seasons. Always do."

"Me too, but I'm ready for business to pick up. Holidays are a big time for the bakery."

"I can imagine," Art said, casting a glance out front.

Gwen followed his gaze. Workmen were maneuvering a forklift to carry the new flowerpot that would replace the one Del and Dr. Spiegleman had demolished.

"Must have left my wallet in the car-damned uncomfortable when you drive-better wrap those up for me. I'll be back soon as we get this thing set in place."

"I'll put them in a box-with a red ribbon-it'll be a nice gift."

"Don't think they'll keep till Christmas." Art chuckled to himself on his way out.

Gwen glanced at the wall. A photo of Art-coffee in one hand, biscotti in another-hung across from the counter. Beside it, a watercolor of a clam shell, its pearlescent interior revealed beneath its unembellished exterior.

She smiled and went into the back room to find a box and resume the conversation she'd been having with Andy when Art arrived. Gwen found him cutting out cookies from dough she'd been rolling.

She watched as he worked over the sugary shapes of leaves and pumpkins. Andy was several inches taller than her with short non-descript brown hair. His usual attire of jeans and a flannel shirt flattered a body he worked to keep in shape, despite a trucker's schedule and his wife's pastries. A baker's apron was slung over his neck and wrapped loosely around his waist. The world might tend to overlook this man, if it weren't for his outgoing nature and genial heart. His simple shell held great treasure.

Gwen knew Andy liked helping out whenever he was in the bakery. He said it made him feel a part of the business, and since the business was so much a part of Gwen's daily life, it made him feel part of that, too.

In Andy, Gwen knew she had found the mate her soul had ached for during her first, failed marriage. Some wives might like their husbands working more and home less. Gwen wasn't one of them.

"Are you sure about this?" she asked, pulling unfolded boxes from a shelf.

"You know it's not my favorite job, but it's the smart thing to do. Pay's good and we could use a little extra savings, just in case." Lately, he'd been taking more and more work, trying to save up, in case there was a strike.

"I know," she said, "but you haven't taken these long runs for a few years."

"Are you calling me old?" He smiled at her. Andy drove a truck for Aero Post, a global delivery service. When he and Gwen first met, nearly eight years ago, he'd been driving the long hauls, from the hub in Denver to out-of-the-way mountain towns and the far reaches of the southwest that weren't serviced by air. After a couple of years they decided to try living together. Another year and they made it legal and Andy switched to local day routes.

Andy came along in time for her son, Jeff's, teen years. Back then Gwen realized Jeff was going into that age when he'd need a man's influence more, and Gwen's ex lived back East. Jeff's dad and Gwen emailed more than talked, and only with regard to their son. Jeff took the occasional trip to visit, but his father was removed, like a great-uncle whose generosity came in infrequent spurts. He was out of touch with his son's day-to-day life.

There had been some rough spots after Andy moved in, but, as time went along he and Jeff formed a solid bond. Not father/son, not friends, but somewhere in between that worked for both of them.

With Jeff in Wyoming for his first year of college, their cozy family had become a cozy twosome. While Gwen enjoyed the intimacy with her husband, she missed her son. There were odd moments in the middle of the day-or worse, the night-when she wondered how he was. It was a strange, disconnected kind of worry. And now her husband was going back on the road.

"I just worry about you, out alone at night."

"Honey, I am never alone on the road. We keep an eye on each other. Think about it. Do you ever hear about truckers getting hurt on the road?"

"Well..."

"Almost never. I'll be fine. I'm more concerned about you staying home without me. I know you don't like it."

"Well..." Gwen hated it, but if it had to be, she didn't want him to worry.

"All I hear is *well* and *well*-that's a very *deep* subject." Andy wrapped his arms around her, dusted his hands against her bottom to knock off the flour, and then pulled Gwen closer.

"Hey, don't you have an apron? And that's a very old joke, and a bad one."

"Kiss me," he said with mock sternness.

She kissed him and buried her head beneath his chin. "*I* worry about *you*, but I'll be fine."

"Worrying about you is a part of the package. You want me to love you, you'll have to put up with being worried about."

"It's a burden, but I guess I can bear it." She smiled and he hugged her tighter.

"Baby, if you don't want me to do this, I won't. That's all

there is. We'll figure out a way. Who knows? Maybe we won't strike."

"Stupid union."

"Stupid company, you mean. You're a union wife now."

"Stupid everybody."

"I'll figure something."

"No, no. You're right, this makes sense. It's what you do, after all, and I'm a big girl. I'm used to being alone. I was alone before I met you."

"Hey, don't get too comfortable with the idea."

"Ola, Senora Gwen!" a voice said, and Cammi swung open the door to the kitchen. "And Senor Andy!"

"Hey, Cammi," Andy said, "how goes Spanish class?"

"I should be bi-lingual in time for spring break." Cammi hung up her backpack and coat, pulled long blonde hair into a pony-tail, grabbed an apron and began washing her hands.

"Every parent's dream for their child's college education," Gwen said, smiling at Andy as they parted. He returned to cutting out cookies and she began folding the box she'd pulled from the shelf.

"Hey, Senor A., want me to take over cookies?"

"I like cookies," Andy protested.

"Here." Gwen handed her the box. "Pack up a dozen hazelnut biscotti for Art; he'll be back in a bit to pay for them."

"Yeah, I saw that production. What a mess that was. You ever hear how that lady's doing?"

"Nope, it's a couple weeks and I haven't seen her since."

"Claire said the same thing."

"You know Claire?" Gwen asked, surprised.

"Sure, she's in here all the time."

"What? I see her now and then, but not since the accident."

"Naw, she comes in late; two, three times a week, at least.

'Bout the time you go up to su casa-your house," she trans-
lated, "right before close."

Gwen had gotten into the habit of going up to the house,
which sat on the hill behind the bakery, every evening
around five. She'd turn up the heat if it had been a cold day,
maybe pop something in the microwave and check the mail
before she went back to the bakery to close up by six.

"I didn't think she was that hooked on pastries," said Gwen.

"She doesn't usually get anything but uno cafe'. The bakery is on the way to *her* casa, and she'd rather come in for a
cup to take home than make it when she gets there."

"Decaf?"

"Nope. The real thing and a grande one, too. Sounds to
me like she is muchos busy. Always workin' late. She pumps
up the caffeine to make it through."

"Surprised she can resist the goodies," Andy said, licking
sugar off a fingertip. "Must have a lot of will power."

"Don't lick!" Gwen admonished him with a smile. "The
health department will shut me down if they find out I have
a *licker* on staff!"

"Technically, I'm not staff, so you're safe. But see what I
mean about irresistible?"

"Claire's built like a model, Senor A. You can't look like
she does without muchos grande willpower."

"Some people are naturally slender," Gwen said diplomatically. "As for Del-that's the gal who crashed her car and
demolished the flower pot," she said to Andy, "maybe she's
hiding out. She was pretty embarrassed by the whole thing.
I felt sorry for her."

"Yeah, I think Claire did, too. Calls her, *that poor kid who
whacked the flower pot*. She even bought tickets for her in the
snow pool."

"For the first snowfall?"

"Si, Senora Gwen, she said she bought some from you,

too?"

Gwen nodded at Cammi.

"She bought five more for the pot killer. She said she figured the *poor kid* could use a break, being such a whacked out mess and all."

"Huh," said Gwen.

"I know," Cammi said, "Claire's weird that way. But this Del, she sounds like a case."

"That doesn't mean she's like that all the time. We all have our moments when we don't pay attention," said Gwen, glancing at the clock, "when we forget what-oh shit, I've gotta go."

"What's up?" Andy asked, trying to lick tell-tale sugar from his lips.

"I'm supposed to meet the manager at the ShopCo in Green Valley. She's gonna work with me on a better price for some of my supplies."

"Green Valley's kinda far. Can't you go through the ShopCo in town?"

"It's not that far, half an hour away at most, and besides, the jerk who runs the Blue River store never gives anyone a deal. 'Course, that means he's losing sales from local businesses, but it doesn't seem to bother him."

"He is el loco!" Cammi declared.

"Are you sure this is a *real* Spanish class?" Andy asked.

"Hyperbole is the spice of life!" Cammi retorted and left to pack Art's biscotti.

"I might be a little late getting home. I'm gonna hit rush hour on the way back." Gwen bent over her desk, making little stacks of the invoices she'd been working on earlier in the day in hopes of trimming even more expenses. Maybe she could come in early tomorrow to finish going over them. She picked up a notebook she used to keep track of costs and grabbed her coat and purse.

"Call me when you're heading home, Babe, and be careful on the pass. It could be slick up there this time of year." Andy held up his sugar and flour crusted hands and said, "Come here."

"I'll be careful–don't touch" Gwen said, pushing his arms away with her hands. "No, you don't. Kiss only–I don't need a sugar coating for the road." They kissed. It was just enough more than a peck to count for something. "You taste sweet."

"Want more? I could wash up first?" Andy smiled.

"No time...maybe later." She smiled back and was gone.

Seven

GWEN SAT ACROSS THE DESK from Terrie, the manager of the Green Valley ShopCo. Her windowless office was as nice as you could make a fluorescent lit cubicle furnished in serviceable steel and vinyl. Family photos mixed with framed sales awards on the wall, and a vanilla scented candle burned on the desk beside a silk plant.

Everything about Terrie, Gwen thought, was petite except her personality. Her curly black hair was cut short around an older version of the same china doll face she'd had in high school.

"This looks great." Gwen scanned the price list Terrie had given her. "In fact, this is *really* great. You sure about this? What's the catch?"

"There's no catch, you idiot." Terrie laughed. "If I could give it to you for cost, I would."

"I wouldn't let you!"

"For as long as I live I will never be able to repay you for dumping John the week before senior prom."

"I did not *dump* him."

"Gwen, you were nice enough about it, but you're," she held up her hands, making quotes in the air, "always nice."

"Stop, don't remind me," Gwen said, recalling the tag line beneath her picture in their senior yearbook: *Always Nice.* "I took so much shit for   that," she said, laughing.

"Jesus, it was true! You were practically a nun. I remember one very bitchy, well, bitch-ha!-who used to call you Sister Gwen when your back was turned because you were always saying things like-"

"It's not nice to talk about people behind their backs."

"That's it! Exactly that." Terrie pointed both hands her direction. "You were so *nice*."

"Well, now we know what they'll put on my headstone. Thanks, in part, to the senior yearbook staff."

"I can think of worse things to be called."

"Unless it's the seventies and everyone's loosing their virginity, except you. Then nice is not the reputation you necessarily want following you around."

"You shouldn't have dumped John. He might have accommodated you on that."

"No, he wouldn't have," Gwen said. "Besides, we weren't in love."

"See? How nice is that? How many of those ex-virgins do you think were ever in love?"

"Not the bitch, that's for sure. You ever hear what happened to her, anyway?"

"She's a congresswoman from one of those little states back east."

"No way."

"Her husband's with the state department."

"How do you know these things?"

"I helped put together the alumni book for the high school. I'm a freakin' font of alumni trivia. Ask me anything."

"I don't know what to ask."

"Come on, there must be someone you want some dirt on. I'm practically the cleaning lady, Gwen. Ask away. I owe you, after all."

"Terrie, you know I didn't dump John. I let him go. Who did he go to prom with the next week?"

"Well...me."

"Exactly. Every time you walked by he was trying so hard not to let me see how hard he was trying to see you. It was painful to watch. As much as I wanted to go to prom, I was starting to feel like a character in Shakespeare, keeping star crossed lovers apart."

"I barely knew he was alive."

"You walked by my locker every day at the exact time John would meet me between his physics and English classes. I checked. You're next class was on the other side of the school." Gwen smiled at her friend.

"Yeah, well...I really wracked up the tardies in that class. Sorry, just couldn't help myself. One day John was just any other guy and then, the next day, he was *the* guy. It was like a switch turned on. I knew you, and you were dating him. It was a safe way to talk to him. I didn't mean to take him away, only be close to him."

"And if we happened to break up one day..."

"I wasn't *trying* to break you up, honest."

"Hey, no apologies needed. John's switch turned on just like yours. Once I figured that out, I knew I was fighting fate. Besides, Carl Landelly was home from college. He took me as a favor to his sister,

Carol. She was my best friend and wanted to double date. Carl and I had a great time, platonically speaking."

"I remember Carl," Terrie smiled at Gwen. "He never responds to alumni mailings. Whatever happened to him?"

"Married a great guy. They live in L.A."

"Ahh." Terrie nodded. "So, now I've got the skinny on Carl. You sure there's not someone you wonder about?"

"Well," Gwen said, a thought occurring to her, "there is this gal, but I don't think she went to Blue River. At least, I don't remember her." She felt awkward, worried that her curiosity might be misinterpreted.

"What's the name?" Terrie asked, pulling up something on her computer screen.

"Del Rufino. But that's her married name, and I think her first name is actually Adele." A touch of guilt nagged at Gwen. Maybe she shouldn't be snooping around about Del. Wasn't she being a little too nosy, after all? "You know, I don't want to put you to any trouble."

"It's no trouble at all," Terrie said, giving her a wink, "we're cross-referenced."

"Oh, very impressive." Gwen watched Terrie tap away at her keyboard, a smile half frozen by her concentration on the task, and realized it was too late to stop her.

"State of the art. My teenage son put the program together for us as extra credit in his computer class." Terrie flashed a proud mother's grin. "Okay, let's see, Adele Rufino. Ahh, here she is. Adele Donahue Rufino."

"She's part of the Donahue family? I thought I knew all the Donahues in school."

"Big Catholic family, that's for sure. But I think Adele's the baby of the group. She wasn't even in high school yet when we were seniors. She graduated several years after we did."

"You're kidding. I didn't think she was that much younger than me."

"Rufino...hey, she's Micky Rufino's wife, right?"

Gwen nodded. "I think he's an attorney. You've heard of him?" Now her guilt gave way to renewed interest.

"Sure, I know who he is. Didn't go to Blue River High, though, he's a Denver brat."

"How do you know him?"

"People think a big place like ShopCo has deep pockets they can dig around in. We get a lot of *accidents*," she said, adding air quotes again. "He's been on the defending side a few times. ShopCo usually settles out of court. Even though everyone knows these crooks are lying, they still walk away with a lot of money."

"So you've seen him in action?"

"In *many* ways." Terrie sat back in her chair and rested her hands, fingers entwined, atop her head.

"Huh?"

"A couple years ago there was a claim from a man who said he slipped on a wet floor and damaged his spine. Rufino was his attorney. In the process of defending the slime ball with the bad back, he interviewed several of our employees. He spent a great deal of time interviewing one employee in particular. A very well endowed redhead who used to work in the bakery."

"Really?" Whether that police officer had been the *girlfriend* or not, Gwen thought, apparently Del really did have good reason to be suspicious when it came to her husband's fidelity.

"Yep," Terrie continued, "I heard just enough to know he made out really well, in a non-monetary way, on that deal."

"Is she still here?"

"Nope. She met some guy and moved to Aspen. She'll fit right in there. Does his wife know what a piece of shit he is?"

"Oh, she knows. They're getting divorced."

"Kids?" Terrie asked.

Gwen nodded.

"That's too bad. I hope they're good about the kids."

"Me, too." Gwen picked up the paperwork and stood. "Thanks again, Terrie. You've been a great help."

"Honey, if you hadn't ditched my poor John, I would not be the happiest married woman in Blue River today. I owe you."

"You do not owe me. We've covered this," said Gwen, smiling.

"Well...more than that, then. I guess, you get a little older, you start thinking about the big picture. We're all part of the same story, know what I mean? And I like happy endings."

"I know what you mean."

"So." Terrie stood and walked to the door. "You can start purchasing today, if you like. Show the checker that card I gave you, and they'll give you the discount."

"That's great. I'm already swamped with orders for Thanksgiving pies. Terrie, you're a life saver. I mean really, you really are saving me–more than money, you know?"

"Sure."

"You come by before Christmas and pick out something. A pie, a cake–I'm making Yule logs, too. It's on me."

"That won't save you anything, Gwen."

"It's a gift, not an expense."

"See, always nice."

Eight

★★★

DEL SAT IN HER CAR watching the entrance to the ShopCo. She'd lain in bed the night before, trying to decide where to look for a job. She could go back to the library, but there would be so many people she knew. Del wasn't ready for that.

No, she had to look outside of Blue River for now. It wasn't forever, after all. Just for a while. Just to get her feet wet. Green Valley was far enough to be safe, but not so far that she'd be on the road too long. One of her friends had moved here during high school, but they'd lost touch long ago.

Del started with the Green Valley library, but they weren't hiring. Then she'd driven around town looking for 'help wanted' signs. Cottrel's Stationary was hiring, but they needed her to be there at eight in the morning. Del couldn't get the kids to school and get all the way to Green Valley by eight. The owner suggested she try ShopCo. They had so many shifts, she said, and they were always hiring.

ShopCo. Not exactly what Del had had in mind. Still. Now she sat in her car, repeating to herself, *it's not forever, it's not forever.*

She watched the entrance for half an hour. People came and went. Lots of people. Del didn't know any of them, which was a very good sign.

Del played absentmindedly with her wedding ring, twist-
ing it around her finger. It was an old habit she fell into
when she was anxious. She'd never really thought about it
one way or another; just a habit. Now, however, as she sat in
the car watching the ShopCo and playing with the ring, she
looked down and thought, for the first time, about taking it
off.

Isn't this my fresh start? Del thought. She nodded to herself,
took a deep breath and pulled. It surprised her how easily
it slipped off, didn't even put up a fight. Memories of her
wedding day brought tears to her eyes. "No," she said firmly
under her breath. "No." She bit her lip and blinked hard.
"No more tears."

Del opened her change purse and dropped the ring inside.
She looked at it for a moment, lying so casually among the
pennies, dimes and quarters as if she were only taking it off
for a manicure. Then she snapped the purse shut.

Finally, she took three deep, cleansing breaths, and got out
of the car. Not forever, not forever...

A gentleman in a green ShopCo vest smiled at her as she
approached the entrance. "Card?" he asked.

"Oh." Del paused. She'd forgotten she needed to show
her ShopCo member's card to get in. Of course, she had
one. Everyone did. But finding it in her purse, standing in
the doorway, with others coming and going wasn't easy.

"Sorry, I forgot, but it's in here somewhere." She held her
purse in one arm and dug with her free hand, glancing about
her every few seconds to be sure no one she knew walked by.

"No problem, ma'am."

"It'll only take a second."

"Take your time."

"Here!" she said at last, waving it before her.

"That's great. Shopping cart?" he asked, reaching for a

cart from the line behind him.

"No, I'm not shopping. I'm, well, I'm only going to the customer service desk, I guess." Del wasn't sure where to go, but she was uncomfortable asking.

"You don't need a card for that. Go on in."

She stared at him for a moment, then tucked her card away and shut her purse. At the desk she waited for several minutes until one of the women behind the counter was free.

"May I help you?" the woman asked. She also wore the standard issue green ShopCo vest, which contrasted strikingly with unruly red hair held in a loose bun. Stray hairs, some gray, Del noticed, wisped loosely about her face.

"Yes, I mean, well, I was wondering if you're hiring?"

"You have a teenager looking for a job?" the woman asked, pulling a sheet of paper from under the counter.

"No, actually, it's for, well, for me."

"Oh. Want a discount?"

"Huh?" Del wondered what the woman's point was. Had she dressed too nicely? Did she not seem serious about a job? What was she doing that wasn't right?

"We get a lot of gals ask about working part-time to get the store discount."

"There's a discount?"

"In your dreams. Would a big company like this give their employees a discount? Fat chance. People don't know that, though. Sorry to disappoint you." She started to put the paper back.

"Wait, I'd still like to apply, if you're hiring."

"You would?"

"Yes."

"Okay then." She gave her the sheet of paper. "Fill this out. You can sit over there." She pointed to the seating area clustered around a small hot dog stand near the front of the store. "Need a pen?"

"No, I've got one."

"Okie, dokie then. Bring it back up here when you're done."

Del eyed the tables. She sat at an empty one off to the side, but, sitting alone at the table with only the piece of paper before her, she felt uncomfortably exposed.

She walked to the refreshment counter and ordered a medium diet Coke. Back at the table she set the drink to her most exposed side. She picked it up and took a sip, eyeing the application as she did. She set the drink down again, dug through her purse and pulled out a pen. Del worked slowly, thoughtfully, filling out the form, sipping her drink, and trying very hard not to be noticed.

GWEN PUSHED THE ROLLING FLATBED of a cart up to the register to check-out. She pulled the discount card Terrie had given her out of her back pocket and set it on top of one of her large, stacked sacks of flour and sugar.

She hadn't run the numbers out to the final figures yet, but Gwen knew the discount she was going to be getting on her basics like sugar, flour and spices, would help. Not big, huge, winning the lottery help, but modest, extra cash, being able to pay another bill or two help. Still, every bill she managed to pay was one step closer to the future.

Gwen was never sure exactly what the future held, but in her mind it was a place of second chances and promise. These days, she dearly hoped it didn't hold a trucker's strike.

She paid for her items and, waiting for her receipt, glanced toward the refreshment counter. The ride back to Blue River was just long enough, she reasoned, to make the purchase of a soda, and maybe a hot pretzel, acceptable.

As Gwen stood at the condiment counter, filling a little cup with mustard for her pretzel, a familiar face caught her eye. It took a moment to put the face together with the accident. A moment more and her name-Del.

Del, Gwen noticed, was concentrating, apparently with some difficulty, on filling out a piece of paper. Every few seconds she either glanced around or took a sip of her drink. Again she glanced, then picked up the cup and sipped and their eyes met.

Gwen smiled. Del froze. Gwen walked closer, obviously intent on greeting her. Del placed her cup and her hand over the sheet of paper.

A drop of Coke slid down the side of the cup and formed a small brown puddle on the paper. Flustered, Del swept it away with the palm of her hand, accidentally hit the pen and sent it flying onto the floor in front of Gwen.

"I've got it!" Gwen said, juggling her drink and pretzel in one hand and picking it up with the other.

"Oh! You don't have to-oh, thanks," Del said as Gwen handed her the pen.

"You mind?" Gwen asked, taking the seat across from her and spreading out her drink, pretzel and mustard cup.

"Um, no, ahh, that is, well," she pulled the paper closer, "sure."

"Del, right?" Gwen asked.

Del nodded.

"I'm Gwen."

"I remember."

"You sure this is all right? I could sit over there." Gwen nodded toward another table.

"No, no, this is fine. I'm, that is, I guess I'm glad to have a chance to thank you again, for, well, everything."

"Don't worry about it. How are you?" she asked, still wondering if maybe she shouldn't have sat down. Del seemed so anxious at her arrival. She noticed the paper beneath Del's hands, and thought it looked like a job application.

"Great..." Del said, shaking her head slowly, side to side and smiling.

"Good." Gwen dipped a piece of pretzel into the mustard and popped it into her mouth.

Del watched her chew. "Are you shopping?" Del asked, and instantly realized how stupid the question must sound.

"Yeah."

"I just mean, it's not as close as the Blue River ShopCo."

"True. But the manager here is an old friend from high school. She kind of owes me-well, she *thinks* she owes me-long story. I don't think she does, but she offered me a discount awhile back, if I wanted it, and now I do. It's worth the drive."

"That's nice of her."

"She's a nice person. And you?"

"Huh?" Del hadn't expected the conversation to turn back on her so quickly and was caught off guard.

"Looks like you're filling out a job application." Gwen nodded at the paper.

Del wanted to say she was just picking it up for one of her kids, but Gwen could clearly see, between her fingers, that she'd been filling it out herself.

"Oh, this, well, yes. I was thinking, maybe, you know, it would be something...to do."

Gwen nodded, "Sounds good. Kinda far from town, isn't it? Or don't you live in Blue River."

"Oh, I do." Del kicked herself mentally. She could have said otherwise.

"I see." And Gwen did. She had gathered enough from their first encounter and put together the pieces. "Do you shop at ShopCo much?"

"Some." Del didn't want to admit that she was not a regular customer.

"It's just, you don't look so comfortable." Gwen thought one ought to at least feel comfortable in the place one wanted to work.

"I suppose I'll get more comfortable."

"Probably." Gwen wondered if she ought to leave. Who was she to give Del advice anyway? It wasn't like they were good friends. In fact, Del's body language practically screamed out, *go away.*

That was why it was so odd when she asked Gwen, "Do you think I...*shouldn't* work here?"

Now Gwen definitely regretted saying anything. What if working here was the perfect job for Del? What if Gwen's opinion mattered? "I really couldn't say. I'm sure it's a fine company to work for."

"But, do you think I'll like it?" Even if it's not forever, Del suddenly thought, shouldn't she like it?

"Del, I don't know you well enough to say one way or the other. I know–here's what I told my son, Jeff, when he went looking for his first job. Work someplace you like to be. Take me, for instance. If I didn't own a bakery, I'd probably work in one. Or a restaurant. Certainly somewhere where I'd work with food, and with the public. I like that. What's your favorite store? Where do you shop when you want to have fun?"

"The outlets." Del loved puttering through the outlets that had sprung up a couple miles outside of Blue River at the intersection of two highways leading to several ski resorts.

"Then why not look there?"

"I don't know." Of course she did. All her friends shopped there, too. "It's just..." Del rubbed the thumb and forefinger of her right hand against the base of her left ring finger. Her wedding ring was gone, but its impression remained.

Gwen watched Del's hands. "Too many familiar faces?"

"Yes, how-"

"Hey, you're not the only person who ever got divorced. Been there, done that, as they say."

"Really?" The rubbing slowed.

"Yup. Been a few years, but, let me tell you what I learned. It's your life. Half the people you think are your friends will say all the right things, but then they'll disappear. Have you told anyone yet?"

"Not really."

"Yeah. It's weird, I remember. But Del, it's not as weird as you think. That half, it doesn't matter what you say or do, or what they say, for that matter. They are gone. Down the road. And you know what?"

Del swallowed, but her eyes were glued on Gwen.

"You don't want them. Really. You don't see it now, but you will. It will be so clear. You'll wonder why you ever cared what people like that thought. Why you cared what anyone thought, really, because in the end, the people who are worth caring about, they care about you. It's great. More people than you know understand what you're going through. You'll find that out, too. For now, though, focus on you. Think about what *you* want. What will make *you* happy."

Del sighed and looked at the paper on the table. She looked around her. The store smelled like hot dogs and popcorn. The floor was cement, and she remembered she was always cold in these big warehouse stores. She was cold now. It was loud and cold, and she didn't like the smell.

"You're right," she said, and crumpled up her application.

"Only you know that for sure," Gwen said, frowning. She hoped she hadn't made more trouble for this woman she barely knew.

"Thank you, Gwen."

"You're welcome. Want some of my pretzel?"

"Thank you, but...no. Actually, I promised myself I'd get this done today, so, while I have the courage, I'm going over to the outlets."

"That's great, Del. Stop by the bakery and let me know how it goes, okay?"

Del took a deep breath. "Okay."

"Hey, it'll be fine. You'll be glad when it's done."

"Yeah. Then I have to tell my mom about it."

"She doesn't want you to work?"

"I don't know. I don't think she'll really mind my working."

"Good."

"I don't think she'll be too happy about the divorce though."

"You haven't told your *mother*?"

"No, not yet."

"Oh."

She gathered her things and stood. "It's only been a couple weeks, and Micky's gone all the time anyway. Nothing new there."

"Kids haven't told her?"

"Not yet. I made them promise not to say anything until I did, but..."

"Not fair to them."

"Right."

"Come here." Gwen stood up and wrapped her arms around Del. "You need a hug."

"And then some." Del laughed nervously. It was funny, she thought, to laugh about it, but it felt better than crying. "Thank you so much, Gwen."

"Hang in there."

D EL DIDN'T HAVE TIME TO think about how uneasy job hunting made her as she drove back toward Blue River. She punched in the speed dial on her cell phone.

"Hi, sweetheart," her mother answered. Del knew she screened her caller I.D.

"Hi, Mom, will you be around later? I thought I'd stop by."

"On a Tuesday?"

"What?"

"Since when do you ever stop by on a Tuesday? What's wrong?"

How did her mother do that? Make her feel guilty just for dropping in. "What's wrong with Tuesday?"

"You always wait for the weekend."

"Well, I thought I would today. Is that okay?"

"Are you bringing the kids?"

"No, Cara is going home with Becky to work on a school project and Nate has soccer practice. It's at the school, so I'll pick him up after practice, then-"

Why, she thought, did she feel compelled to explain her schedule to her mother? "Then I'm picking up Cara. So, I thought I'd come by before I have to pick them up."

"Why?"

"Do I need a reason to visit my mother?"

"Is this about Micky?"

"What?" Del hadn't said a thing to her mother about Micky or their marriage. "Why would you think this is about Micky?"

"I heard something at the club, Adele. Has he left you?"

"*What?*" Great, Del thought, her worst fears were realized. A complete stranger had told her mother about Micky. She would never be forgiven. "Mother, I–I don't want to get into this now, I just want to know if you'll be home if I stop by. Will you?"

"I will. I don't think you should bring the children, if we're going to talk about *him*." Micky had never been her favorite person, though Del couldn't understand why.

"I told you, they're not coming. I have a few things to do, but I'll be there later." Traffic picked up as she approached the turn to Blue River. "I have to go, Mother."

She wrapped up the conversation quickly, before her mother asked what she was doing. Del could feel her heart racing and strength drain out of her shoulders. Was this an anxiety attack, she wondered? Dr. Spiegleman had asked if she had had them. She didn't think she did, but who knew? She tried to calm her breathing, but the traffic didn't help so she pulled the car to the shoulder of the road, turned on her hazard blinkers and sat for a minute, her eyes closed, trying to soothe her speeding heart, thoughts, and worries.

She opened her eyes and saw the familiar 7–11 sign just off Highway Eight ahead. Gwen had said to focus on what made her happy for now. Not forever, just like the job she was looking for. She pulled back into traffic and headed for the sign.

Del didn't want to buy cigarettes where someone she knew might see her. It wasn't that she was a regular at the local 7–11, but she did take the kids in there now and then for Slurpees. She knew the clerk in the same way she knew the checker at the Safeway or the owner of the local dry cleaners. But no one knew her at this store; she could be anyone.

She was nervous making the transaction, as if her mother were watching. Del kept telling herself, *you're an adult; you can do anything you want.*

A stand at the end of the counter held a selection of condoms in colorful foil packets, available for purchase in emergency situations, just like the individual packets of aspirin or antacids. She could even buy condoms, she thought. Be prepared.

Though she thought this, she could feel an inkling of panic at the idea that she, Adele Donahue Rufino, might actually take the two steps required, reach out and pick a condom from the little condom tree. And even if she did, which one would she pick? The varieties in which pleasure came were even more intimidating. She would rather die than stand there in public contemplating a condom purchase.

"May I help you?" A young clerk smiled across the counter at Del. Startled from her unnerving thoughts, she froze. He looked like a kid. Could he sell her cigarettes? "Ma'am?"

"Camels," she said, thinking her voice must be quivering but the clerk didn't seem to notice. He ran his hand along the selection stacked against the back wall.

"Which one?"

"That one," she said, not even bothering to notice where his hand hovered. *Just buy them, just go*, she thought.

"You want a Super Ball ticket, too?" he asked, referring to the local lottery.

"Ummm."

"Sorry, don't mean to push you; owner wants us to ask everybody. Besides, if the big winner buys their ticket in our store, we all get a bonus."

A gentleman in a dark grey suit set a cup of coffee on the counter beside Del and pulled a well endowed money clip from his pocket. He peeled a ten dollar bill from the top. "I'll take ten, when you get to it."

"Want to pick the numbers?" the clerk said, pointing to a stand of Super Ball forms.

"Surprise me," he said.

"Surprise me, too," Del said. There was something about the guy's attitude. Micky would have picked the numbers. He liked to be in control. Del was fed up with control, she realized. Now that she was in control, she would do what she liked. She liked surprises.

"Ten?"

"No-three." Three was her favorite number. "And-and, I'll take one of these, too," she added, stepping to the condom tree, she pulled the most colorful packet she saw and set it beside the camels. She glanced at the gentleman beside her. He smiled. Del paid for her purchases and left, quickly. Camels and condoms and Super Ball tickets, oh my!

Nine

"MADISON. THIS IS INAPPROPRIATE BEHAVIOR. Get down right this moment," Carol said in a stern but calm voice.

Madison was three years old, precious and occasionally incorrigible. Claire knew this because Carol, Madison's mother and Claire's client, had told her so.

At the moment, precious Madison was working on her incorrigible side by jumping up and down on the beautifully made, king-size bed in the impeccably appointed master bedroom of the high-end mountain home in an exclusive gated community. Claire was hoping her clients would write an offer on the house, and then take their children and go back where they came from until closing.

The chances of that happening fast enough for Claire seemed slim. Downstairs she could hear the pitter patter, or more accurately, banging and slamming of Jordan, Madison's six year old brother. He, according to Carol, was a *pistol*. Claire thought a pistol would come in handy right about now as her choices of targets were numerous.

"Mommy is very unhappy with her Madison," Carol said as she stood beside the bed, less than an arms length away from her giggling, jumping bundle of joy.

"Carol!" Alan, Carol's husband, yelled from downstairs. "Would you please come down here and stop your son? He's going to break something!" Alan must have had psychic powers, Claire thought. The ensuing crash came only seconds later, followed by the shrieking sobs of a little boy. "Carol!"

"Oh." Carol looked from her bobbing Madison, to the bedroom door, to Claire.

"I'll watch her," Claire said.

"I will be right back, Miss Madison," Carol said sternly. "Thank you so much, Claire, you're a gem."

What Claire was was pissed, but she said, "Don't worry about it."

Carol blew her an air kiss as she ran out the bedroom door and downstairs. "Mommy's coming!"

Carol and Alan were in town on their third and final trip before their move. They had to buy a house that weekend and Claire was going to find one. She just prayed nothing expensive had broken in the process.

Madison was trouncing the pillows now. At this rate, Claire thought, she'd be jumping from side table to dresser any minute. And this was only the second house of the day. They had six more to see. She squared her shoulders, took a deep breath and walked to the bed.

"Madison," she said quietly but with menace, "get down now, or I will get you down."

Madison stopped bouncing and looked her in the eye. Claire looked back. Apparently Madison didn't get the whole staring thing, giggled and resumed bouncing. From downstairs she could hear Madison's other family members still sorting out that mess. The coast was clear.

"That's it," Claire said. She grabbed little Madison's arm and pulled her off the bed, landing her right in front of Claire. The little blue eyes grew instantly wide and her mouth popped open in surprise. Claire knew what would be next, so she acted fast.

"Absolutely no crying allowed," she said in her best "wicked witch" imitation, stooping before the little girl with her face so close to hers that tendrils of her mussed brown curls tickled Claire's cheek. Madison's chin quivered, uncertain if it would give in to tears.

Six houses to go; Claire knew what to do. "There will be no more running around," she continued, "and no more jumping." The quiver increased and Claire could hear Carol wrapping up downstairs. Only a minute or two left; time to finish her off.

"Otherwise, I will make sure that *your* bedroom is in the basement."

Precious Madison's mouth snapped shut, her eyes grew even wider.

"But if you behave," Claire continued, her voice softening, "I'll find a beautiful bedroom for you." Claire knew that for her client's kids the bedrooms were the biggest bargaining chip.

A little smile grew on Madison's lips. "Utterbys?" she asked.

Claire had already heard how much the little girl loved butterflies and knew a bargaining chip when she saw one.

"I will personally make sure there are butterflies. But only if you behave and only if you keep it a secret."

Claire wasn't crazy about blackmailing a child. It wasn't as if she was going to hurt her, after all, she reasoned to herself. She just wanted to make little Madison happy, without losing her sanity trying. "Promise?" She added a smile, for effect.

"Pwomis." Madison giggled and threw her arms around Claire's neck in a hug just in time for Carol to catch the touching moment.

"How precious," Carol said.

CLAIRE SAT BACK IN HER chair. The glow from the computer screen washed blue light across the room, reminding her that the sun had set long ago. Madison's parents had finally decided to make an offer on one of the homes she had shown them, so Claire had taken them back to their hotel late that day, then gone home to write up the paperwork in anticipation of meeting with her clients first thing the next morning.

Claire was nearly finished when the phone rang. It was Carol. Of course they loved the house. Of course they completely planned to make the offer. *But.* Claire hated that word; it always meant more work. In this case, her clients were ready to go with their offer, but they were hoping she might be able to find two or three more homes to show them first. Just to make them feel *certain* this house was the one.

"We simply need to be certain there isn't another house out there that we'd be happier with," Carol explained.

Claire wanted to point out that over the course of their two house-hunting trips she had shown them a total of thirty-two different homes. The home they finally decided on was nothing like the home they originally told her they wanted.

They were the sort of clients who couldn't say what they liked until they saw it. Claire showed them almost every home available in the area in their price range: big homes, many on large parcels spread out over miles of mountain roads, with two small children in tow every inch of the way.

And so, Claire said, "No problem." Which was exactly

what it would be if she had any say in the situation. The pickings were getting slim, and she chose three homes that were totally wrong for little Madison's family, but she'd show them nonetheless.

It was late by the time Claire printed up sheets of statistics on each house, decided which order to show them in, and mapped out the route. Come morning she'd call the real estate offices to set up the showings.

Meanwhile, she printed up a blank contract, in case they decided to make any big changes to the offer. Then she printed out triple copies of the prepared contract and attachments on the house she already knew they would buy. The one they decided on late that day.

It had been the third house Claire had shown them on their very first trip. She knew it was *the* house the moment they walked in the door. Claire could always tell these things. From that point on, every house was compared to number three, but they needed to see twenty-nine more before they were convinced.

In the end, Claire took them back to that house late that afternoon and, magically, her clients finally also knew it was the one, at last.

Claire licked her index finger and pressed it against the few remaining crumbs of coconut tart on her plate. She sucked at the last drop of coffee from the Styrofoam cup she'd purchased from Cammi at the bakery on her way home. Hot coffee and the last tart: dinner.

Claire liked Cammi. She reminded her of herself, a long, less complicated time ago. Funny how life changed one's priorities.

She hadn't seen Gwen since the day of the accident. Gwen seemed like a nice gal, someone Claire might like to know, if she had time for that sort of thing. If she *made* time, she corrected herself. Did she really want to go down that road again?

She had to admit she missed the companionship of a close girlfriend more than a loving relationship with a great man. Were there any great men left? At forty-two, had she managed to avoid commitment just long enough to let all the good ones get away? She thought she'd found a good one once, but... She had learned that lesson long ago, and she enjoyed being single, didn't she?

Maybe the next time she saw Gwen she'd try a little harder to strike up a conversation, though she imagined Gwen was probably one of those people whose lives were overflowing with little room for more.

Claire winced and pushed against her abdomen where a sharp, uncomfortable feeling returned. Lately her stomach didn't like being empty, and it let her know in a most uncomfortable way.

"Shit," she said and, picking up the empty cup and plate, went to the kitchen, turning lights on in the dark house. She filled a bowl with the last of a bagged salad, sprinkled it with low fat vinaigrette and tore a plain bagel in half.

As she ate she flipped through a travel magazine intended for her neighbor, but that had ended up in Claire's mailbox. She'd get it to them, eventually. Claire thought back to the last time she had traveled for pure enjoyment. It was an old memory. These days she was too busy and she found her enjoyment in short, sweet, uncommitted relationships.

Hadn't she learned the lesson about girlfriends, too? she wondered. She rinsed the dishes, put them in the dishwasher and, popping her customary two antacids before bedtime, turned out the lights.

Men lied, men cheated, wasn't that to be expected? But your best friend should never be disloyal. Claire had learned that truth the hard way and the memory still burned even after ten years...

Ten

Nine Years Earlier

BUSINESS HAD BEEN SLOW THAT summer, but it was Cindy's turn to treat, so Claire was looking forward to lunch with her friend. Ironically, when home sales had been so brisk in the spring, they hadn't managed anything more than a few phone calls. Why was it, Claire had thought to herself, that when you could afford to take a friend to lunch you never have the time, but when you have the time, you couldn't afford it?

Claire's career in real estate had started a few years earlier when she moved to Denver from New Jersey, trying to forget a former fiancé and make a fresh start. She'd worked hard to build client loyalty and it was starting to pay off.

Still, when it came to finances, half the time she felt like that little kid holding up the cracking dam, and the rest of the time she was saving nuts against the day the dam cracked. Would she ever feel she was ahead of it all? Would the tension between her shoulders, and that nagging fear of financial catastrophe ever go away?

"You'll never guess what we did this weekend!" Cindy bubbled over as soon as Claire joined her at the table overlooking the eighteenth green. Lunch was at Cindy's country club. Cindy was, as usual, a vision of affluence, from her perfect hair-blonde on blonde highlights-to her Manolos, and every bit of DKNY, Cartier and Chanel in between.

"What?" Claire sipped her favorite chardonnay that Cindy had ordered for her. How nice, she'd thought, to have a friend who knew you so well that she ordered your drink for you.

"You've got to guess!"

Claire smiled. They'd been college friends who scrimped together to buy second-hand furniture for their first apartment, rented to escape dorm life.

But Cindy married Tom, a rising corporate star, moved to Colorado and quickly forgot what it felt like to worry about paying the electric bill. Cindy's priorities revolved around her family, her home and her favorite malls. Claire's choices were limited, but Cindy's extravagances were always entertaining.

"Did you go to the mountains?" Claire asked.

"Not even close."

"Brandon's already walking and talking and even taking piano lessons. He didn't perform at Carnegie Hall, did he?" She laughed at the scowl her friend gave her. Obviously Claire wasn't taking this seriously enough. Which probably meant it was more expensive. "I know. You got new living room furniture. You've been threatening for months and you've finally gone out and done it. What did you get?"

"Closer, but that's not it." Cindy arranged the napkin on her lap, reached for her wine glass and waited for another guess.

Too bad about the furniture, Claire thought. She wanted a new couch and had considered offering to buy Cindy's old one, when she finally replaced it.

"Let's see...not travel news, not kid news, not even furniture news. That can only mean one thing. But you're too young for plastic surgery!"

"Claire, don't be silly!"

Claire shrugged her shoulders. "I give up, and I've guessed three times. That's the limit; you've got to tell me now."

"Okay." Cindy reached into her purse, pulled out a glossy sheet of paper and handed it to Claire. It was a brochure for a very expensive home in a very exclusive neighborhood. Claire knew the area; she'd been marketing to the home-owners, trying to get her name in there. One sale in that neighborhood would pay bills for months, plus she could make a nice contribution to that breaking-dam fund.

She hadn't known Cindy was thinking about moving up, after all, their current home was a spacious showcase of Cin-dy's good taste. Still, Claire's real estate brain kicked in fast. The sale of Cindy's home-even with the great discount she'd give her friend-combined with the purchase of this one felt almost like a miracle.

That paycheck could literally change Claire's life, and the lives of those she loved back home. Plus, it could give her the profile she needed to finally break into the high-end home market. But her friend hadn't said anything about moving...maybe it wasn't what she thought.

"Are you thinking of buying a new house?"

"Nope!" Cindy actually giggled.

Of course, Claire thought, too good to be true. Must be something else, but what? "Well, what then? I give up," she said at last, taking another sip of her wine.

"We *bought* it!"

"What?!" Claire sputtered, almost choking on her wine.

"We were in the neighborhood and the agent was holding it open. We had some time to kill so Tommy said, let's look around. And we did!"

"Since when have you been looking for a new house?" Claire couldn't believe the direction this conversation was taking.

"We've been thinking about it for a while."

"You never said anything," Claire realized she was shaking and set her glass down.

"You've been so busy, we didn't want to bother you." Cindy smiled.

She actually smiled, Claire thought. She didn't get it at all. Okay, damage control, damage control... "Well, so, you need to get your house listed. We can get that going right away." Cindy may have been stupid and ignorant and many other things Claire wanted to say aloud, but she was a friend, so she'd still give her a discount on her commission. And it was still seven figures, after all. It wouldn't be a life changing sale, but at least-

"No, that's the best part!"

"What is?"

"We sold our house too! Isn't that great?!"

"You-you-" Claire couldn't say anymore. She felt the heat rising to her face, but the words were all stopped up.

"I know, it's amazing!" Cindy chirped, totally misreading her friend's reaction. "We wanted to move into something bigger, and the seller wanted something smaller. The agent even closed the open house right away, just so he could take the seller over to see our house!"

I'll bet he did, Claire thought.

"Of course, our house wasn't as tidy as I would have liked, but the agent said that didn't matter-"

Cindy, Claire knew, had a housekeeper who came in three times a week and a part-time nanny who kept Brandon's sprawl confined within his bedroom walls.

"All the pieces just fell into place so perfectly, and by dinner time, we'd all signed contracts!" Cindy's smile was bigger than ever. "We did it right over there," Cindy pointed to a table in the corner. "Tommy and I were so delighted; we treated them all to dinner, too."

Claire stared at this person she'd thought was her friend. Was it possible for a college educated woman to be so utterly clueless? "Did you even *think* about calling me?" she asked at last, her voice almost choking with emotion.

Cindy's smile deflated slightly. "Well, I did, sweetie. Remember? I left you a message."

Claire remembered. Cindy's message had been: *Hey, call me, I need to ask you something.* Claire had been in the mountains for the weekend, *trying to relax.* She'd been out of cell phone range and hadn't gotten the message until she came home on Monday. All Cindy had said, when she'd called back, was that she had some news, and she was taking her to lunch.

"You didn't say you wanted to buy a house!"

"Well, every time I've talked with you lately you've been busy. You told me a few months ago that things were simply nutty; you barely knew if you were coming or going. I didn't want to bother you with...this!"

"This? Did you even know that agent before you went in that house?!"

"No..." Cindy said, a touch of defensiveness creeping into her voice.

"So," Claire said, trying to get a grip, "let me see if I got this right. Instead of calling your...*best* friend to help you buy this new house, and sell your present home-which, I might add, I would have done for a discounted commission because you're my-" she took a breath and forced the word out, "*friend,* instead of doing that, you did it all through this one guy-a complete stranger!

"You gave him both ends of the commission on your purchase, and his sale, of your *new* home-*and*-you gave him both ends of the commission on the sale and purchase of your *old* home-the home I sold you! You know what's the called, Cindy? Double ending-times two! It's four friggin' sides, for Christ's sake! It's *huge*. You made his year. Maybe his decade! He'll be telling friends about this for the rest of his career! What the hell is he charging to sell your home?" Claire demanded.

"Six percent. He said that was a good rate for that price range."

"Sure, he probably charged the other guy seven percent; it usually takes a lot of time and money to sell big, expensive homes. Not an afternoon! So basically,

you bought him a new car, sent his kids to college-in state, of course-and made a down payment on his mountain get-away, all in one weekend, right?"

"Well...I suppose. He's handling it all, he was so nice about it."

"I'm sure he was. You're his new best friend! And he's a *complete stranger.*"

Cindy shifted uneasily in her seat, a small pout on her lips. It was clear, Claire thought, that it was beginning to dawn on her that she'd screwed up, but she didn't get it, not really.

"I thought you'd be happy for me, Claire," Cindy said, forcing her smile back into place. "I thought it would be such a nice surprise. And it's a wonderful place," she pointed at the brochure on the table in front of Claire but accidentally knocked Claire's wine glass over as she did. "Oh!" The wine splashed over the brochure, melting and fading the colorful photos of Cindy's beautiful new home.

An attentive waiter arrived with extra napkins, blotting the wine. "I'll get more napkins-and another glass of wine for the lady," he said before leaving.

"Thank you," Cindy said, giving him her trademark smile.

So sweet, Claire thought. At that moment, if someone had asked her to describe how it felt to have your heart broken by your best friend, Claire would have said it felt like a cold steel door shutting on a warm, sunny smile: so sweet, so shallow and so, so sad.

"Really," Cindy said to Claire, "it's going to be so much fun to fix up. I can't wait for my friends to see it." She was past the moment and back to her bubbly self.

But Claire wasn't. She picked up her purse and stood. She looked at the green golf course beyond the window, calm and sedate, and at the other diners, adrift in their own worlds. "I'm sure your friends will love it," she said and turned to leave. She stopped a moment and added, "Good-bye, Cindy," because she thought she should. She walked out, and never looked back.

Three months later a business associate of Claire's called to say she was opening an office in Blue River. Claire moved within a month. And when she did at last look back, it was to remember never to get that close again.

Eleven

★★★

GWEN RESTED THE SHELL ON the little mound of sand
she'd poured into a neat pile atop the small table beside
her easel. She didn't know where the sand came from; the
bottle didn't give a location, only *Fine Grained, White Beach
Sand*. Gwen had ordered it online, along with several more
shells to add to her collection.

She contemplated the tableau briefly, then shook her head
and picked the shell up off the sand before placing her grand-
father's old, leather bound cigar box carefully on her lap.
Gwen lifted the lid, replaced the shell and surveyed her other
choices.

The cowrie's turtleshell colors always attracted her, but
she'd painted it before. The tulip shell. Its classy exterior
came to a sharp point, revealing a smooth and beautiful interior. It was multi-layered and perfect but she would get back
to that one another time. It wasn't what she was thinking of
tonight. Tonight she was thinking of Del.

One by one she held each treasure in her box. Not this
one or that, and certainly not the one she picked up next.
Or was it?

Every person was a shell to Gwen, and finding the shell
that symbolized a person was her secret pleasure. On the
walls of the bakery were displayed pictures she'd taken of
some of her favorite customers. They loved seeing themselves on the walls, even if some of the women complained

that they never took a good picture. Inevitably, however, one of Gwen's watercolors hung nearby.

So far, no one seemed to have figured out the connection, which was just as well, since some of the connections were less than flattering. A local councilwoman who was a frequent customer, smiled smartly beside a painted hooked mussel. The shell's striated exterior commanded attention, while its interior, dark ambers fading to black, combined with the two- sided nature of the double shell, told much more, Gwen thought, about the woman's character.

Only Andy knew what she was up to. He sometimes joined in the selection process, when he knew the person. They both agreed, for instance, that Art, of hazelnut biscotti fame, who could always be depended upon to take charge when maintenance jobs needed doing around Blue River, was a simple, common clam. Its nondescript exterior might catch few eyes, but upon opening, it revealed a stunning mother-of-pearl interior whose beauty was worth the effort to see.

The phone rang. Gwen quickly set the box on the floor.

"Hello?"

"Hi, Babe," said Andy, his voice thin through a haze of static.

"You're hard to hear."

"I'm parked at a truck stop in the middle of a snowstorm. I'm lucky to get through at all."

"Are you all right?" Gwen asked, old worries about Andy's long hauls returning, particularly when his route took him through the mountains.

"I'm fine, I'm fine. Don't you start worrying about me. I've got plenty of company here. Gonna join a poker game when I hang up. Not much to do but sit it out."

"I wondered how the weather was up there," Gwen said, looking out her window at the soft flakes that swirled in the

glow of the street light below. The weather man had pre-
dicted an inch, at most for Blue River, and then a return to
the prolonged Indian Summer. Gwen knew the snow might
be heavier higher up.

"What's my baby up to tonight?" Andy asked, changing
the subject.

"Oh, I'm shelling."

"You haven't done that for a while."

"Too busy," she said. The truth was that she hadn't painted
much since Andy gave up the overnight hauls. Her painting,
and her mixing of people and shells that Andy dubbed *shelling* was something she'd done to fill her nights alone.

"Who's the subject?"

"Del–that woman who ran into the flower pot. I saw her
again today. She was job hunting."

"How's she doing?" Gwen had filled Andy in on Del's
circumstances.

"Okay. I guess she's still finding her way."

"Remind you of yourself, once?" he asked, his voice growing even fainter with static.

"In a way, I suppose."

Andy said something, but Gwen couldn't understand.

"Honey? Honey, you're breaking up."

"Sorry, it's–worse, I'm still–, but I–go." His voice cracked
in and out.

"I love you!" Gwen shouted through the noise.

"–you too. I'll call. Okay, I'm–" The line went dead.

Gwen tried not to worry. Storms happened. Andy knew
what to do, he'd be all right; but still...

She deliberately turned her thoughts back to the box, not
allowing herself to worry. Wasn't this why she'd started
painting in the first place? To fill the time. No, to fill
her thoughts, really, to push out loneliness and fear. Gwen
picked the shell out of the box.

For each person, a shell, and for each shell, a certain sort of person. But this one she held in her hand was different. She stroked the smooth, winding surface of the moonshell, contemplating its simplicity. Still, she'd always seen it as so much more; the opposite of Del, but Del all the same.

She nestled it in the sand, turning it to its best advantage. Then she laid out her paper on the flat easel and began to draw Del's shell.

"THE RIVER INN ALWAYS RESERVES a suite for our guest of honor, Carolyn. I booked it for this year right after last years' luncheon. But you should call to confirm."

After seven years as Director for the Ladies League Holiday Luncheon, Del had handed over the reigns to a very nervous Carolyn. After half an hour on the phone answering Carolyn's anxious questions, Del wondered if the committee had done the right thing by putting Carolyn in charge. But what could they do? Del felt compelled to step down when it was clear her marriage was over and her future uncertain. And Carolyn, as her assistant, seemed the logical choice.

"We finally decided on our menu a few weeks ago. At least, the committee did. We tasted so many things-desserts too, Del. I can't believe I'm saying this, but I actually didn't want any more chocolate after that meeting!"

"It can be overwhelming," Del said. She smiled, remembering how she used to complain about the long days she put in volunteering for the Ladies League. But because they were her days-her choice-they flew by, and she loved them. And she missed them.

"Sally picked out the centerpieces for the tables. She did a great job; I'm glad you recommended her for my assistant."

"She was always a great *worker bee*. I knew she'd be a lot of help."

"Oh, she is!"

"Be sure you call the florist a few days before-to confirm the details," Del said. "They are so busy during the holidays; it helps to go over everything with them one last time."

"I will." Carolyn paused. "Del?"

"Yes."

"How are you doing? I heard, well..."

"That Micky and I are getting divorced?"

"Uh-huh."

"It's true."

"I'm so sorry."

"Thanks, Carolyn."

"My sister got divorced a couple years ago. It was rough for a while. But she's really happy now."

"Really." Del had known Carolyn for five years. She realized she must have known her when the divorce was happening, yet Carolyn had never said anything. Was it because they didn't know each other that well? she wondered. Or because the women of the Ladies League didn't talk about those sorts of things. Shouldn't the Ladies League be just the kind of group a woman could share such concerns with?

"Barb-that's my sister-she had a friend who got divorced. Her friend kept telling her there was light at the end of the tunnel. She told her she'd see the light eventually. Barb says it took a while, but her friend was right. I just thought, well, I thought you ought to know about the light, too."

Del felt overwhelmed. All this time she imagined that her friend's lives were so different. That they'd never understand. But Carolyn did, and so did her sister.

She swallowed hard and said, "Thank you so much, Carolyn. You don't know...how much I appreciate...well..."

"I know. Hang in there, Del. Maybe, when this holiday insanity is over, you and I could get together for lunch."

"I'd like that."

"And thank you so much for all your help. I'm going to tell Angela that your name should still be on the program-Honorary Director-how's that? Because you are!"

When she'd finally hung up, Del wondered how many other friends understood but never spoke about divorce. How many were fighting to keep their own marriages together?

It was late and the kids were asleep. She went into each room, stood beside their beds and listened to their even breathing, whispered their names and got no response. Sandy was curled up on a couch cushion, snoring softly. The coast was clear.

Del quietly pulled the back door closed behind her and turned the collar of her coat up around her neck. She wrapped a cashmere scarf loosely around her head, partially shielding her face from the gentle snowfall. It wasn't expected to amount to much, she knew; a light dusting before the clear cold of a November mountain night. She walked to the swing-set, digging the pack of cigarettes from one pocket, matches from another.

The first drag made her cough; out of practice. The second was better, and felt warm inside.

Already the weather was breaking up and Del could see the moon, half revealed by a gap in the clouds. A generous break between the pines looked down upon Blue River reservoir; its icy, black waters glowed with the reflected moon.

It was late, and few lights remained on in her neighbor's homes. The yards were large in her subdivision, over an acre a piece, so no one's house sat too close to another. Generous stands of pine dotted the area, obscuring the view even more. Just as well, Del thought. She didn't need neighbors gossiping about her new bad habit.

She was beginning to understand, however, what Gwen had said about not caring quite so much what such people thought. Her day had left her with enough cares; she didn't have time for any more.

The outlet stores had seemed unpromising at first. Del walked up and down the courts, looking for 'help wanted' signs. With the holidays coming up she'd expected to see more of them, but the few she spotted were stores that didn't appeal to her: children's shoes, athletic gear, and a store that catered to teenagers.

Finally, she decided to ask if they were hiring at the stores she liked. Hadn't that been Gwen's suggestion after all? Surprisingly, three of them were. Del filled out applications at each of them and interviewed at two. The manager wasn't available at the third, but he would call her.

She was nervous to begin with, particularly in the first interview at Imagine, her favorite women's clothing shop. The female manager seemed so professional, Del actually stuttered two or three times out of sheer intimidation.

Del's nerves frustrated her. Hadn't she chaired numerous committees over the years for the Ladies League and the PTA? She'd made a point of putting that on her applications. Even though she'd never been paid, she knew what it was to put in long hours and work with difficult people. Didn't that count for something?

The second interview, at a high-end purse store, went much better. The woman treated her like a friend and they'd actually chatted about their children. After that, Del felt more at ease. She thought she'd made a good impression at her third stop, a bookstore, but she still needed to interview there.

The whole experience left her feeling more confident than she had felt in quite a while. If only she'd gone straight home it would have been the best day in a long time. Instead, she'd gone to see her mother, and now it felt like the worst.

"I always knew Micky would turn out to be trouble. I'm not at all surprised," her mother had said.

"Mother!"

"How can you defend him? Obviously, he thinks with some part of his anatomy other than his brain!"

"That's not fair, really." Del felt compelled to defend Micky. But considering his behavior, she wasn't sure why.

"Is it fair that his actions will hurt your children?"

"Actually, the kids seem to be doing pretty well with–"

"Of course they seem that way now. But you should get them into counseling; they will need years of counseling."

"Well, I've considered the possibility, but I thought I'd see how they did first, and so far–"

"You should be seeing someone, too, Adele. This sort of experience could devastate your self esteem."

"Well..." Del didn't want to say that her mother wasn't exactly helping, but that was par for the course.

"And Micky should pay for your therapy and the childrens'. It's his responsibility, after all, since his actions are the cause of your mental instability."

Del wasn't sure how to respond to that. "I don't think I'm mentally unstable, Mother!"

"The unstable never do, dear. And how could you remain psychologically intact after such a personal assault on your very character?"

Del thought her mother's anger and outrage were growing exponentially, like a tsunami hitting the shore and smothering her. She had to get out of there before her mother really lost it.

"What is your attorney doing? You do have an attorney, don't you?"

"Yes, Mother, of course I do." Del didn't want to mention they had a mediator, not two separate attorneys. "She's–"

"*She*? Don't you think you should get a man?"

"What?"

"Really, Adele, you are so naïve. You can't let him get away with this. You need a warrior in your corner, not Florence Nightingale."

"She's hardly Florence Nightingale. She's very good and I'm very happy with her."

"I hope you don't live to regret those words. You just can't let him get away with-he hasn't hurt you has he? Have you been abused, Adele?"

"Mother!"

"What? He has? You must call the police, you can't let him-"

"No! I have not been abused, and I am not calling the police."

"Have you at least talked with Father Frank?" Her mother referred to the priest at their family's church, St. Benedict's. But Micky wasn't Catholic and so they'd given up regular attendance years ago, much to her mother's disappointment. Even so, Del's mother knew she still went on her own, occasionally.

"Father Frank probably doesn't even remember me."

"Of course he remembers you-he's known you all your life! You absolutely must call him."

She paused, then shrieked, "Oh, God!"

"What?" Del thought she'd hurt herself.

"What if you can't take communion anymore? You'll have to get the marriage annulled. What if that makes my grandchildren illegitimate?" Del's mother's hysteria reignited. "That's it," she said reaching for her phone. "You've got to call him immediately." She held the phone out to Del.

"Mother, please. My children are definitely not illegitimate and I'm not calling Father Frank!" she said. Seeing the distressed look on her mother's face Del added, "Not now,

at least. I've got to pick up the kids. Good-bye, Mother."
Del left, exhausted.

She took one last puff on her cigarette and snuffed it out
in the damp sand beneath the swing. Later, she would toss
it in the trash, pushing it beneath the top where the kids
wouldn't spot it.

Del sat, her head leaning against the swing's chain, and
watched the moon move back and forth on either side of
the opposite chain as she swung slowly. She breathed in the
crisp, snow-spiked air and blew a steamy cloud back out.

A little yip drew her attention to the back door where
Sandy stood, her paws against the glass. Nice to be missed,
Del thought. She stepped in the door and Sandy scrambled
to greet her, sniffing at the hem of her coat.

"Shoot." Del realized that even if she'd done her smoking
outside, she still had the lingering smell. It was one thing
when the kids weren't home, but she couldn't risk their finding out. She didn't want to give the impression she approved
of smoking, after all.

She hung her coat to air out from the edge of an arbor on
the back porch, draped her scarf beside it and, shivering, ran
back inside. Once the lights were out and Sandy comfort-
ably snuggled atop her bed pillow, Del turned on the hot
shower and washed away the evidence.

Twelve

ANDY RELAXED AT A TABLE in the bakery, the morning crush long gone. He was alone to enjoy a day off with his thoughts and the day's sports section. Unseasonably warm Chinook winds blew gusts at the windows, soft accompaniment to Gwen's occasional humming as she worked in the bakery's kitchen.

"Sweetie, you want another coffee?" Gwen called from the back room where she was mixing cake batter.

"Naw, Babe, I'm fine."

"How 'bout some coffee cake?"

"Stop worrying about me. You keep on with whatever you've got going. I'm checking up on my boys."

Gwen's husband was a football fanatic and she knew *his boys* were the local team. He enjoyed catching up with the news after a few days on the road. "Let me know if you want anything," she said, delighted to have him safely home again.

The door chimes jangled, and Gwen heard another male voice. She came out front to see who her customer was.

"Look what the Chinooks blew in," Andy said, patting the man beside him on the back.

"Bob! When did you arrive?" Gwen walked around the counter to give the man a hug.

"Drove in this morning; can't find a decent chocolate éclair in Grand Junction." Bending his husky, six-foot frame, he enveloped her in a bear-like hug.

"I'll get you one. Have a seat. You can keep Andy company. Want a coffee?"

"You bet." He folded himself into a chair beside Andy's. Though a large man, Bob was not out of shape. Like her husband, he favored blue jeans and flannel shirts. His boots had a thin crust of mud, and beneath short dark hair was a weathered but pleasant face with dark brown eyes and a day's growth of stubble.

"How's the wine business?" Andy asked.

"Great. Finished up the harvest, 'course, so now we're enjoying a little down time. Still things to do–always something to do. But that's usual with the winter season coming up." Bob owned a winery in Palisade, over a hundred miles west, but he split his time between the mesas of the western slope and the mountain scenery of Blue River.

"Are you staying through the holidays, then?" Andy asked.

"Pretty much. My employees won't mind getting the boss out of the way for a while. Never do, and things run fine enough every year."

Gwen placed Bob's coffee and éclair on the table just as the door chimes jangled once more and Claire walked in.

"Gwen, I'm glad you're here. I keep missing you when I come by." Claire glanced at the men, smiled curtly and moved over to the counter to talk privately with Gwen.

"Cammi told me you've been in."

"She's a good kid. Glad I caught you though, I was curious–have you seen Del, the pot killer?

"Yes, I saw her at ShopCo yesterday. She was looking for a job."

"ShopCo. Really? She doesn't seem like ShopCo material to me."

"I'm sure she'd be fine there," Gwen said, somehow feeling a need to defend the abilities of someone she barely knew.

"I suppose..."

"Well, actually, I don't think her heart was in it. I think she was going down to the outlets."

"Holidays are coming. Half the stores ought to be hiring."

"I hope so. She seemed kind of–I don't know."

"Deer in the headlights?"

"Exactly. Like the one she almost hit." Gwen smiled at Claire.

"That was one more problem she didn't need. Maybe she'll get lucky and find something great at the outlets."

"Speaking of which, I hear she has a benefactor who bought her five tickets in the snow pool."

"Yeah, well, I was planning on drinking my winnings. She can use it to pay her attorney fees. Not gonna win today, though. Friggin' nice out." Claire glanced at the window and again noticed Andy and Bob. "Boys," she said, nodding.

"Oh, Claire, this is my husband, Andy. Honey, you remember me mentioning Claire?" Gwen asked. "Sure," Andy said, standing and shaking Claire's hand. "You two were good Samaritans."

"Felt more like we rescued a puppy, don't you think, Gwen?"

"Maybe. She's getting tougher, though, I think. She may turn out to be more of a Rottweiler than a poodle."

"Poodles are smart, bred to hunt, you know," Bob said, extending his hand to Claire. "Bob. And you are...Claire?"

"Yes." Claire looked him over a bit warily.

"Sorry, forgot my manners," Gwen said, "Bob's an old friend–just got back in town."

"Ah. Well, then, nice to meet you, Bob. Are you moving back to Blue River? Looking for a house?"

"No, I've got a little place up in The Range."

"Nice." Claire knew The Range was an exclusive area

of not-so-little and quite expensive homes that sat up high enough to have killer views of the reservoir and mountain ranges beyond.

"Claire's in real estate," Gwen said.

"You probably know my neighborhood."

"Yes, I've been there quite a lot lately." Madison's family would be moving in soon, she thought.

"Maybe I'll see you around," Bob said, smiling.

"Yes, well..." Claire looked at Gwen and then the bakery case.

"Can I get you something?" Gwen asked, thinking Claire's reception toward Bob was a bit cool for such a warm day. Especially after some of the comments she'd made about other males at their last meeting.

"A coffee. And I think a chocolate éclair, perhaps. Just one."

"No problem. Bob's having one, too," she added.

"I'll take mine to go. I'm between clients."

"Sure." Was it Gwen's imagination, or had it gotten suddenly chilly?

Claire smiled at Andy and Bob. "Nice to meet you both. Excuse me," she said and, taking a Styrofoam cup from a stack on the counter, walked to the baker's rack in the back to fill it. Gwen bagged her éclair and met her at the register.

"How have you been?" Gwen asked.

"Ah–fine."

"How's it going with that guy you were meeting with the morning of the accident?" Gwen wondered if perhaps Claire was involved with the *Asshole* after all. She'd thought he was attractive, in spite of his behavior. Yet, Bob, who was his usual charming self, practically got the cold shoulder.

"He was right, of course. They took the offer. Still..."

"An asshole?" Gwen asked.

"*Friggin'* asshole," Claire emphasized.

"Hope it works out."

"It'll take a while for the deal to seal, but it'll get there. Just gotta work it."

"Cammi tells me you work late a lot."

"She should know, she's my connection; your caffeine gets me through many late nights."

"Goodies, too," Gwen added, holding up the bag with the éclair.

"Takes me a while to go through those. Only eat a third or a quarter at a time. That diet crap, you know?"

Gwen nodded, handing Claire her change.

"Thanks again," Claire said, glancing toward Bob, who was moving casually along the bakery case in her direction. "Gotta get moving," she said, and brushed past Bob, toward the door. "Nice to meet you," she said over her shoulder as she reached the door, juggling her purse, coffee cup, and éclair.

"Let me get that for you," Bob said, jumping ahead of her to pull the door open.

"Oh, thanks...Bob." Claire turned toward Gwen. "If you see Del, tell her I hope things are improving for her, will you?"

"Sure," Gwen said, a slightly amused smile crossing her face.

"Okay." Claire looked up at Bob and added, "Thanks again," turned, and was gone.

The door blew a warm gust into the bakery as it shut, tinkling the chimes anew. Bob took his seat and Gwen brought his éclair over.

"Nice gal," Bob said.

Gwen glanced at Andy, who was smiling up at her.

"Friend of yours?" Bob asked her.

"More of an acquaintance, really."

"On the shy side, huh?"

"Ohhh, I'd, ahhh..." Gwen shook her head, unable to find the right response for that one.

"She drop in often?"

"Yeah, mostly later in the day, though. On her way home."

"Interesting. Hey, this éclair looks great." Bob took a bite and knocked down a third of the éclair, a big grin on his face as he chewed.

"FUNNY," GWEN SAID LATER, AFTER Bob had left and Andy mentioned Claire.

"What do you mean, *funny*?"

"Her behavior, I just thought it was...funny, that's all."

"How so?"

"With Bob."

"Bob's a big guy, Babe, and the ladies probably think he's good looking-I could see that. Probably tongue-ties a lot of women when they meet him."

"That's what I mean. I don't know Claire well, but I would never think of her as someone who got tongue-tied, especially around good-looking men. Quite the opposite, in fact."

"Well, maybe she had something else on her mind, you know? Maybe she was distracted, wasn't prepared for Bob."

"Maybe."

"Sure. Probably worried about that Del. She was asking about her, right?"

"Actually, now that you mention it, it did seem like that was why she dropped by."

"See?" he said, snuggling up behind her as she rinsed dishes, his arms around her waist. "She was being thoughtful."

"I guess it never occurred to me that-"

"That she could be thoughtful?"

"I guess."

"Not like you to be so judgmental," he said, teasing as he nuzzled her neck. "Maybe you need to get to know her better."

"Maybe," Gwen said, as he kissed beneath her earlobe. "Wanna get to know me better?" he whispered.

"Cammi should be here soon." She dried her hands on a dishtowel and turned around to kiss him back. "Maybe I could go back to the house a little early today, to turn up the heat."

"I like how that sounds," he said, and kissed her in return.

Thirteen

SEVERAL DAYS PASSED BEFORE DEL received any response from her job interviews. The first call came from the delightful manager of the high-end purse shop. Since her interview, Del had thought how much she would enjoy working with such a pleasant woman. Unfortunately, the woman didn't have the same thought. She'd hired someone else.

After three follow-up calls to the bookstore, she still hadn't managed an interview for a position there. Del was high-lighting want ads in the paper when the phone rang.

"Ms. Rufino?" said a vaguely familiar woman's voice.

"This is she," Del said, trying to place the voice. The caller ID gave no clues.

"This is Bella, at Imagine. We spoke last week?"

"Oh, yes," Del said, after a pause. She had given up hope of obtaining a job at Imagine almost from the moment she'd finished the job interview.

"I'd like to offer you the position in our store, if you are still interested." Bella was as business-like as she had been during the interview. Though Del wished she felt warmer toward a future employer, she was happy for any employer at all.

So it was that two days later, Del found herself nearing the end of her first official workday in years.

She'd arrived early, before the store opened, so that she

could fill out the necessary forms. Bella was older than Del, but it was hard to tell how much older. She could be anywhere from mature forties to well preserved sixties. She wore her brown hair in a chignon, and her style was classic, with a tasteful elegance; all business, but no rough edges here.

Bella ran Del through a tutorial on the cash register. Del had never used one before and was more than intimidated at first, though she made her greatest effort to conceal that fact.

At noon a second employee, Mary, arrived to help with what Del had been told was the lunchtime rush. Mary's personality was the polar opposite of Bella. Del guessed she must be mid-thirties. She dressed like she poured her paycheck back into the store, wore her black hair in a short, perky style that highlighted bright blue eyes and an ever present smile. She sparkled with personality.

"Is it always busier around lunch?" Del asked, neatly folding a coral shaded cashmere cardigan for a customer as Mary rang up the bill.

"It's the best time for a working woman to squeeze in a little extra shopping. Unnoticed, of course," she said, giving their customer a wink that made the woman smile.

Del wrapped the cardigan in Imagine's trademark powder blue tissue, sealed the tissue with a white sticker embossed with a pearlescent "I", and tucked the package into a beautiful, powder blue, lacquer-finished bag with powder blue ribbons for handles. Across the front of the bag was another, larger pearlescent "I". She inserted the customer's receipt into a small matching envelope and added it to the bag.

"Thank you for visiting Imagine," Del said, smiling, as she passed the bag over.

Bella had specifically instructed Del to use those words. "Our customers are our *friends*, and they don't shop, they *visit*. Always remember that."

"I think you're getting the hang of this," Mary said, "want to ring up the next *friend*?"

"Okay..." Del smiled nervously as she greeted the next customer. Mary took over wrapping duties and Del only needed help once, entering an item that was on sale.

"Not bad," Mary said when they were done.

"I wasn't sure about–"

"Oh, that sale stuff can be tricky. You'll have it down in no time."

"Mary!" Bella called from the front of the shop where she was working hard to encourage one of their *friends* to spend a large amount of money on a holiday ensemble.

"Yes, Bella?" Mary smiled.

"Could you see if we have a size eight in this, for Mrs. Roberts?" She held up an emerald green, sequined tank.

"Of course," Mary said and, grabbing Del's arm she whispered, "come help."

The back room was the size of a large living room. One corner was set with a partition to enclose Bella's desk and files. The remaining space was equally divided between a processing area for new merchandise, and rows of racks and shelves for overflow merchandise.

Mary found the eight almost immediately, then leaned against the shelf behind her. "So, how's your first day going?"

"Pretty good. But I have to admit, I feel more incompetent than competent most of the time."

"That's probably more Bella's fault than yours. She can be tough on new employees. Thought you looked like you could use a minute off the floor. Have a seat." She pointed to a folding metal chair against the wall.

"Thanks. Actually, I was surprised she even hired me. I mean, it's not that I don't think I can do the job–"

"Sure, sure." Mary nodded.

"But my interview, well, I didn't think Bella even liked me," she said, then added quickly, "I'm sure it's all in my head."

"No. It's not you. It's her. I'm sure she didn't like you, either."

"Oh." Del had no idea what to say to that. She wasn't used to not being liked.

"No, no, I don't mean it that way. She doesn't like anybody who applies. At first. See, this is a pretty popular store with a certain group of women. This stuff's not cheap, that's obvious. Some of these women, they want the discount, not the job. See what I mean?"

"I guess." Del remembered the woman at ShopCo saying the same thing. Was she the only woman in this town that actually *needed* a job? It was a silly thought, but it gave her a solitary chill all the same.

"Especially before the holidays," Mary was saying. "All this gorgeous stuff and none of it marked down in time for the company party. And all the other parties. We get women who don't have to work, but they don't want to tell their husbands how much they spent on that special dress, see? So they think, why not come to work for us just long enough to use the discount, buy the dress they want and maybe use their paycheck to cover the cost. Hubby never knows, you know?"

"Yes, I guess that would make Bella kind of suspicious."

"Of everyone! You can't blame her, really. I mean, there's a lot of work to do. We don't want to hire someone who won't work hard and then, just as we get her trained, she hits the road. Make sense?"

"Completely. It makes me...wonder."

"Why she hired you?"

"Yeah."

"She told me. She said nobody gets that nervous in a job

interview if they don't really need the job." Mary smiled. "I know she seems like a terror. But really, she's not so bad after you get to know her."

"How long have you been here?"

"Since the place opened, six years ago."

"And you and Bella..."

"I'm telling you, she's not bad. But at work, she's all about the job."

Del nodded, then remembering the tank top, "shouldn't you get that out to her, then?"

"Hmmm..." Mary looked at the clock. "Yep, I think it's been long enough."

"Huh?"

"Oh, I forgot, let me explain. If Bella needed it fast, she'd get it herself. When she asks you to get it, she's still working the sale. Bella thinks that if the customer has to wait a little longer than expected for me to find it–and I come out saying, *You're so lucky, it's the last one*!–then they *feel* lucky, and they want it even more. See?"

"So, even though we might have two or three of them..." Del said, pointing to the emerald green tanks on the rack in front of her.

"Still lucky. I know, you're thinking, it doesn't seem right. Maybe kind of a lie?"

"Well..."

"I suppose, but it's like telling someone they look great on a bad hair day. Or like they've lost weight, when they look like they haven't. It makes them feel good about themselves. We're not lying about the price, or the quality–this stuff's not cheap for a reason, it's top drawer. We're just giving them one more reason to feel good about their shopping experience. See what I mean?"

And Del did see what she meant. It wasn't completely honest, but it wasn't really a lie, was it?

"And that's why they come back, because they always feel good when they leave."

Mary winked and walked back out front. Del could hear her say, "You're so lucky! It's the last one!" She tried to remember if they had ever used that tactic on her when she had been a customer. But all she remembered was that she always felt good when she left.

Fourteen

ANDY WAS ON THE ROAD again and Gwen was avoiding her empty house. She sent Cammi home early to study for finals. She'd close the shop herself and shave an hour off her night alone at home.

DEL RAN THROUGH A SHORT list of errands on her way home from work. It was Friday night and the kids were at Micky's for the weekend. Maybe she'd pick up a video on the way home. Or there was that book she had wanted to read. When she passed the new flower pot it reminded her of Gwen, so she pulled the van, just back from the body shop, into a spot in front of the bakery.

MADISON'S NEW BEDROOM DIDN'T HAVE butterflies. At the closing, earlier in the day, the little girl had sat, pouting and grim in the corner of the conference room as her parents signed the papers and handed over the check that would make the house in The Range theirs.

Claire chose a moment when her assistance wasn't needed to take Madison down the hall in search of a juice box from the title company's fridge. She poked the straw through the hole in the box and promised little Madison that she would bring butterflies for her room. It had taken a couple of hours searching local shops, but she'd found them at last, in a garden shop just down the street from the bakery.

THE JANGLING WIND CHIMES DREW Gwen's attention away from the last of the coffee pots she rinsed in the sink behind the front case.

"Del," she said, a little surprised. Had she really expected to see her again? Gwen noticed Del's appearance had improved since the first day they'd met. Beneath a mid-length black wool coat were gray slacks and a nicely fitted antique rose blouse. Her hair was cinched in a tasteful chignon by a silver and pearl clasp.

"Hi, Gwen. Are you in the middle of something?" Del asked, pausing at the door.

"No, no, come on in, I'm just cleaning up. Almost time to close."

"Oh, well, I don't want to keep you." Del started to turn.

"No, really. It's just me, anyway. Come on in."

Del shut the door and ran her hand down to silence the chimes.

"Coffee's done for the night, but I've still got a few things in the case." Gwen nodded toward the pastry case as she wiped a pot dry.

"Thanks. No, ummm, no, actually, I was driving by and, well, I thought I'd drop in. Just to let you know, ummm-"

"The job?" Gwen asked, remembering their conversation at the ShopCo.

Del nodded. "I found one."

"Fantastic! That's really great."

"Thank you," Del said, smiling shyly.

"So where'd you find it?"

"At Imagine-the dress shop at the outlets."

"Oh yeah, I think I've been in there. I don't get dressed up too often, but...it's fun to look, right?"

"Yeah." Del stood awkwardly, as if now that she'd delivered the news, she thought perhaps she should leave.

"Tell me about it."

"Well, it's not bad. Listen, I don't want to keep you, I can leave-"

"Sit, sit, please," Gwen said. "I'm just wiping down the counters, you can keep me company. Actually, company would be good."

Del sat, her coat still on, her purse in her lap.

"So...it's not bad?"

"No, you know, I had to learn to use the cash register. Never used one before. It's fun. Who knew?" She smiled up at Gwen.

Gwen stopped and looked at Del. A warm little spot fed with memories of her own past percolated with a bit of joy for this woman who was surmounting challenges so like ones Gwen had once known well. "It is kind of fun," Gwen said. "I forget that, sometimes."

Del nodded.

"And of course," Del continued, "I have to check in the new items, steam the wrinkles sometimes, and update price tags. I even vacuum before we open. At least I knew how to do that."

"How about the people? Do you like the people you work with?"

"I do. At first, well, I wasn't sure. Bella-the manager-I wasn't sure about her. She's all business, but she's not bad. She's even taught me a lot about putting together my own wardrobe."

"That's good, I mean, that she's not bad to work with."

"You're nice, but I think, maybe I did need a little help

putting clothes together. Haven't really had to think about it much before. I guess I was kinda stuck...wearing jeans, or jumpers all the time."

"Hmmm." Gwen nodded.

The chimes jangled again and in walked Claire. "Well," she said, looking from Gwen to Del. "This is just like old times!"

"Hi, Claire," Gwen said.

"Hi," Del added, clutching her purse tighter.

"How you doing, kiddo?" Claire said to Del.

"Pretty good."

"Del was just telling me about her new job. At Imagine. You know the place?"

"I love that place. You work there?" Claire asked.

Del nodded.

"I'll stop in."

"Coffee's gone for the day," Gwen said, wondering if Claire was stopping in for her caffeine fix before working late into the night. "Sorry. I could zap some water in the microwave for tea. Anybody want tea?"

"Don't' worry about it," Claire said as she joined Del at the table. "I'm done for the day. I had some shopping to do and was nearby, so thought I'd stop in.

Glad I did," she said, looking at Del. "It's been a long week, figured I'd hide out at home from my voicemail with a glass or three of wine."

"I should probably go home..." Del rose from her chair.

"Hot date?" Claire asked.

"No."

"Gotta pick up kids?" Gwen asked.

"No. They're at Micky's for the weekend."

"Kids are gone and you're just going to hang out at home?"

"Well..."

"Say," Gwen said, realizing that it might be nicer to take

some time getting to know these women, than to spend the evening alone again. "Andy, my husband, is out of town tonight. I was going to go home and put a pot pie in the oven. Watch the news. How about, instead, I'll open a bottle of wine, get out the crackers and cheese...for the three of us? I live in the house on the hill–right behind the shop."

"Don't you have to close up...some more?" Del asked, looking around the store, as though uncertain exactly what that entailed.

"I'm done here, really. All I have to do is turn out the lights and lock up. You could pull your cars around back, in front of the house and I'll meet you there."

"I'm game," said Claire. It wasn't quite the night she'd planned, but it wasn't like she'd really planned anything at all. And hadn't she promised herself she'd work on a friendship or two? Could it hurt to try it again?

"Del?" Gwen said.

Del didn't have to be at work until early the next afternoon. Sandy had food and water and a little doggie door for nature's call. She didn't have to go home right away, she supposed.

"Just for a little while." Gwen said. "Keep me company, you know?"

"I suppose, for a little while," said Del.

"What the hell," said Claire.

"SO THIS BELLA BABE, SHE'S tough, but she's not really a bitch?" Claire asked Del as she accepted a glass of pinot grigio from Gwen.

The women were settled in front of Gwen's fireplace, watching the logs respond to the tinder and matches Gwen lit when they'd first arrived. Outside, a light snow fell.

Inside, Gwen passed full glasses around and set cheese and crackers, chips and salsa, and a plate of small sugar cookies from the bakery within easy reach.

Del was in the midst of recapping her new job to Claire. "No, she's...fair. It's not that she's mean, only serious about her job."

"She's run the store for several years, right?" Gwen asked.

"Since they opened."

"Is she the owner?" Claire asked.

"I don't think so. I mean, there are a few other stores in the chain, but this is the only one in an outlet mall."

"Yeah, but it's not like they really cut the prices, right?"

"For sales, they do. And there's always a sale rack. And almost all the prices are marked down ten percent from the regular stores."

"I've been to the regular stores," Claire said.

"Ten percent from God awful expensive is still expensive, but hey, when you want something special, you can't beat the quality."

"Bella's very proud of the store."

"I bet she gets a piece of the profit," Claire said. "Nobody sticks around that long with that much loyalty without the bottom line. So, it sounds like it's working out for you."

"I guess so. I mean, for now."

"But not your dream-come-true, life-fulfilling job, right?"

"Right. Thing is, I'm not sure what that is. For me, anyway. Like you Gwen, I can tell you love your bakery."

"I love to bake...and eat, unfortunately." Gwen said, smiling as they both laughed.

"And Claire," Del said, "you must love real estate. I always thought it would be fun to be a real estate agent."

"Oh, don't go there, you are way too nice for this business."

"You seem...nice," Del said, afraid of insulting her new

acquaintance.

"Thanks, kiddo. You're sweet. And I am nice. At least I don't bite." They laughed. "In fact, I can be friggin' nice all day long. It's funny, I probably started out that way, haven't thought about that in a long time. Yeah, I was nice, and I still want to be.

"Over the years, you put up with so much shit. I'm the target. Buyer's offer is too low, sellers want too much, loan didn't come through; you name it, my fault.

It's always easier to blame the person who's getting paid for whatever shit comes along. Clients think we make too much-easy money-they don't have a clue."

"I love going to open houses, seeing the decorations, the floor plans," Del said. "I always go if there's one in my neighborhood, just to see."

"*Looky-loos*," Claire said. "That's what I call the neighbors who drop by."

"They're a problem?" Gwen asked.

"Oh, no. It's a curiosity thing and I totally get it. Hey, I like looking at houses, too. Besides, every once in a while one of those neighbors becomes a new client."

"That's nice," Del said, sipping her wine, enjoying the warmth from within as well as the growing warmth of the fire.

"Used to be. I don't do many open houses anymore, though."

"Too busy?" Gwen asked.

"No, too risky."

"You mean liability?" Gwen asked. "All those strangers going through the house?"

"Sure, there's that. Anybody in the world can come through. I can only keep my eye on so many at a time. And you wouldn't believe the stuff-valuable stuff-people leave lying around in plain sight. Sometimes I've got to tuck jewelry, cash–even condoms–into drawers before I open up."

"Condoms?" Del coughed on her wine and felt her cheeks flush. She still had the condoms in her purse that she'd purchased at the 7-11.

"But that's not what I mean by risky. Last year I did a deal with a gal who was assaulted in a house."

"Oh, my God!" Del's eyes grew wide, and she took a larger sip from her glass.

"Poor woman," Gwen said. "She was still selling homes after that?"

"Yeah, and it wasn't pretty. Though it took guts, I had to give her that. But she really shouldn't have stayed in the business. She was terrified of talking to strangers."

"It seems like that would be part of the job description," Gwen said.

"You've got that. I worked through her office, over the phone, when I could get her to answer. The only time I saw her in person was over the closing table, and it was bizarre. She couldn't look at me or talk to me directly, had to hold a notebook or papers in front of her face, never addressed my client."

"What did your client think?" Gwen asked.

"He didn't get it at all. I'd explained the situation early on, told him that was why it took forever to get simple answers, but he had no patience. Even at the closing table he was his delightful, aggressive asshole self. And you can imagine how, being in a small, closed room, freaked out the poor agent. What a nightmare for all of us. No, I don't like taking chances, just too freaky out there. That's why I carry a Taser."

"You have one of those?" Gwen asked.

"What's that?" Del asked.

"It shoots out wires that carry fifty-thousand friggin' volts. I like it better than my gun."

"You've got a *real gun*, too?" Del asked, shocked.

"Used to. Traded it in for the Taser. Every gal should have one. It's easy to use and less messy-and no blood. It's the size of a small pistol." She reached down for her purse and unzipped it. "I stick it in one of the inside pockets of my purse," she said and pulled out a black leather case. "See, it's in a case." She snapped open the end of the leather holder.

Gwen and Del stared, but neither moved to touch the case, or the black and lavender stun gun inside.

"Isn't that dangerous?" Del asked.

"Naw, I don't always turn it on-it's not on now-and even then, I put the safety on."

"I like the color," Del added warily.

"Ever use it?" Gwen asked.

"Not on a person." Claire said, tucking the case back inside her purse. "I had a friend show me how it worked. I zapped the air for a second or two."

"Friend?"

"Very sweet police officer over in Breck," Claire said, referring to the town of Breckenridge.

"That was nice of her,"

"Him. Yes, he's *very* nice." She smiled wickedly and laughed. "Very fit, too."

"I'm going to remember to be nicer when I go to open houses," Del said. "Well, if I ever go again. It doesn't seem like I ever have free time anymore. I've only been working a short while, but between the kids' schedules, work and all the other things I have to do, there's not much free time."

"It's overwhelming sometimes, but it'll get better," Gwen said reassuringly.

"*You* will get better at juggling it all, you mean," Claire added.

"Exactly," Gwen agreed. "Some days are still insane for me-especially during the holidays. With Thanksgiving only a couple weeks away, my workdays are getting longer."

"I think it would be fun to own a bakery during the holidays," Del said. "Everyone's so happy, and all your wonderful cakes and pastries, they must make people happier."

"That's true. But during the holidays they want so many *more* of them, and they want them all at the same time. It can be crazy, lots of long days, but I can't complain about holiday income. I make a lot to carry me through the leaner times of the year, so I appreciate that a lot. Especially this year."

"What's this year?" Claire asked.

"Oh, it's Andy." Gwen saw the worried looks on their faces. "No, everything's fine-with us, that is. *We* are not the problem. It's Andy's company. Looks like there may be a strike, we don't know for sure, and it could be months yet. These things sometimes drag on like you would not believe, but if they strike..."

"Gotcha," Claire said. "My father was in management, but strikes aren't fun no matter what end you're on. Nobody wins."

"Exactly. So he's doing these long hauls, like he's on tonight. He doesn't enjoy them anymore than I do, but they bring in extra money. Just in case."

"And you're home alone at night, too," Del said.

"Hmm-mm." Gwen nodded.

"Do you...like it?"Del asked.

"Being alone? Not much. Well, sure, sometimes it's nice to have the place to myself, but..."

"Gets quiet," Claire said. "I've got a few places around town I don't mind hanging out, when it's too quiet. In fact, I was thinking about dropping by the Dockside tonight, before your offer." She toasted her hostess, sipped and then watched the light from the flames play off the rim of her glass.

"Isn't that a bar?" Del asked, a little surprised.

"You've got something against bars?"

"No-no," Del said, taking a large gulp of her wine. She usually didn't drink anything as dry as this wine, but she was amazed at how much better it got the more she drank.

"Don't worry, Del, I'm not offended. I get you. That's not your thing; you're home with the kids, doing family stuff. I totally get that. It's nice, in fact."

"I like the Dockside, it's a restaurant too, Del," Gwen said. "Andy and I go there once in a while. I love their nachos."

"Great nachos," Claire agreed. "Jimmy, the owner, he's a good guy." It was Claire's turn to see a look on their faces and she added, "just a friend."

"Really," Gwen said.

"He's good conversation, and he keeps the drunks at bay. Besides, he's too old for me."

"Really?" Gwen asked, thinking Jimmy seemed about their age, but she recalled Claire's interest in the young paramedic who attended Del after the accident.

"Mature men are highly overrated. Not that I'm into robbing the cradle, but..."

"Boy toys?" Gwen asked, smiling.

"What?" Del's eyes grew large.

"Not *little* boys, Del." Claire laughed. "Believe me, they're big enough to go out without their mommies! Plenty big enough!"

"Claire!" Del said.

"You cannot be that naïve, Del. And if you are, well, now I know why God sent you to me. Next time I go to the Dockside, I'm taking you with me."

"Oh, no, I don't think I'd...I mean-"

"You'll have a blast. Maybe we'll come get Gwen, too, if she's alone."

"Maybe. I do love those nachos."

"So, that's what I do when I'm home alone. What do you

do Gwen?"

"Well, there's chicken pot pie and the news," she said.

"And you paint?" Claire said, nodding at the easel in the corner. She had looked it over while Gwen was getting the wine, noticed the half finished watercolor of a smooth, cylindrical shell, an open box filled with more shells, and a small collection of photos of people, some familiar from around town.

"Yeah," Gwen said, hesitantly, realizing that her watercolor of Del's shell was displayed on the easel.

"It's nice," Claire said, walking over to look at the painting. "You're very good; did you study art in school?"

"No, I picked it up on my own. Seemed like fun."

"How pretty," Del said, looking, unknowingly, over Claire's shoulder at her own unfinished self.

"Thank you," Gwen said, smiling.

"How nice to be able to make something so beautiful."

"It is nice," Claire agreed.

"It helps pass the time, that's for sure."

"So I visit Jimmy, and you paint," Claire said, standing with her back to the fire, enjoying the warmth. "What about you, Del? What do you do when you're home alone?"

Del thought a moment, looking out at snow drifting past the window, "I guess-" A loud pop from a log in the fire made her jump. "I guess I'm still figuring that out."

"THANKS FOR YOUR HELP, CLAIRE," Gwen said. Del's level of inebriation had kept pace with the falling snow throughout the evening. Gwen tried to get her to stay over, but Del insisted on going home to Sandy. Claire thought she was nuts to worry about a dog, but she'd agreed all the same to follow Gwen as she drove Del home in

Del's van, then Claire had returned Gwen to her own home.

"What are you gonna do," she said, pulling up in front of Gwen's house, "let the poor kid drive herself home and get in another accident? Nah, she's had it tough enough lately."

"Big learning curve."

"She'll get tougher with time. We all do."

"Or at least we seem to," Gwen said, smiling.

"Just don't go telling everybody what a softie I am for little lost puppies."

"And newly divorced friends," Gwen said, opening the door. "Thanks again!"

"Hey, thank *you*. It was a nice change from the Dockside."

Claire watched as Gwen ran up the snowy walk and let herself safely into her home before driving away.

Friends, Claire thought, were they friends? She supposed they were, or at least they were on their way to becoming friends. She wanted to feel good about that, but there was always that reserve. Old habits die hard and old wounds leave scars.

Fifteen

✦✦✦

HER FIRST AWARENESS UPON WAKING the next morning was of the snug warmth of her bed on a chilly morning and Sandy's soft breath against her ear where the dog had curled up on her pillow. Then she noticed the headache and remembered the night before when Gwen and Claire had driven her home.

"Ohhh," she moaned into her pillow. What must they think? Del really liked Gwen. What must she think of her? She wasn't quite sure what to think of Claire, but still, she was mortified that they had seen her in such a condition. She was mortified she had been in such a condition. What had possessed her to drink so much? How could she face them again?

But of course, she would have to. At the very least, she would need to stop by the bakery and apologize to Gwen. As for Claire, well, Gwen would probably pass it on to her. Then she wouldn't have to face her at all.

If only she could spend the day in bed with Sandy and her humiliation. Instead, she had to work. At least, she thought, she had a few hours to get herself together before she had to be there. That's when the phone rang. The sound pierced through her like a physical sensation.

"Ohhh..." Del put one hand to her head, as if that would hold it together, while she reached for the phone. Not since college had she paid so painfully for the night before.

"Hello?" she said, hoarsely, making an effort to keep her voice low. The voice on the other end, however, was far less soothing, and far more chipper.

"Hey, Del. It's Mary!"

"Hi...Mary." It took Del's handicapped brain cells a few seconds to process that Mary was her fellow employee at Imagine.

"We are really snowed in up here."

"Oh?" Del knew Mary's home, several miles outside of Blue River, was high up, overlooking Elk Creek Canyon.

"How's it look down there?"

"Snow?"

"The white stuff. Did you get much down there?" Del remembered snow from the night before. How much snow?

"Ummm..." Del swung her legs out of bed, "I'd say about..." She walked over to the window. It was, indeed, a winter wonderland. But the layer of white didn't look like a serious accumulation. "Maybe four or five inches."

"That's not bad at all. We've got close to a foot and a half! What a difference a thousand feet makes, huh?"

"Sounds like it."

"Listen. I've got a big favor to ask. I was thinking that if you got hit as hard as we did, the shop would open late and it wouldn't matter. But, there's no way I'll be able to dig out, *and* be presentable for work in a couple of hours. Would you mind very much taking my early shift? Then I can come in late morning and you'll get off earlier. What do you think?

Del looked at the clock: seven-forty-five. The store opened at ten. Of all mornings to be pulled from her soft, warm bed, she thought. But Del knew the old saying: what goes around comes around. Years of volunteer work had taught her that. Someday she'd need a favor from Mary. And besides, tomorrow was Sunday. She had Sunday's off.

"Sure."

"You're fantastic! I'll hustle and be in as soon as possible."

"Don't worry. Take your time and be safe on the road. I'll explain to Bella when I get in."

"You're a doll. I owe you!"

Del sat down on her bed, and Sandy hopped into her lap. "Well, sweetie, looks like mommy has to get going." Sandy stood to lick Del's chin, her front legs propped against Del's chest. "Tomorrow we sleep in. I promise."

A LONG HOT SHOWER, FOUR IBUPROFEN chased down by a strong cup of tea at home, and a triple latte from the coffee shop at the outlets had improved Del's hangover enough to make her reasonably functional.

Del and Bella arrived at the same time, and together they opened up the shop. Bella was never happy with the work of the janitorial staff, so Del gave the carpets a fresh once over with the vacuum. Del noticed that the brisk morning air, combined with productive activity perked her up even more.

Bella, who liked the impression fresh flowers made, arranged a bouquet of white lilies on the counter while Del counted out the cash drawer.

"Del, I know you haven't worked here for a while, but I think you are truly getting the knack of it."

"Thank you, Bella," Del said, genuinely appreciative. She didn't think of Bella as the sort to idly hand out compliments.

"Well, I mean it. And I just want you to know that, when your first month's review comes up, there will be a positive adjustment in your hourly, and an increase in your store discount."

"Really?" Bella had promised regular raises and an increased discount over time, but Del hadn't expected anything so soon.

"I know, it seems early. But I can tell you're serious about your commitment to Imagine, and I don't want to lose you. I make it a point to appreciate employees who appreciate their position here."

"I do, and thank you again."

"Don't mention it. Reliable employees are hard to come by. Now, I need to take that linen suit–the one Mrs. Andrews returned–out to the dry cleaners before I put it on the sale rack."

"Is it in bad shape?"

"No. But it's clear she wore it; probably the plan all along. Some of our *friends* do that sort of thing now and then."

Some friends, Del thought.

"Nevertheless, a fresh press should make it more than presentable. I'll be back shortly."

With Bella gone, Del passed the time refolding cardigans on the front table. Funny, she thought, she never would have guessed she would enjoy her new job, but she really did. There was something comforting in having a place and a purpose.

The door chime rang and in walked Ted from the shoe store next door, stomping a thin layer of snow from his shoes as he entered.

"Hey, gorgeous, can I trade you a couple bucks for some quarters? The bank screwed up our bag this morning."

"Sure," Del said, taking the dollars to the register. Ted was forty-something, three piece suit, slightly graying, and more than interested in any available woman within walking distance of his shop. Since he'd discovered Del, his bag seemed always short of change.

"So Del, you got any plans for tonight? Saturday night and

all. Want to meet me for happy hour?"

"I'm sorry, Ted, family plans tonight," Del lied. The kids were with Micky for the weekend. She just couldn't bring herself to be so rude as to actually tell Ted she wasn't interested in him, but she was determined to always have an excuse.

"Kids, eh? I like kids. Do you have a sitter? Ellen's daughter babysits."

Del knew Ellen. She worked at the luggage shop across from Imagine and she'd already mentioned her daughter's babysitting business, but Del had her own babysitters. Not that she had babies anymore. Nate and Cara were nearly old enough to be home on their own. Nearly.

"Thanks, but, like I said, we already have plans."

"Okay, but I'll catch you another time. We'd have a great time together, know what I mean?" He leaned in beside her as she counted off the quarters, resting his arm along the top of the register and closing the gap between them to something less than what Del considered acceptable personal space. His cologne, administered with a heavy hand, hung in the small void between them.

"Del. What's that short for?"

"Adele," Del answered in as friendly a tone as she could, trying to ignore his increasing efforts at intimacy.

"Adele. That's gorgeous, just like you."

"Thank you." She smiled tightly.

"So, I heard through the grapevine that you're getting divorced."

"What?" Del was shocked that he knew personal details, and also wondered who would have talked about it. Who knew? Bella and Mary, but would they talk about that? "How..."

"Not important. What's important is that you and I, I think we could have a great time. I can help you get back out there, be a transitional figure, so to speak."

"Excuse me?" Del had been so busy wondering if Mary or Bella had said something, she hadn't been paying much attention to Ted.

"No worries, gorgeous. No STDs; I'm a safe bet. We can have some fun, get you back out in circulation, know what I mean?"

It was finally dawning on Del just exactly what he meant and she stood there, her mouth slightly agape, amazed that he was proposing what he was proposing, and in the manner he was proposing it, when she was literally saved from comment by the bell.

The front door chimed and in walked two women, chatting amiably as they began picking through the table of cardigans Del had been folding.

"Here are your quarters," Del said at last, handing them over, careful not to let her hand linger close to his.

"Guess I'd better get back," Ted said, taking his quarters, but then leaning close to whisper in her ear. "Don't forget my offer, A-Del. Baby, you won't regret it."

He winked, turned and left. Del went into the bathroom in back, took a washcloth and washed her ear and the side of her neck where his breath had touched. Then she sprayed a mist of air freshener heavily before her and walked through it to remove the lingering scent of his cologne before she returned to help her customers.

BY LATE AFTERNOON THE HIGH altitude sunshine had melted most of the snow from the sidewalks and streets, but clumps still clung to the grass. Though the descent of the sun brought a nip of late autumn to the air, it was still so warm that Claire was hot in a sweater set and slacks.

She waved goodbye once more as she walked to her car. Madison was still standing in the doorway, giggling and waving, holding a pink and lavender stuffed butterfly in one hand, clutching a butterfly book in her other arm, her tiny fingers dancing in a wave from the edge of the book.

"Score one for the realtor," Claire said under her breath. Madison's parents were thrilled to see their previously pouting princess smiling with delight at the butterfly gifts Claire had brought for her room.   Carol held a delicate butterfly mobile, as well. Her son was happily pushing a bulldozer-another gift from Claire-through the woodchips in the front garden of their new home in The Range. Happy children and happy homeowners hopefully meant many referrals.

Claire glanced over her shoulder once more, catching a last glimpse of Madison's smile. So like another little smile she never could resist.

BOB HAD BEEN SITTING ON his front patio, tasting a new white from an Oregon vintner and enjoying the late afternoon, when Claire had pulled up in front of the new neighbor's house.

He's watched her juggle an armful of packages from the back of an expensive black SUV-ette, watched the new neighbors let her in, happy greetings all around, and then he sat, waiting. He refilled his glass, swirled and sniffed, savored and watched.

Finally the front door opened. A little boy raced out with his truck; a little girl laughed.

Bob set down his glass and stood.

Claire waved goodbye and walked down the sidewalk toward her car, parked in the street out front.

Bob walked diagonally across his lawn, toward Claire's car.

Claire turned to wave one last time before Carol shut the door.

Bob reached the sidewalk.

Claire, still smiling, dug through her purse for her car keys.

Bob walked across the street.

Claire reached her car, looked up and saw Bob coming across the street. Her smile froze.

"Hello again," he said, approaching the car.

She knew the face. What was the name? She turned her keys in her hand, still smiling at him, felt the small pepper spray canister that was part of her keychain and nonchalantly placed that hand behind her back. Then it came to her. "Bob."

"Claire," he said, rounding her car and shaking her free hand. "You mentioned you had clients up this way. The new neighbors?"

"Yes. You live..." She let that hang, wondering for a second if he'd been stalking her.

"Just there," he said, pointing to a stone and wood contemporary she'd always admired from the street. "I was on the porch, having a glass of wine and getting ready to enjoy the sunset. Never know how many opportunities you'll get to enjoy fine weather this time of year."

"Hate to pass up a good chance," Claire agreed.

"I never pass up a good chance when it comes along."

"Hm." Claire nodded curtly.

"So, I don't suppose I could tempt you to join me on the porch? Don't like to drink alone, and it's a very good wine."

"Well, I'd love to..." she said slowly, planning her escape and switching her grip from pepper spray to keys.

"Now Claire, I hear the word *but* coming in that sentence. Hard to believe I can't get a professional such as yourself to join me for one glass of a very fine chardonnay. I might want to discuss selling my house."

"*Do* you want to sell your house?" she asked, walking around to the driver's side.

"Not really. It's a nice house."

"I agree. And besides," she said, unlocking the door, "I prefer red. And I have an appointment." She didn't.

"Maybe another time? I have reds, too."

"Maybe. Thanks anyway. Nice to see you." She got in the car and left. She might have wanted to look back, but she didn't, not even in the review mirror.

Claire loved red. And white. And many shades in between. But what she didn't love, and what she prided herself as an expert on avoiding, was a man like Bob, who had commitment written all over him.

"FUNNY THING HAPPENED WHILE I was on the road," Andy said, sharing a glass of wine with Gwen as they sat, cuddled together on the couch in front of the same fireplace she'd shared with the girls a couple nights before.

"I don't like *funny* when you're on the road; I like dull and boring, same old same old." She kissed his earlobe and then began to nibble.

"No worries there, babe, it was all of that. But Bob called me on my cell."

"Back-in-town Bob?"

"The very same."

"What, he was lonely? Bob's not-"

"Don't worry, Bob likes the ladies."

"Then how come we never see him with any?"

"Well, he doesn't talk about it much, but from what I've picked up, I'd say his divorce was pretty nasty. He's taking it slow."

"More like a prehistoric crawl. Hasn't it been six or seven years? Isn't that why he bought the vineyard and moved out here from wherever it is he's from?"

"Chicago. Yeah, it's been a while. I think he's had some lady friends, but nobody special, nobody long term."

"That's pretty cautious, all right."

"Like I said, it was nasty."

"So, he called you for therapy?"

"Cute-hey!" He jerked his head and rubbed his earlobe.

"Too hard?" She giggled and then, moving her hand to other regions, added, "no, just right."

"Let's move this reunion into the bedroom," Andy said, slipping his hand beneath her shirt.

Later, her head nestled in the crook of his naked shoulder, Gwen's mind drifted easily over the events of the day, and her curiosity returned. "So what about Bob?"

"Bob? How can you talk about another man right after we've made love?"

"It's all the testosterone in the air. What about Bob?"

"Okay." He pushed his hand through her long, straight hair, flowing a silken brown wave of it over her shoulder. Then he ran his hand slowly down her arm, pulling her closer. "You remember the other day-when he stopped by the bakery?"

"Sure."

"Well, you went back to the kitchen and Bob and I were talking. He wanted to know what was new, one thing led to another, I mentioned the long haul I'd just gotten back from and that brought up the strike."

"Bob have a thing for unions?"

"No, he has a thing for business. Thinks I seem like the sort of person who can take charge of things-work kind of independently, if I need to."

"I'd agree with that. You're always the one in charge no matter what you're doing." She played with the hair on his chest, swirling it with her fingers, forming peaks, brushing them away and reforming them. Gwen remembered when she first met her husband, how stray hairs peaked alluringly from the collar of his shirt. The desire to find the source had teased her interest.

"Guess Bob thinks so. He offered me a job."

"Is he starting a business here?"

"No, at the winery."

"On the western slope?" Gwen lifted her head up to look into his eyes. "And you said?"

"I said I have to talk with my wife." He softly pushed her head back down.

"Good answer. You win points for that answer."

"We're counting?"

"Sometimes. Is this like, in case of a strike? Something part-time?"

"Well, yeah, if we strike, but not part-time. Things are slow there right now, not so much to do. But in spring, it gets busier. If I went before, he'd give me some training. I don't need to be an expert on wine.

I just need to be good at organizing people, and I like physical work. You know I like working outdoors, and working with my hands."

"Hmmm-mm," Gwen nodded. She didn't want to jump right in and protest; she'd learned from her own experience that one had to keep an open mind about life's possibilities. Still. "Still..."

"I know. I don't need to decide anything right away. But it would be a big change, Babe. A new career."

"What about the bakery?"

"We'll open another one there. Something tells me if Bob is your cheerleader, you'll draw customers."

"Maybe," she said, thinking about her customers in Blue River. Gwen didn't like change, but her divorce had forced her to get good at it. With the bakery's growing success, and her new life with Andy, she'd grown comfortable. She'd begun to assume the days of change were safely over.

"It's just an offer, just something to consider. I was surprised he offered. I thought at first it was a pity thing but, well, one of his best managers is leaving."

"He really needs help?"

"Yep."

"It's nice of him to think of you. Now."

"He said he felt he'd be doing himself a favor, just as much as doing one for me."

"Nice."

"Yeah, but, like I said, we've got time to think about it. He understands, and he wouldn't be ready for me for a while anyway."

"Okay." Gwen rolled over and spooned up against her husband in the dark. He wrapped his arm around her and she pulled it tight.

They lay quietly, holding each other. She heard his breathing fall into an even, deep pattern and felt his grip loosen and her anxiety surrender as a wine-infused exhaustion washed over her. "Can't hurt to think about it, I suppose," she said, almost to herself.

"I love you," he whispered in her ear, and pulled her close again.

Sixteen

SUNDAY WAS HER DAY OF rest. Del didn't have to work, and the kids were still at Micky's, so she wouldn't have to encourage them out of bed in time for church; an old habit she was trying to get back into. In fact, she realized, she wouldn't have to encourage herself out of bed for church either. She slept in. When she finally got up, she made chocolate chip pancakes, sipped her coffee slowly, and read every cartoon in the comics section.

Around noon she gave in to civility and took a shower, did her hair and make-up, and was considering the rest of her day when the doorbell rang.

"Father Frank?" she said, startled to find her pastor at her door on a Sunday afternoon. Tall and stout, he'd clearly been athletic in his youth, but now, in his mid-sixties, time and the cares of his flock were taking their toll. He looked thinner than she remembered, though she saw him most Sundays. And his once bright red hair was fading into silver.

"Good afternoon, Adele. May I come in?"

She offered him coffee, which he declined. Something about saving room for a late lunch after their *visit*. She picked the scattered Sunday paper off the couch, feeling like a criminal hiding the evidence, and offered him a seat. The last time Father Frank had visited her home she was organizing a bake sale. And Micky still lived there.

"I apologize for dropping in unexpectedly."

"You're always welcome," Del said, smiling, though inside she couldn't imagine why he'd visit her. Maybe they needed help with another bake sale. Del had a reputation at her church as a successful chairperson for any fundraising need.

"Well, it's Sunday afternoon and I'm sure you have plans," he said, eyeing the newspapers she'd piled on the coffee table, "so I'll get right to the point. Your mother asked me to stop by."

"Oh, God!" Del was immediately embarrassed by her reaction and promptly followed up with, "Father, I'm so sorry."

"Don't be; perfectly natural reaction." He smiled.

"What–what did she...say?"

"Adele, in my vocation, I am frequently called upon to help others during their darkest times." Del opened her mouth to speak and he quickly silenced her. "No, wait, let me just say this. It is not always the person themselves who requests my help. Sometimes it is a well meaning third party. I stress *well meaning*, because it is not at all uncommon for parents to ask me to intervene in situations where I realize I may not be welcome. But I often respond because I understand the request is made out of concern for a loved one."

Del had known him all her life, and felt comfortable in his presence. For a man in the business of God, he had a remarkable ability to refrain from judgment. "I'm going to kill my mother," she said.

"And you would not be the first to feel that way." He smiled and gave her a fatherly pat on the hand. She was blessed, she knew, that in spite of the death of her father several years ago, there was still one person in the world who felt a paternal inclination toward her. "Your mother is simply worried."

"She always disliked Micky," Del said, slumping back on the couch and holding her arms tight around her. "I almost feel like this whole situation gives her satisfaction."

"I've known Evelyn many years, and I would not describe her as one who is cautious in sharing her thoughts and feelings-"

"Oh, you've got that right, Father Frank."

"Exactly. But nevertheless, I know how much she loves you and your brothers. She's very protective. And sometimes people who are protective try too hard to solve the problems of those they love. They forget that they shouldn't try to solve a person's problems until, and unless, they are asked."

"That's Mother, all right."

"And that is why I am not coming by to offer solutions to your problems either-not that I could-and I'm not even presuming you have problems. I recognize that it's possible you're satisfied with how your life is progressing. Still, I promised Evelyn that I'd drop by and I have. Beyond that, I want you to know that you are in my prayers and, if you ever want a sympathetic ear, well, you know where to find me."

"Father Frank, you are a saint to put up with my mother. And I appreciate the offer." Then, remembering her mother's concern, she asked, "I did want to find out about one thing..."

"Yes?"

"Annulments."

"Have you decided to apply for annulment of your marriage?"

"I'm sure Micky couldn't care less. He wasn't raised Catholic."

"And you?"

"I don't know how I feel. I guess when I really get down to it, well, divorce is the real world. And annulment deals with some other world that I'm not so sure I connect with anymore. Does the church still take this sort of thing all that seriously? Mother says the kids will be illegitimate-isn't that kind of old fashioned?"

"The church takes it seriously, but in this modern world different parishes have their own approaches. I can assure you, Adele, you will never feel in any way betrayed or ostracized in our parish. If you decide to pursue that line, I'll be happy to go over the details with you. It has its formalities but it's not the medieval process it's often made out to be. And no, the church does not consider the children of annulled marriages illegitimate."

"At least that's one less thing she can stop worrying over. I'll consider the annulment, Father, but for now, I think a plain old divorce is all I can handle, with or without my mother's two cents." Del sighed and some of her tension eased. "She loves me, and that's why she worries. I just wish..."

"She'd trust you more," Father Frank said.

"Yes. I'm not always sure myself. Still, it would help if I had her support. Not gonna hold my breath on that one, though!"

"Different people show their support in different ways."

"I know. She supports by worrying. I'll try to be comforted by that thought. And I'll try really hard not to think of it as interference."

"A good plan, I think. Of course, I couldn't leave without at least asking you how you are doing."

"Well, I think I'm doing pretty well. In fact, maybe better than good; at least, better than I was doing at first."

"I'm glad to hear that. It makes me think prayer works."

"If you didn't think that, I'd be worried! I do appreciate the prayers, Father Frank, really I do, and I'll keep the offer in mind."

"Sounds like a plan. Now, I'd better go. A few of the women in the auxiliary are taking me out to lunch. I believe they have desires with regard to renovating the vestry."

"No rest for the wicked?"

"At least you didn't say, *from* the wicked. Well, Sunday *is* a work day for me, after all."

The Father bestowed a long, loving hug before leaving her. It was better than a trip to confession. She felt cleansed.

THE PREVIOUS DAY'S SNOW WAS a distant memory marked only by random damp patches trickling onto the pavement. Del dodged most of them, but Sandy stopped occasionally for a drink. Sunday had turned into such a lovely day, Del couldn't resist a long walk with her loyal miniature poodle. As winter's approach loomed inevitably, the lure of warm sunny days became more irresistible.

Though she dearly missed being intimately involved in her children's coming and goings, she was increasingly aware of simple, new found luxuries like an evening alone with a good book, or a long walk on a beautiful day. Full-time mothers seldom had time for such solitary pursuits.

Micky had planned to take Cara and Nate to dinner before bringing them back home. That left Del with only her own dinner to plan, and she was seriously considering something take-out when her door bell rang. Two visitors on one Sunday. She hesitated when she reached the door, wondering if her mother had decided to follow up on Father Frank's surprise visit. But her visitor was an even bigger surprise.

"Gwen," Del said, the ease of her day suddenly washing away in the memory of her hangover the previous morning.

"Hi Del, I'm not dropping by at a bad time, am I?"

"No, I ummm..."

"I would have called first but, well, I don't have your number. I tried to look it up, but it's unlisted?"

"Oh, yes. That was Micky's idea. Being an attorney, he didn't want his number to be public."

"Makes sense."

"I guess I could change that now."

"I suppose you could."

"I don't mind people having my number."

Gwen nodded her head and smiled. "So, anyway, I knew where you lived...after the other night."

Del flushed with embarrassment at the memory. "Thank you, again," she said, "I really feel badly about that."

"Don't. Really. Everybody has those days–God knows if anyone deserved to kick back and have a few glasses of wine, it was you."

"But to have you and Claire out in bad weather driving me home..." Del clasped her hands together and tapped them anxiously to her chin. "I don't know what to say."

"You said it already, remember? *Thank you* is more than enough. What are friends for? So, the reason I stopped by–"

"Oh–I'm so sorry." Del shook her head as if coming to her senses. "Please, come in. Would you like something to drink? I just came in from taking Sandy for a walk; I was going to have a cup of tea."

"Tea sounds good, thanks."

Del set a basket of assorted tea bags on the coffee table in the family room for Gwen to pick through while she filled cups with water and put them in the microwave. "Cream? Sugar?" she called from the kitchen.

"A little of both would be great. Your home is lovely, Del." Gwen looked around the room, admiring Del's décor. It was a comfortable mix of contemporary sectional and chairs in pale, creamy earth tones with handcrafted wooden accent tables clustered around a river stone hearth.

"Thank you," Del said, carrying a tray of tea cups, cream and sugar. "The house is me," she said, handing Gwen her

cup and settling in beside her. "I know it must seem sometimes that Micky made all the decisions in my life. Before.
But the house, that was mine to do. He wasn't home that
much anyway."

"You did good," Gwen said, stirring cream into her tea.
"Anyway, the reason I came by..." she picked up her purse
and pulled out an envelope and handed it to Del. "This is
yours."

"Huh?" Del took the envelope, wondering if she'd left
something at Del's house, but couldn't imagine what.

"You know the snow pool?"

"Ummm..." Del thought it sounded familiar.

"Not sure we ever talked about this, but I have this contest
every year: the snow pool. Folks buy dates on the calendar
at the bakery-dollar a date-and the lucky winner is the one
who buys the date that the first measurable two inches of
snow falls on the edge of my flowerpot out front. You had
the winning date!"

"I don't remember buying a ticket." Del sipped at her cup.

"You didn't, actually. I guess she never told you, but Claire
bought a few tickets for you, after the accident. She said she
thought you could use some good luck."

"You're kidding. That's so...nice."

"I know. I'm starting to discover that Claire is sometimes
not what you expect."

"In a good way."

"That's it. So look inside; you did pretty well."

"Wow," Del opened the envelope and counted the twenties and change.

"One hundred and seven dollars. Not bad for a buck a
day. Lucky for you I have some customers who expect the
snow to start in September-which it could-and others who
don't expect much until December-which could happen too.
Luckily for the skiers that doesn't happen too often."

"I ought to split this with Claire."

"Naw, I'm sure she wouldn't let you. But she'd probably let you buy her a drink sometime."

"That's the least I could do. Maybe I can host the next girl's night out. I'll have to call her."

"Good idea. I'm sure she's in the book." Gwen, in fact, *knew* she was. She'd called Claire to tell her, and ask if she wanted to personally deliver Del's winnings.

"That's great!" Claire had said, sounding happier than when she had, at first, thought she might have been the winner, herself. *"But I'm with buyers all day today. Could you drop it off to her? She could buy herself something nice at Imagine. What with that employee discount, might be worth at least one nice top."*

"Maybe some night later in the week," Del said.

"Andy's going to be on the road Thursday through Saturday, so any of those nights work for me."

"How is that whole strike thing going? I thought I saw something about a vote on the news last night."

"The vote's been delayed again, more negotiations."

"Is that good?"

"Who knows? It may just be delaying the inevitable."

"Will you be...okay?" Del asked, touching Gwen's arm.

"I think so. I hope so," Gwen patted Del's hand. "We're planning as best we can, can't do much more." Gwen thought about sharing her concerns regarding Bob's job offer, but her friendship with Del was new and Del's plate was full enough. Did she need to worry about losing a new friend, on top of everything else? Gwen wondered. "We'll figure it out. How about you? How's your new job?"

"It's great!" Del's face lit up with enthusiasm. "I didn't expect to like it so much, but I do."

"Even Bella?"

"Even Bella. She's all business, but she's fair. She told me yesterday I'm even getting a raise after my first month!"

"That's wonderful, Del. First the snow pool, now a raise. What's next?"

"I don't know," Del said, "maybe the worst is over."

"I definitely think your luck is turning. Maybe you should buy a Superball ticket!"

"I tried that...but I didn't win anything. I even bought condoms!" Del blushed. "I can't believe I told you that!"

"Well...I bet if Claire were here, she'd tell you there's more ways than one to get lucky!"

Del's blush grew deeper and they both laughed at that.

Seventeen

Del
Sunday

WHAT A DAY! MOTHER SENT Father Frank to visit me-and on the day I skip church! But he was very nice. I think I felt better after his visit than I feel after services. I relaxed all day and did what I wanted. I'm getting used to this. I need to ask Father Frank if he thinks enjoying my "alone time" so much could be sin-especially on Sunday!

Gwen came over later to tell me I'd won her little snow pool thingy she has. I didn't even enter! Claire entered for me!! I still don't know what to think about her. I'm starting to think she doesn't seem like what she really is.

Micky brought the kids home. I didn't realize how much I missed them until they came running in. He didn't come in with them, just let them out of the car and drove off. Part of me was relieved, but part of me was sad. After all these years...

Gwen
Sun.

I took Del her snow pool winnings today. I couldn't think of a better person to win. Not that it's a lot of money, really. It's the luck that matters this time. Del's such a sweet person, and I'm beginning to think she's a lot stronger than we give her credit for.

Andy got home from a long haul this afternoon. He doesn't have another one of those until Thursday, thank goodness.

It's funny, I used to like it when Bill went out of town on business. Jeff and I would get Whoppers at the Burger King for dinner-his dad hates fast food-and we'd let the clutter build up a little longer than usual, because we could. We'd do our own, non-Bill thing. Guess I should have seen the handwriting on the wall there. Bill was doing his own thing too. Who knew? Not Jeff and I.

But, Andy. I don't want him to leave. I like having him home. Even Jeff likes hanging out with him. If we moved to the western slope, if he took that job at the winery, if I opened a new bakery...Jeff says he'd like that. Would I?

Claire
11-13

10am: Meet Chandlers at IHOP. Breakfast, review properties we've seen so far, tour remaining seven homes.

Contract??

To-Do:

Paperwork if Chandler's finally make an offer.

Make to-do list for Monday: Chandler's lender, call title on Regency closing, pull comps for new listing in Cottonwood Estates.

Call Sally-send Jordan's birthday present on Monday!

Call Del.

WHEN CLAIRE GOT HOME ON Monday night there was a message on her voicemail.

"Hi Claire, this is Del. I wanted to thank you for purchasing tickets for me in the snow pool. You are *so* nice. You didn't have to do that. Anyway, I wanted to show my appreciation by having you and Gwen over sometime later this week. You know, a girl's night out, like the last time, at Gwen's. Only this time, if I have too much wine, you won't have to drive me home." Del laughed nervously, but plowed on.

"Not that I'm going to drink that much again, oh no, I've had my night of indulgence. I'll stick with my one glass of wine, thank you very much. So, anyway...," more nervous laughter, "well, I never know how to end these recorded messages, so just, ummm, call me, okay? Gwen thinks she could meet later this week. Oh, did I say that already? Well, anyway, call, okay? Thank you again. So much. Talk with you soon! Bye-bye!"

Claire smiled, deleted the message and listened to the next message.

"Hi again. It's Del. Well, you probably figured that out. Anyway, I realized as soon as I hung up that I didn't give you my phone number." Del left her number, mentioned Gwen would be free later in the week and thanked Claire again before hanging up.

Claire compared the number Del had left with the one on her caller ID; they were the same. It was after ten and Claire decided that was too late to call Del. She'd call the next day.

On Wednesday night when Del got home she checked her messages. She'd decided she'd try Claire again if she didn't hear from her soon. She wondered if Claire was mad at her for winning the pool, instead of Claire. Or mad because she'd had to drive Del home after she had one too many glasses of wine. Or mad for something else. Del imagined many possibilities as she pushed the button for her messages.

"Hey, Del, it's Claire. Sorry I didn't get back to you sooner. Didn't know what my schedule was gonna be and

I had a couple of late nights. I'm free Thursday or Friday night, whatever works for you. Give me a ring and let me know. Are you sure you want to go to the trouble of putting a spread together for all of us? Why don't we go out somewhere? Nothing fancy. I've got an idea. Call me. Bye."

Del was a little flustered at the thought of going out somewhere. It's not that her budget was so tight. Even though her final settlement was still pending, she had assets. But she tried to watch her pennies, and that wasn't it, really. The fact was she hadn't actually *gone out* since Micky left. Sure, she'd stopped by Gwen's for tea and a pastry, or picked up take-out. But actually *gone out*? No. And what kind of place would Claire have in mind? Still, she thought, Claire had purchased the winning ticket for her. If Claire wanted to go somewhere, she ought to honor her request. It was only polite.

It was early evening so she called Claire. The answering machine kicked in and she left a message.

"Hi Claire, it's Del! I got your message. Ummm...I suppose it would be fine to go out somewhere. Nothing fancy. If *you'd* like to do that, I'll see what Gwen thinks. I'm sure she'd enjoy that too. I guess, yes, I'll call Gwen and see what she thinks and then I'll call you back. Bye-bye!"

When Claire returned home later, she listened to that message, and the one that followed.

"Hi Claire, it's Del again! Listen, I talked with Gwen, and she says going out is fine with her. Nothing fancy. So, where would you like to go? That cute little creperie on Crestline might be nice. I know they serve wine, so we can have a drink with our crepes. My treat, remember. It's dressy casual, by the way. Gwen says tomorrow night-Thursday-works best. Let me know if that's okay. Bye-bye!"

Later that evening Del was in the backyard on the swing, smoking and listening to music that drifted in from a neighbor's outdoor stereo. She could hear the soft mumbles of conversation and intermittent laughter that always told her they were in the hot tub. Del loved hot tubs, but she didn't own one. Micky thought they were a waste of money. He said everybody uses them at first, but then they don't. Then they were another thing to pay for and maintain. Del thought she'd use it. And she wouldn't mind maintaining it. The kids said Micky's townhome had a hot tub that they used almost every night.

Del heard the phone ringing and debated running in to get it, but decided not to. Cara and Nate were asleep, after all, so she wasn't worried that anything had happened to them. That was really the only time she felt she had to answer the phone, when she wasn't with her children. She'd check for messages when she went in, and now there was a Michael Buble song on the neighbor's stereo.

Later, as Del climbed into bed, she saw the message light flashing on the phone and remembered she'd forgotten to check for messages.

"Del, it's Claire. Sorry I missed you. Thursday sounds good. Why don't we meet a Gwen's at seven. I'll reveal our destination at that time. Same dress code as the creperie, by the way. And Del, you're only allowed to buy me one drink. That's it, kiddo. I want you to spend the rest of your winnings on yourself. Got it? See you then. Bye."

Thursday afternoon Gwen checked the messages on her home phone.

"Hi Gwen, it's Del. I know you must have gone to work already, but you mentioned you always check messages in the middle of the day, so I thought I'd leave you a message. I didn't want to interrupt you at work. Anyway, Claire called last night, well actually, she left a message. I don't know why it's so hard to connect! But she said tonight is fine, she wants to meet at your house at seven. I hope that's all right with you. If it's not, call me on my cell, you can leave a message." Del gave her the number. "Claire has somewhere in mind she wants to go. Dressy casual, she says. Don't know where...well, I guess we'll find out at seven. Should be fun!" she said with what sounded like a nervous laugh. "See you then. Bye-bye!"

"This should be interesting," Gwen said to herself, pressing the delete button.

Eighteen

"HERE COMES CLAIRE!" DEL CALLED out to Gwen who was still changing for their girl's night out. "Tell her I'll be right down."

Del opened Gwen's front door, the chilly night air sweeping in around her, and Claire rolled down her car window.

"I've got to finish this call," Claire said, holding her hand over the cell. "You two come out when you're ready. I'll drive."

Del checked herself again in Gwen's hall mirror. A few weeks with Bella and Mary had revived her appearance. Bella, in particular, would point out styles and colors that complimented Del. Mary had been more up front. During her first week at Imagine, Mary recommended a new shade of lipstick and a particular line of hair care products. The results showed.

She'd tamed the blonde frizz of her long hair creating lush waves of curl that framed her face. Her dressy casual attire included a chocolate brown turtleneck layered atop matching slacks. Over the turtleneck she wore a short jacket of cream silk that was embroidered with a pattern of autumn hued leaves. Del had purchased the jacket that day at Imagine with her winnings from the snow pool. The total, even with discounts, had actually come to more than she'd won. But the savings was enough to finally justify the purchase of the jacket, which she'd fallen deeply in lust with upon first sight.

"I'm ready," Gwen said, running down the stairs. She wore a comfortable pair of khakis dressed up with a beige and black sweater set. Her straight auburn hair hung long, with only the front pulled back and fastened by a gold barrette. Gwen's hair was still a bit damp after a quick shower to remove the fine layer of flour from her day at the bakery.

"Where's Claire?"

"She's waiting in the car; she's driving."

"Well, let's get this show on the road and find out where our mystery destination is."

"Gwen, you don't think she'd pick somewhere..." Del searched for an appropriate word and could only come up with, "loud?"

"I don't think we're off to play pool at Sharky's, if that's what you're worried about," Gwen said, mentioning a bar that had a rowdy reputation.

"Oh, no, I'm sure she wouldn't...no." Del reached for her coat and *hoped* Claire wouldn't.

The Dockside had a reasonable crowd, even for a weeknight. Del had never been there before but she knew Micky frequented it for business lunches. That alone was enough to color her opinion before she even walked in the door.

Gwen, however, liked the casual feel of the bar/restaurant. She and Andy had eaten there many times, preferring a table by the window overlooking the reservoir and the docks to the south. Gwen noticed Del's muted reaction when Claire pulled up in front.

"Believe me, it's no Sharky's," she whispered to Del as they got out of the car.

Del wasn't sure what she expected, but she liked what she found. It wasn't fancy, but it was nice. From the entrance, a long porch wrapped around the back for diners to sit outside in sunny weather and watch activity on the docks, or enjoy the lapping of the waves against the shore. Inside, the décor was heavy wood, from wall to floor to tables to the chairs with their earth toned upholstered seats. On the walls hung many black and white photos of sail boats, and stained glass lights above the tables cast a warm glow.

"Let's sit at the bar," Claire said.

"Oh?" said Del.

"Sure, you're buying me a drink, after all. We can share some appetizers instead of ordering big meals. How about it?"

"Sounds good to me," Gwen said. "I love their quesadillas."

"And the crab dip–let's get that, too."

Two young men moved their beers and buffalo wings to make room for the three of them at the end of the bar where it curved, offering a view of the moonlit reservoir.

"Too bad we weren't here for the sunset," Claire said, laying her coat over the back of the chair closest to the men.

"Andy and I love sitting on the porch in the summer and watching the sun go down. It's so beautiful, how it sparkles on the water." Gwen folded her coat over the seat of the chair next to Claire, adding an extra inch to make her more comfortable at the bar.

"This is...very nice," Del said, standing beside the last chair.

"Have a seat," Claire said. "Gwen, let's see the appetizer menu."

Gwen pulled a small menu from between the salt and pepper shakers in front of her, and they looked it over.

Del put her foot on the brass rail that ran along the bottom of the bar and hopped onto the chair. She took her purse off her shoulder, set it on her lap and unbuttoned her coat until she got to the point where her purse covered the buttons. She paused, placed her purse in front of her, in the middle of the bar, then pulled it a few inches closer. She finished unbuttoning her coat and pushed it off her shoulders, over the back of the chair, picked up her purse and put it back on her lap. She looked at the bar and the wall behind the bar with its shelves of multi-hued bottles and jumped when she heard–

"What'll it be ladies?"

Del looked nervously toward the bartender.

"Why don't you give us a second, Jimmy," Claire said.

"Just holler when you need me."

"Del," Claire said, "you don't usually sit at the bar, do you?"

Del smiled nervously. "Does it show?" she whispered.

Gwen looked up from the menu and saw the death grip Del had on her purse. "Here," she said and, reaching over, picked up her purse and hung it from the strap over Del's knee. "Gets it out of your way but keeps it close."

"Thanks."

Gwen handed her the menu. "Pick an appetizer–we'll each pick one and we can share."

Del read through the list. "I like nachos...but if you don't–"

"Love nachos!" Claire said. "Sounds like a plan. Jimmy!"

Jimmy rinsed a glass, set it out to dry and, wiping his hands on a white bar towel, walked over to them. "Claire, ladies," he said. Mid-forties, with a lean build, Jimmy's jet black hair was giving in to salt and pepper. He manned the bar like he owned the place, which he did.

"Jimmy," Claire said, "this is Gwen–"

"Jimmy DiSanto," he said, shaking her hand. "Nice to meet you Gwen, I think I've seen you in here before."

"My husband and I come in once in a while for dinner. We like your view."

"Hope you like the food, too."

"Besides being the bartender," Claire said, "Jimmy's the

owner. And that's Del, down there."

Del smiled and offered her hand for him to shake. His hand, she noticed was cold, but his smile was warm.

"Del. Nice to meet you; don't think I've seen you in here before." He continued holding her hand.

"No, ummm...this is the first time."

"I hope you don't make it the last. It makes my day to see such a beautiful face at my bar."

"Oh. Thank you."

Jimmy smiled a little bigger, released her hand and said, "So, what can I get you lovely ladies this evening?"

Claire placed their appetizer order, adding, "and a vodka martini with–"

"Two olives," Jimmy said.

"Am I that predictable?" Claire asked.

"No, ma'am. You're a classic, like a fifty-five T–Bird, very cherry. Hard to forget a classic. How about you Gwen?"

"Malibu and Coke sounds good."

"And Del?"

"I'll just have an iced tea...for now."

"Why don't you have one glass of wine, Del," Gwen said. "Then switch to iced tea. What with the appetizers, you'll be fine."

"Oh...I don't know."

"Low threshold," Claire said aside to Jimmy. "One won't hurt, Del."

"Well...," Del scanned the mirrored wall, unsure what to choose.

"Like it on the sweet side?" Jimmy asked.

Del nodded.

"Let me see what I can find," he said and then left before she could stop him.

"Don't worry," Claire said, "Jimmy's good at figuring out what people like. Time to lose the uniform."

Claire peeled off the jacket portion of her black suit and hung it neatly over the back of her chair. She rolled up the cuffs of her white silk blouse, straightened her knee length skirt and crossed her legs to better reveal the soft black leather of long boots. The day had started with another frosting of snow, so Claire had chosen a pair of boots with a more serviceable two inch heel. Her spikes only came out in dry weather.

"I guess I'm sort of awkward at this," Del whispered to Gwen. "You and Claire are so much more...comfortable."

"More practice maybe."

"I can't imagine Claire being uncomfortable anywhere."

"I'm sure she has her moments. We all do. When Jeff's dad and I were first divorced I felt awkward too-getting out there, you know? Everyone does. You feel like there's a neon sign over you that says "failure", but you're not a fail- ure. You're moving on to the next phase. I think it's not so much about success or failure, but about change, and what you take away from it."

"I hope I can handle this all half as well as you have, Gwen. I always feel so clumsy, like I'm trying to get my bearings, trying to figure out which way to go. But you're so calm, so in control. I wish I could be like you."

"Del, you're great, really. We all feel awkward when something is new. Some of us just have a calmer shell. And besides, what are friends for, if not to stand beside you when you trying something new-like sitting at the bar!" Gwen gave Del's hand an assuring squeeze and her friend smiled. "You might find you like it."

"I suppose. Micky always liked to sit at a table," Del said. "*Full service*, that's what he called it. He liked having a waiter or waitress take care of him. I guess it seems silly, that I've never sat at a bar, I mean."

"Never?"

Del thought. "No. That makes me sound so old, doesn't it?"

"Or young."

"When I was young, and went out with my family, my mother would *never* have allowed me to sit at the bar."

"What about your father?"

"Daddy didn't get involved in that sort of thing. He left discipline to Mother. I guess he expected us to know the rules and follow them. She must have done a good job. We didn't go out to dinner as a family that much–I have five older brothers–but when we did, everyone knew how to behave."

"I didn't realize you had that big a family. I knew a couple of your brothers in school. I never see them around, now."

"I'm really the only one who lives in the area. Isn't that odd? Three of them live out of state, one's in Denver, and one lives outside Durango. Just Mother and me left in town now. I remember my oldest brother saying he couldn't wait to grow up and get out of Blue River. Maybe it's different, for girls. I love Blue River."

"Before the divorce, Micky talked about moving to Denver. Every time I thought of that, I felt like there was a hole in my stomach and all the life was seeping out. I suppose it's silly to get so attached to a place. Places are like things, don't you think? It's really people we should be attached to. If you're with people you love, you should feel whole no matter where you are."

"I suppose," Gwen said, thoughtfully. She couldn't help but think of the places and people her future might hold.

"You know," Del continued, "I never really thought about it before, but don't you think, if I really loved Micky, I wouldn't have minded moving?"

"But moving away from your family is a big step for anyone."

"That's true, but I think I should have been excited about moving to Denver with him. It's not that far, after all. I think that should have out-weighed my other feelings. It's like my gut knew, before my head did, that Micky wasn't my...home. Even before I knew about his...girlfriends...*part* of me knew."

"Women's intuition?" Claire leaned over Gwen's shoulder to listen in on their conversation.

"Maybe," Del said. "But if that's true...you know what it means?"

"What?" they asked in unison.

"My intuition is part of me, and part of me was making a choice: choosing not to go with Micky. It means," Del's face lit up, and then her shoulders visibly relaxed and tears formed in the corners of her eyes, "it means I chose first."

"Huh?" Claire asked.

"I get it," said Gwen. "Your gut knew the marriage wasn't right. When Micky asked for the divorce, when the truth came out, it wasn't really thrust upon you. In fact–"

"I was already there!"

"Looks that way," Claire said. "You just weren't prepared for the details. That's what swamped you."

"And going public," Gwen said. "That's the part you can't control. That's the biggest unknown."

"You're right. It was scarier than all the concrete details."

"And now?" Claire asked.

"The details are almost sorted out. The divorce will be final in early January. I found a good job. Not my dream job, but good for now. I've made some nice new friends, and some of my old friends still call...some don't."

"Screw 'em if they don't care enough about you to pick up the friggin' phone."

Del laughed. "Yeah. Screw 'em!"

"Ladies?" Jimmy said, placing drinks in front of them.

"Who's getting screwed tonight?"

Del felt like melting off her chair, but her friends were laughing so hard, she had to join in.

Nineteen

★★★

"I DIDN'T ORDER THIS," DEL SAID as Jimmy placed a tall glass of white wine beside her iced tea.

"On the house...Del, right?"

"Yes. You really didn't need to-"

"I don't need to do anything, but the pleasure's all mine," Jimmy said, holding up both hands to stop her. "Have a sip, see what ya think."

Del raised the glass hesitantly, aware that she was accepting a free drink within fifteen minutes of her first time sitting at a bar. Yes, he was the bartender, she thought, but what would Father Frank say? What would her *mother* say?

She took a sip, surprised at the result.

"You like the bubbles?"

"Champagne?"

"Moscato. A sweet Italian with a little fizz." He wound one hand up into the air to emphasize the fizz part.

"Oh, it's very nice, and sweet. But champagne...it..."

"Goes right to your head, eh? That's why I pick the moscato-special for you, half the alcohol."

"Really?" Del said, taking another sip. "I never knew."

"We Guineas have our secrets."

"Guineas?"

"Italian. That's slang. Not so nice slang, I guess. You never heard that before?"

Del shook her head. "Are you from Italy? You don't really

sound...foreign."

"I'm from Providence. Rhode Island. Little Italy Providence. My folks were old country. I've got plenty of family back there still, but I got out a long time ago. Good food, but for me, myself-not so good company, if you know what I mean. Colorado was like the other side of the world, and that's what I was looking for. You from here originally?"

"I grew up in Blue River."

"A native. Don't meet too many of those."

"My great-grandfather came over from Ireland."

"Irish. I should have known from the lovely hair, and freckles, too."

"Oh, well, t-thank you," Del said, flustered and unaccustomed to flattery from bartenders.

"What, are you a Kelly, an O'Brian, one of those?"

"Donahue."

"Del Donahue."

"Well, yes, that's...right." Del considered mentioning it was her *maiden* name, and adding Rufino to the end, but decided to leave Micky out of their conversation.

"Is Del short for something?"

"Adele."

"Adele. Now that's a lovely name. How'd you end up with Del? You pick it?"

"No. Friends in school."

"What do they know? I like Adele. Okay if I call you that?"

"Sure."

"Jimmy! Couple of drafts?" a man at the end of the bar called.

"You enjoy," Jimmy said, tapping the foot of her wine glass. "I'll be back."

"That's a first," Claire said, after he left, "Jimmy chatting it up with a customer for more than a few seconds. He's usually back and forth and all around, seeing to everything in the restaurant and tending bar at the same time."

"Oh," Del said, "I'm sure he talks to others, too."

"Not so much."

"Hey Claire, you want another?" said the young man beside Claire.

"'Scuse me, have to tend to my new friends," Claire winked.

"Looks like Claire makes friends easily," Gwen said.

"They're kind of young, don't you think?" Del asked.

"I suppose. I think Claire likes young men with short commitment spans," Gwen said smiling. Then, looking over Del's shoulder she added, "But here comes somebody who may change her plans."

"Huh?" Del turned to see an attractive middle-aged man approaching them.

"Gwen, nice to see you," Bob said, giving her a small bear hug in greeting. "Am I interrupting girl's night out?"

"Yes to girl's night out, no to interrupting. It's always nice to see you. Del, this is Bob," she said, making introductions.

"Good to meet you, Del." He shook her hand firmly, but not crushing.

Bob's size gave him an imposing presence, but his khakis-and-polo persona and easy smile put even Del at ease.

"And you've already met Claire," Gwen tapped Claire's shoulder to get her attention. "Claire, you remember Bob?"

"Who?" Claire turned from the young man and said, "Oh, Bob. Sure. Nice to see you." The words were pleasant, but the delivery flat.

Bob held his hand out and Claire took it after a moment's hesitation. He wrapped his other hand around hers and held her hand firm and steady for a moment more than usual. "What a surprise finding you here, Claire."

"Well, yes," she said, and started to pull her hand and turn away to speak with the young man beside her, but Bob held on.

"How've you been?" he asked her.

"Fine." She smiled and glanced at Gwen.

"You know," Bob said to Gwen, "Claire was at my house the other day."

"Really?" Gwen said, casting a surprised look at Claire.

"Well–" Claire sputtered.

"Not exactly *at* my house, that's true. But she was across the street, so we stopped and talked for a little while. I think I promised to buy you a drink, didn't I?"

"Not quite..."

"I see you're having a martini, can I buy you another? Jimmy!" Bob called, before she could protest. "Another round for these ladies, please."

Jimmy nodded at Bob's order from the far end of the bar.

"I'm fine, really," Claire said.

"Of course you are," Bob said. "I can tell you're a woman who is always fine with her own resources, Claire, and I respect that. 'Course, I'm the kind of man who enjoys the opportunity to do a good deed for a lady. I'm sure you respect *that*, am I right?"

Claire knew a rock and hard spot when she saw it. To argue with Bob's logic would mean insulting him, and whatever else he might be, Bob was still the owner of a very nice home that he might one day want to sell. "In that case, I'll say thank you and leave it at that," she said as she turned her attentions back to the young man beside her.

Bob, however, wasn't about to leave it at that. In fact, after their last meeting Bob had decided that Claire was more than interesting. He'd determined to put some effort into plowing down the road blocks she was obviously erecting in his path. Claire, he could tell, wasn't about to make it easy, but Bob slid up to the bar between Gwen and Claire.

"How's Andy?" he asked Gwen.

"On the road. He'll probably call later," she added, touching the cell phone she'd placed beside her glass.

"I'll be right back," Del said to Gwen, before sliding off her chair and heading toward the ladies room.

"By the way," Gwen said, leaning in and lowering her voice as she spoke to Bob, "Andy told me about your offer."

"I didn't make it lightly, or out of any kind of pity for your circumstances, what with the impending strike, if that concerns you."

"Oh, no, I didn't mean it that way. I think Andy would be good at anything he tried, if he wanted to be."

"That was my thinking."

"I just wanted to say thanks for thinking of him, and, well," she glanced to here side and back, "I hope you won't mind if I ask that you don't mention it, tonight, here."

"I understand. It's not a done deal."

"Yes, well, and I," she leaned a bit closer and whispered, "I haven't said anything to Claire or Del. I don't want to, until I know for sure."

"Got it," Bob nodded. "They won't hear it from me before they hear it from you. My word."

"Thank you." Gwen sat back, and, feeling the muscles in her neck and shoulders relax, realized how tense the moment had made her. Was it the move, she wondered, or the secret? Maybe both, or maybe simply the unknown.

"Before we drop the subject completely, however, I'd like to say that I respect your hesitation; picking up and starting a new business is always a major concern. In a way, there are more what-ifs on your end than on Andy's."

"Exactly," Gwen said, surprised that Bob understood, and that she'd jumped so quickly to acknowledge it, as if doing so somehow made the move less an idea and more a reality.

"We could use a nice bakery over there. Had a French

couple that ran a place for a long time but they retired last
year. No one's really stepped in."

Jimmy returned to distribute the round Bob had ordered
and placed a Bud Light in front of Bob.

"I'm too predictable," Bob said, smiling at Gwen.

"Makes my job easy," Jimmy said. "Did Adele leave?"

"Ladies room," Gwen said.

"Good, thought I might have scared her off." He picked
up Del's glass, "I'll bring her a fresh one when she gets back,"
and left to answer the call of another patron.

"Is the space still available?" Gwen asked. Bob looked
puzzled. "The space the French couple had their bakery in."

"Oh. No. They've rented it out to a CPA of all people.
Don't think he uses the kitchen facility much, though." "Too
bad...wasting a good kitchen."

"I know they've tried to find a better tenant, but, eventually they needed to get it rented. The location was good."

"Lots of traffic?"

"Definitely. It's on a main route in and out of town."

"I don't suppose that makes much difference to a CPA."

"Probably not. You know, the wife, she mentioned to me
once that this guy was new in the area and, since he wasn't
sure about how business would be, he wanted a short term
lease. I don't know for certain what she signed him to, but
I'll give her a call. It may be the space will open up again
soon."

"I wouldn't want to get her hopes up. And I wouldn't
want him to loose his space..."

"An accountant doesn't need *that* much space, I'm sure
there are office fronts in town that would work as well. I
think she rented it cheap, just to get some cash flow, and
he probably couldn't resist. I'm sure she'd prefer the entire
space be used. Don't worry, I won't promise anything, I'll
just see what's up."

"Well...I suppose it couldn't hurt to ask; just in case." Gwen felt tension wash once more across her shoulders and wondered if she'd ever really relax again.

DEL NOTICED THE SMELL AS she washed the lather from her hands: honeysuckle. She wondered if Jimmy picked the soap for his bathrooms. Would a man pick honeysuckle? She dried her hands on a towel and double checked her appearance in the mirror.

She pulled a small brush from her purse and realigned a few stray hairs, then carefully applied fresh lipstick. For a moment she admired what she saw in the mirror, then the door swung open, a woman walked in, glanced at Del and entered a stall. Del glanced at her reflection again, feeling suddenly like a schoolgirl caught in a foolish moment. How long had it been since she'd felt that way?

"I SAVED THIS UNTIL YOU GOT back," Jimmy said, placing a fresh wine glass in front of Del.

"I haven't finished the first one yet."

"That's okay. This one's different. You give 'em both a try and see what you think."

"Like a wine tasting?"

"Exactly like a wine tasting. You'll be a pro in no time."

Del sipped.

"Whadayathink?"

"This one's nice, too. Not so sweet."

"That's one smart wine; knows better than to compete with sweet Adele."

Del blushed. She hardly knew what to say, so said nothing and took another sip. Thankfully, Gwen's cell phone rang and drew Jimmy's attention from her face.

"That's Andy!" Gwen said, picking up the phone. "I'll take it over there." She answered it as she walked, "Hi honey," a pause, then, "at the Dockside, guess who we ran into..."

Gwen walked around a corner in search of a quiet spot and left Bob alone just as Claire's new acquaintance excused himself to visit the men's room.

"Nice kid," Bob said.

Claire looked for Gwen but found only Del, whose attentions were more than monopolized by Jimmy. Didn't he have a bar to tend? she thought.

"He seems very nice," Claire said.

"You don't like me, do you Claire?"

"Well-I..." Claire, who lived daily with the diplomacy of the deal, didn't like being pressed for her genuine thoughts and feelings. "I don't know you well enough *not* to like you."

"Good answer. Very middle-of-the-road."

"I didn't mean it-"

"Sure you did, but that's okay. And I agree completely. You *don't* know me well enough. So, what can we do to change that?"

"You're assuming I want to?"

"Now, Claire, you're a smart business woman. I can tell that. You know it never hurts to assume the best."

"While preparing for the worst," Claire added.

"I'm already past the worst. You're talking to me, right?"

"Foot's in the door?"

"So to speak."

Claire's acquaintance returned and she hoped to ignore Bob once more, but Bob reached his hand out to shake the other man's. "Name's Bob," he said, "I'm a friend of Claire's." He grinned at Claire as he said it.

"Micky," the young man said, taking Bob's hand.

"Hey, that's funny, huh? Bob and Micky-you could be my son!" Bob laughed and looked to Claire.

She narrowed her eyes and, crossing her arms, sat back in her chair to emphasize her displeasure with his joke.

Micky laughed too, and glanced at the plasma TV over the bar. Bob followed his glance to catch the highlight reel from the previous week's football game.

"Can you believe that guy?" Bob said.

"Totally," Micky agreed, shaking his head and taking a large swig from his beer bottle. "Guy's an idiot! I can't believe they paid him that much. Complete screw up."

"He was the top draft pick. I suppose he could write his ticket."

"Shit, I could throw the ball better than he does."

"You play?" Bob asked.

"Just pick-up, but hell, anybody could throw it better. This guy's a looser."

"Couldn't have said it better myself," Bob said, smiling at Claire, who sighed and reached for her martini.

THOUGH SHE WAS TIRED, GWEN couldn't sleep. She missed Andy's warmth against her and the soft in-and-out of his breathing that lulled her every night.

She added a heavy sweater over her PJ's, pulled on wool socks and padded downstairs, where she turned on the light over her desk and opened her diary.

Thurs.

It's late, can't sleep. I miss Andy. I miss Jeff. The house is too quiet.

We went for girls-night-out to the Dockside tonight. Claire's choice, which ended ironically, I think, as Bob showed up. I finally know what makes Claire uncomfortable.

Bob mentioned a location near the winery that might make a good bakery, if it's available. Part of me is excited–a small part!–but most of me wishes this would all go away and we could get back to normal again.

Poor Del–she was out of her element. But she definitely made friends with the owner, Jimmy. Del said a funny thing, that I'm so calm, that she admires me. People always say I seem calm, but I don't feel it. My sister, Gayle, used to say I was way too mellow-I guess that's what they called *calm* in the seventies.

She thought I was nuts. She burned her bra and attended sit-ins. She was paving *the way*, she told me. I thought *the way* looked embarrassing and not so comfortable. Mom's way looked better, easier. Dad loved her and we loved her. She seemed to love herself and her life. Maybe it wasn't cool, but I was no ground breaker. I needed to follow a role model with a successful track record. So I followed.

Only thing was, nobody told me it didn't work for everyone. Nobody said he doesn't always love you forever. He might not be a bad guy, but that didn't mean he'd be the right guy. Or maybe it was time and growth and change that made us not right for each other anymore. Nobody told me, so I had to find it out for myself.

My sister finally married the young attorney Dad kept sending to bail her out. She worked a couple of years as his secretary, and then she quit and had three kids. She joined the country club and the PTA and volunteers at Democratic fundraisers. She got a housekeeper. She jokes that she sold out, but she doesn't seem unhappy with the deal.

I started over at forty; started a new business and found a new guy, who was the right guy. I work long days, and I don't always know if the ends will meet, but I'm happier now. It's not the same, and not always better than it was, it's just different, and it feels true. Or it did. Now, with this possible move, I just don't know. I want Andy to be happy, but...

My friends say they admire me. My sister says I'm her hero-that I did life my way and that's what her path was all about in the first place.

I don't feel like a hero. I'm just a survivor, looking for a new shell.

GWEN CLOSED HER DIARY, POURED herself a small glass of wine and went to her easel. Del's shell was almost complete. The smooth coils of the moonshell glowed like their namesake, opalescent and creamy white, spiraling and growing outward, creating a larger, newer path as they went.

Gwen picked up a brush, dipped it in water and washed it around in the palest blue pot, loading and adding faint luminous highlights to the shell's coils.

She would put away her paintings for Thanksgiving, she thought to herself. Del had mentioned her children would be with Micky for the day, so Gwen had invited her. She'd invited Claire too...and she knew Andy would invite Bob.

Gwen rinsed the brush in water and admired the final painting. Her skill as a painter had a ways to go, she thought, still, it was good. And it was truly Del. Now, she thought, picking up the wooden box that held her treasured shells, where was Claire?

***

"HELLO, CLAIRE," SAID THE MESSAGE on her machine. "Listen, this is Linda Campbell. Haven't you been able to get any kind of feedback from that agent that showed our house? They were in here for thirty minutes, at least–we were across the street at the neighbors–so we know. They must have liked it if they stayed that long. I just don't understand why we can't get some feedback. Give it another try and let me know, I'm sure they'll want to talk to you. Let me know. Bye."

"Jesus, Linda, I've already left two phone messages and sent a friggin' email," Claire said to her phone as she hit the erase button. "And that was four *fucking* days ago! They don't even remember your house by now!"

She took a sip of merlot, rubbed her neck where the muscles seemed to stay perpetually tight. "Oh, shit," she sighed, "okay, I'll try one more time," she muttered and looked at the clock. Almost eleven-thirty; far too late to call. Claire knew she should have checked messages before she went to the Dockside with the girls...but sometimes it was nice to put voicemail on hold.

She pulled up her email, pasted the real estate agent's address on the *send* line and typed:

Dear Karen,

I am trying one last time to get some feedback on your showing of my listing at 1253 Rockridge. You showed it four days ago, from five-fifteen to five-thirty-five. I know this because my obnoxious client spied on you from across the street!

Claire took another, larger sip of wine, erased the last two sentences and continued.

I realize you may have a busy schedule, but I would truly appreciate some feedback regarding the showing.

She massaged the familiar discomfort and growing pain beneath her ribs. "Damn." Claire pulled a large, nearly empty bottle of antacids from the desk drawer, popped two, then a third, chewed and then rinsed with merlot. "Jesus." She crossed her hands over her chest and bent forward, leaning against the edge of the desk, resting her chin against her knuckles, her forehead tipped over the keyboard. She breathed slowly, in, out, waiting. Finally, the moment passed. She sat up. "What the fuck."

Listen, I went to the trouble to fill out all that fucking paperwork for the listing, take pictures, make brochures, pound that pain-in-the-ass sign into the frozen ground with a sledge hammer, set up the virtual tour, and tell my client twenty million times to pack up all her crap so that your buyers could see the place-you owe me!

She typed her name and told herself she really shouldn't send it, but she knew they weren't interested. She knew if an agent didn't call, if it had been more than a day or two without a word, she knew. Linda Campbell paid her-or would, if they ever sold the house-to know. But Linda Campbell thought she knew better. She was a doctor, after all, so she knew everything. Claire finished off her wine and hit the send button. "Jesus."

She went upstairs, brushed her teeth, washed her face and brushed out her hair. She stripped and put on a silk robe and went down to turn out the lights. She checked her email one last time before turning off the computer: two messages.

The first read: *Sweetie, he loved it-you always know! An official thank-you is in the mail, but here's a snap-shot to get you by. Love you! Call me! S.*

Claire clicked on the link and up came a photo of a twelve-year-old boy, a huge grin on his face, IPad in hand, and all his attention focused on the screen in front of him.

Claire switched photo paper into her printer and hit *print*. She waited as it came out, trimmed the edges and leaned it against his framed, school photo on the bookshelf above her computer.

Then she opened the other email.

Claire,

Sorry I didn't get back to you sooner-clients looked at thirty-seven fucking houses in last two weeks and even I can't remember any of them anymore. Looked up your house/checked my notes. They hated it the moment they walked in-too traditional, said her paint choices sucked-decided they'd seen enough. Delightful people, my clients. But we sat at your client's kitchen table sorting through notes of all the other houses-narrowed it down to two. Made an offer the next day, got agreement yesterday, had inspection today, they flew back to Florida earlier this evening. I'm eating chocolate chip ice cream floating in a bowl of Baileys, and listening to Enya. Thanks for going to the trouble to list the house that finally convinced my clients to buy another one. Good luck, Karen.

"Shit." Claire tapped out one last email.

Linda,

I finally heard from the buyers who toured your home. They thought it was "charming...though a little cluttered," but felt they had to have one more bedroom and really needed to be closer to his work. Sorry it took so long to get this feedback, but these things sometimes happen. Don't worry, the right buyer is out there. Let me know if you need more packing boxes.

She sent the email, turned off the computer, the lights and went to bed. Finally.

SHE REALLY NEEDED TO THINK about giving up this habit, Del thought to herself as she puffed and swung beneath the night sky. As beautiful as the stars were, the crisp mountain air was growing cooler. As this rate, she'd find herself swinging and puffing in a blizzard one night. Besides, Sandy had taken up the habit of sitting at the backdoor, watching and whimpering for her to either let the little dog out or go back inside.

The kids hadn't taken Sandy along this weekend. Micky complained that she kept peeing on his dining room carpet. Del smiled at the thought. Good dog.

Yes, she'd give up smoking soon, but not tonight. Tonight she was overflowing with conflicting emotions, and she didn't feel she was up to adding withdrawal to the mix. One second she felt sixteen again and couldn't stop smiling, the next she chastised herself for being so easily swayed by a man's attentions.

She blushed at the thought of how attentive Jimmy had been. Even Gwen had commented when Claire had, again, pointed it out on the ride home.

"I don't really know him," Gwen had said, "but I have to admit, he seemed much less interested in your order than he was in you."

The quarter moon faded behind a cloud, making the dusty stream of the Milky Way stand out against the darker sky. A chilly breeze danced down her collar and across her shoulders. She pulled on the cigarette, inhaling the warmth, and wrapped her scarf tighter.

She blew smoke at the cloud and it floated slowly on, revealing the glimmering sliver of moon. Del knew Gwen was right, but what, if anything, should she do about it?

Twenty-One

IN THE WINTER, BLUE RIVER'S fortunes were tied to the local ski resort, Blue Mountain, and their fortunes turned on the weather. Late November nights were more and more frigid, but Del's winning snowfall had been the last considerable precipitation. If God wasn't going to make snow, men could, and would.

Nightly, the slopes of Blue Mountain glowed with the eerie, mist filled light of the busy activity of making snow. Each morning, the residents looked to the expanding white slopes, oddly contrasted against the brown and green of the dry surrounding mountain sides. Tourists arrived, filling hotels and lodges, though not to the capacity that heavy snows inevitably brought. Some found the contrast between snowy slopes and the dry streets of town odd but acceptable. At least they could ski. Others grumbled, unhappy without a total winter wonderland.

For the residents, life went on, with or without the snow. The week leading up to Thanksgiving was a busy one.

Bella had Mary and Del working overtime preparing for the day after Thanksgiving: Black Friday, the retail world's make-or-break, hottest shopping day of the year.

Claire had out-of-town clients coming in over the holiday and needed to prepare for their arrival.

Gwen was overwhelmed with holiday orders. She didn't

mind the long days–and nights.   Every extra order was money in their strike fund.   Even Cammi didn't mind the extra hours, but she'd be leaving the day before Thanksgiving to fly home for the holiday.   Good thing Andy would be back by mid-week.   He wasn't off again until the Monday after, and could lend a hand at the cash register if needed, and that would free her to bake.

Holiday profits felt like extra money, but they weren't, really.   Gwen knew it was all part of the same *kitty,* making up for slower months.

Gwen's holiday would truly begin Thanksgiving morning, when Jeff's flight arrived.   The bakery closed late the night before, and Gwen worked even later finishing up preparations for her own big meal.

She started Thanksgiving at dawn with a triple latte as she rinsed and stuffed the turkey.   The large bird would take all day in her oven, cooking low and slow to moist perfection. Andy made her a second latte as she accomplished one last task, her favorite, putting clean sheets on Jeff's bed.

"I could drive down by myself to pick him up, you know," Andy said, handing her the additional caffeine.

"I know, but I love being there.   I love...greeting him. Sounds stupid, I guess."

"No, babe, it sounds nice."   He wrapped his arms around her and kissed her forehead.   "You're a good mama bear."

"Grrr," she growled softly.   "Maybe papa bear will get lucky tonight.   If he doesn't hibernate after he eats all that turkey."

"I'll pace myself," he said and kissed her just long enough to stimulate her imagination.

"How long to get to the airport?" she asked, dreamily. The trip into Denver to pick up Jeff would take all morning, and then some.

"Too long to stop for what you're thinking about...but I'll

remind you later."

"Promise?"

"Definitely. Okay, mama, let's go get your cub. If we're lucky, we'll be back before kickoff."

D EL WHIPPED THE WARM SWEET potatoes, adding butter, maple syrup and spices. She spread the creamy mixture into a large, flat baking dish and sprinkled miniature marshmallows across the top. Sandy sniffed the air and, standing on her hind legs, pawed softly at her leg.

"Okay, here's one for you." She placed a small marshmallow in his open mouth and patted his little head. "That's all though, don't want you getting sick." Sandy licked his lips and sat, looking expectantly up. "Sorry, I don't have any turkey for you this year."

She scooped him up in her arms and looked at her kitchen. "I don't think it's ever been this clean on Thanksgiving. And it doesn't smell right, does it?" she said, realizing how odd it was to be alone in her kitchen on Thanksgiving morning, watching the Macy's parade and preparing only her special sweet potato casserole and nothing else. No scent of onion and sage from her stuffing, no fresh green beans to be cleaned, no cranberry sauce bubbling on the stove.

Soon, the smell of cooking turkey should fill the air. She'd have to wait til she got to Gwen's house later in the afternoon for that. Was it really so bad to skip making the entire meal? Next year, she thought, she'd have to make it all, maybe make some new traditions for her and the kids. This year was Micky's turn for Thanksgiving.

It would be fun to have the meal with Gwen and her family, especially dessert. What did a baker bake for themselves on such a special day? Del looked forward to finding out, but knew she'd have to be careful to save room. Her mother was expecting her for dessert at her house in the evening. At least she'd let her off the hook about dinner.

"You're not coming for the meal?" her mother had asked.

"Well...we don't usually come until dessert anyway, Mother." Though some of her brothers and their families always came home for the holiday, Micky had insisted they have their own Thanksgiving at home and then visit her family for dessert. While Del enjoyed making their own meal, she didn't savor the guilt her mother inevitably served with her pecan pie.

"I know, but I thought this year..."

"Me too," she said, suddenly feeling genuinely sorry she hadn't put her mother's meal before Gwen's. "I'm sorry, I guess I wasn't thinking. Gwen asked and, well, since Cara and Nate are at Micky's, I thought it might be fun."

"I wouldn't want you to miss having fun just to spend time with me, dear."

From anyone else, those words might have been genuine, but Del knew her mother, whether deliberately or not, picked this sword with two edges.

"Mother, please, I didn't mean it that way."

"Neither did I, dear."

"I promise I'll be there for dessert. In fact, I'll probably be there before dinner is even over. I'll save room...you know how much I love your sweet potatoes." That was the truth, she thought, looking at the filled dish on her counter. She was making her mother's recipe. She thought about telling her that, wondered if her mother would appreciate it, maybe even be flattered, then, unsure why, decided not to.

"I'll make extra, so you'll have some to take home. And some turkey–you'll want leftovers."

Del put the casserole in the refrigerator and went to shower. "Don't worry, Sandy," she said to the little pitter patter that followed her up the stairs, "Mother is saving leftover turkey for us...well, for me, but we're a team, right?" Sandy jumped onto the bed, danced a circle or two and curled up on Del's pillow.

***

"HEY, MOM, CAN YOU FIX these?" Jeff walked into the kitchen holding a pair of jeans with a large, "L" shaped rip in the back of one leg. He was taller than Gwen, not hard to be, but taller than Andy too. Jeff had straight brown hair like his mother's, growing scraggly over ears and shirt collar, and a lean and muscular body that moved with lanky elegance.

"I'll try," she said, and hugged him.

"What's that for?"

"Because I can. Moms don't need an excuse. Besides, I've got months of hugs to make up for."

"I should have known you'd be like this," he said, "hang on," he set down the pants and wrapped her in a big hug, lifting her off the floor.

"Whoa!" she laughed, half afraid he'd hurt himself, but joyous her grown son would still hug his mother with such enthusiasm.

"Now that's a hug!" Andy said, walking into the kitchen.

"She wanted a hug, she got one." Jeff smiled as he set his mother down, and then opened the refrigerator door. "What's to eat?"

"I've got a whole Thanksgiving dinner almost ready, mister," she said.

"I know, I mean right now. Any appetizers, or stuff like that? Some dip or..." he shut the frig and went to the pantry, "how about chips? I'm starving."

"There's chips and salsa, if you'll dump the salsa in a bowl for the company. Don't eat too much though."

"Who's coming this time?" he asked, accustomed to his mother's habit of inviting friends for holiday dinners.

"A couple of my friends you don't know yet. You'll like them. And Bob."

"Bob's coming?" Jeff had known Bob since he'd first arrived in Blue River and discovered Gwen's éclairs.

"Yes, but you can't talk to him about the move," Andy said.

"*Possible* move," Gwen corrected. "At least not while Del and Claire are here."

"Del and Claire?"

"My friends who are coming. They don't know about it yet."

"What kind of friends can't you tell about important stuff like maybe moving?" Jeff asked, pouring salsa from a large jar into a green pottery bowl.

"New friends. I don't want this to get in the way.""Of what?"

"...friendship, I guess."

"That's stupid."

"Jeff!"

"I agree," Andy added, "well, not about the stupid part, but about the not telling friends part."

"I'll tell them when I'm ready. It's just, okay, I know it's stupid, but I don't want them to feel like, you know, like it's not worth being my friend, since I may be leaving."

"Geez, Mom, you're not even leaving the state. It's not that far away."

"Far is kind of relative for friendships. I found that out last time we moved. If you're out of the circle, you're out."

"That doesn't make any sense," Jeff said, taking salsa and chips into the living room.

"Is that what this is about?" Andy asked.

"What?"

"You told me when you and Bill got divorced and you moved up here from Denver that all your old friends stopped calling. That nobody stayed in touch."

"It's true. I might as well have moved to Brazil! You'd think I'd left the country."

"Nobody stayed in touch?"

"A couple did; for a while. But it's too much trouble, you know? They had their lives, in their town, and I had mine. You have to really care to work that hard at a friendship."

"And they didn't care?"

Gwen shrugged her shoulders, turning her attention to a steaming pot on the stove.

"Hey," Andy nuzzled up behind her, wrapping arms around her waist. "And you're worried these gals don't care that much either?"

"I don't know. It's really too early. We're only just all getting to know each other. And all of our plates are over-flowing. Who has time to work that hard?"

"Maybe you'll be one big smorgasbord of friendship."

"Or not."

"You should give them more credit."

"I'm not sure I've known them long enough to give them any credit."

"So negative," he said, kissing her neck. "You sound like one of those friends you left behind."

"Maybe you're right. Who knows, maybe they will be the best friends I've ever had. Maybe they'll be the kind of friends who stick to you like family."

"You would be a friend like that."

"Takes two."

"Or three. We won't say anything, Babe, but you wait and see. It's not location that makes family or friendship."

"Yeah, but it helps."

Twenty-Two

GWEN WAS HELPING DEL UNWRAP her sweet potato casserole and put it in Gwen's oven when the phone rang.

"Gwen, it's Claire."

"You on your way?" Gwen asked.

"That's why I'm calling. I'm trying to get there as soon as I can. Listen, I'm really sorry, but these people, I'd hoped to unload them early and have at least part of Thanksgiving off."

"Are you still with them?"

"Yeah, we're touring the area and I'm showing them all the vacant homes I could find. Who wants to have people looking at their house while they're eating turkey, right? They're inside, I'm outside-told 'em I had to get something from the car. I am so sorry..."

"Don't worry about it. I knew you were busy, that's why I told you not to bring anything."

"I'm hoping another hour or two, tops, maybe I can come by for dessert?"

Bob walked into the kitchen with a large salad bowl. "Where do you want this, Gwen?"

"Over there," she pointed to the counter.

"You need anything else?" he asked.

"Not now, you guys just let me know when we're getting

close to half-time."

"*Dinner* time!" Del clarified.

"Right!" Bob said, pulling a beer from the frig before he left.

"Was that Bob?" Claire asked.

Gwen caught Del's eye and said slowly into the phone, "Yes, that was Bob."

Del put her hands on her hips and tilted her head, trying to decipher the bent of the conversation.

"Oh."

"Bob doesn't have any family in the area. We always invite him for the holidays."

"Well...that's very nice, Gwen. I wouldn't expect any less of you. Sounds like you're taking in all the strays this year, I guess."

"Claire, you are not a stray."

Del opened her mouth, shut it, then took the phone from Gwen. "Hi Claire, it's Del. Another stray."

"I didn't mean it that way," Claire protested.

"I know, but you deserve a nice holiday. You tell those stupid people from Botswana-"

"Singapore."

"Whatever. You tell them to go back to their hotel and eat their own turkey."

"I would, but they're vegetarians. Very, very, *very* wealthy vegetarians who want to spend an obscene amount of money on a house they'll only live in three or four weeks of the year."

"Really?"

Gwen looked at Del, narrowing her eyes and taking her turn trying to decipher the conversation.

"Really. Listen, I'll try, but I...just don't know. Uh-oh, gotta go, they're waving at me from the upstairs balcony-what?"

Del could hear a conversation in the background.

"You can always have one installed!" she heard Claire say.

"What's she want installed?" Del asked.

"You don't want to know. Listen, I've gotta go. The Mrs. is worried about the *Chi* at the front door. Think we've got to throw some coins or something."

"What?!"

"You wouldn't believe some of the shit people do when they're looking at houses, Del. These folks are all about feng shui, good Chi and crap like that. Not that I discriminate against someone's superstitions...but it can get pretty frustrating. They toss coins at the entrance and if they don't come up right, they won't even consider the place. I had a client once who loved a house so much she went back three times to toss the coins–I even asked a friend who goes to Vegas several times a year to find out if there was such a thing as "loaded" coins, you know, like the dice?"

"Is there?"

"No dice. Listen, tell Gwen I'll try...but...well, I'll see. Bye!"

"Bye." Del handed the phone back to Gwen.

"She's not coming," Gwen said.

"She said she'd try, she's really busy, something about chi and coins."

"Chi and coins? What the–whatever that's about, I don't think that's what it's really about. It's about *Bob*."

THE ONLY PROBLEM WITH FOREIGN buyers is that they had no respect for national holidays. Well, Claire-thought, some foreign buyers. And truthfully, the Wangs weren't so much a perfect example of foreigners as they were stunning representatives of that most desired and dreaded of all clients, the uber wealthy, self-centered, fulfill-our-desires-in-three-days-or-we'll-find-someone-else kind of client. They came from all countries and nationalities, even her own.

But a commission like that could buy a lot of breathing room and Claire had to admit–if only to herself–that it was getting harder to breathe every day.

She turned the corner across from the bakery, just down from Gwen's house, pulled to the curb and turned out her lights.

The Wangs had finally given up the search, as least for the day, and she'd returned them to their hotel with the thought that, perhaps, she'd be in time for dessert. Now, almost on the threshold, she paused. She recognized the silver pick-up from Bob's driveway on the day they'd met at her car.

Claire popped the console between the seats, pulled out the bottle of antacids and chewed thoughtfully, wondering if her need was a by-product of her clients or...something else. She was tired. A relaxing evening with friends might be just the thing, but this felt more like a blind date. Bob was nice enough, and persistent.

Still, she'd been on a mission for a long time now, and she remembered that happy young face focused on the new IPad that Sally had sent. She was his chance, she always had been, and she wouldn't let him down now by loosing her own focus.

But couldn't she do her part and still save a part for herself? Claire wondered. What was the compromise between selfless and selfish? And even if she did decide to give Bob a chance, her history in that area was a painful one. She smirked to herself and shook her head. "You're such a hard ass...," she leaned back against the headrest and rubbed the discomfort beneath her ribs, "...maybe you're just full of shit...or just chicken shit!" She smiled at her own joke and then jumped at the sound of a door slamming.

Across the street she saw Bob walk down Gwen's front steps carrying a large plastic bag. He walked out of sight, behind the bakery and Claire heard the clang of a dumpster lid, then he returned without the bag and walked up the stairs. He opened the door, then turned, looking down the street toward her car.

In the darkness she hoped she couldn't be seen. Though she'd doused her headlights her engine was still running and the dashboard lights shined faintly up at her. Could he see her? Did he see her? Was he even looking at her car?

She held her breath, thinking for a second that perhaps she should just give up and get out, say hello and join him and the others for a cozy family-style evening. Then he turned, went inside and the door slammed shut. She sighed. Had she been saved or had she blown it? She took another antacid, put the car in gear, turned around and didn't turn on her lights until she was two blocks away.

WHEN IT CAME TO HOLIDAY desserts, Del discovered Gwen was a traditionalist. "It's nothing fancy," Gwen had said as she handed out the pumpkin pie.

"You're wrong. This is the best pumpkin pie I've ever eaten," Del said after a few bites.

"Mom's pie's the best," Jeff said around a mouth full. "Mom's *anything* is the best-my friends always want to know if Mom is baking anything-for home, you know, not for the bakery- before they decide whose house to hang out at."

"Smart friends," said Bob, enjoying his own slice of pie.

"It's the crust," Andy added, "she's got a secret recipe."

"It's not so secret if you just take the time to figure out the science of crust. You've got to know your ingredients, your environment."

"You shoulda' been a scientist, Mom."

"Baking *is* a science."

"A lot tastier than physics, I'll bet," Bob said.

"What did you do to the pecans?" Del asked.

"They're toasted, then caramelized before I chop them up. It's pretty simple, really, just plop some fresh whipped cream on top of the pie, sprinkle with the pecans and–"

"Pumpkin pie nirvana," Andy said, taking another large bite.

"It's so yummy," Del agreed. "I'm sorry Claire couldn't make it, she would have loved this."

"I'm sorry she couldn't make it either," Gwen agreed, "you'd have liked her," she added to Jeff.

"Maybe she can come for Christmas Eve," Jeff said.

"Yes! Del, you should come too."

"Oh...I don't know, Cara and Nate will be with me."

"Even better, we start at three, and you can come late, leave early, or leave when you're done."

"Done?"

"Ever since I broke my leg," Jeff explained, "Mom invites her friends over to the bakery on Christmas Eve and we make cookies an' stuff, for the firemen, policemen and everybody."

"It's a tradition," Gwen explained, "we started it the year after Jeff broke his leg snowboarding on Christmas Eve."

"I was twelve."

"The ambulance took him from the mountain clinic to St. Francis in Green Valley. We spent Christmas Eve night–"

"*And* Christmas," Andy added.

"Yep, he ended up having surgery and they didn't send him home until a few days after Christmas. I never really thought about all the people who work the holidays until then."

"It was kinda fun," Jeff said, "Mom and Andy brought all our presents to my hospital room."

"And pie and cookies. I gave every staff member who came in a slice of pie or some cookies."

"Seemed like they showed up a lot that day," Andy said. "And they brought Jeff a stuffed animal."

"Some ladies in town made them for kids who spent the holidays in the hospital," Gwen said.

"I was kinda old for that," said Jeff.

"Yeah, but I noticed you've kept it," added Gwen, reaching out to run her hand through her son's hair and brush it from his eyes.

"You've still got it in your room," said Andy. "I remember I was going to carry it for you when you left the hospital, but you wanted to hold it."

"Well...," Jeff shrugged and then, changing the subject, stood up and said, "who wants more pie?"

"I'll have another," said Andy.

"Me, too," said Bob, "I'll help you." He stood and took Andy's plate and followed Jeff into the kitchen.

"That was our first Christmas together," Gwen said to Andy.

"We weren't married yet."

"We weren't even engaged. When Jeff broke his leg I remember thinking, well, I guess I'll really see if Andy's up for the whole family experience now."

"I think I passed the test," he wrapped his arm around her and kissed her cheek.

"He was at the hospital almost as much as I was."

"That's how we got to see all the staff that spent their holiday taking care of Jeff."

"And us! They were so nice. They put up Christmas lights around their work area, everybody brought in decorations and whatever treats were traditional. It made it special for them and it was special for the patients, too. St. Francis isn't that big of a hospital, so it really felt like family."

"That's when Gwen got the idea of making goodies for them."

"But I didn't have time, not that year. Jeff's leg really messed up our schedule."

"So the next year, she decided to make Christmas cookies and pies for the pediatric staff at the hospital, and the paramedics who transported him-and the firemen. We all helped."

"The next year I thought it would be fun to invite a couple friends to help, too."

"That's when the tradition really took off. Now she fills Christmas orders at the bakery until three on Christmas Eve, then closes up and we all come in and start baking whatever she tells us to bake!"

"I'm the brownie guy," Bob said, carrying in fresh pie for Andy and himself. "Can't blow brownies, right Gwen?"

"Right...not that you are a bad cook, Bob."

"Just don't want to find out for sure, huh?" Bob laughed.

"Then we divvy up the results and go off in groups and deliver. We've added a few more people to our list of recipients over the years. The police station in town and the emergency medical staff at the base of Blue Mountain.

"It's a manageable list for now, but if our community gets much bigger...well," Gwen set her empty plate on the coffee table and nestled up against Andy, "it's a lot of goodies!"

"May have to find a smaller community," Bob said, catching Gwen's eye and smiling.

"Maybe." Gwen frowned. The room was silent for a moment. "Anyway, it would be great if you could come. Claire too."

"Maybe she could make it on Christmas Eve," said Del. "Poor Claire, she's missing out on everything."

"Hmmm." Bob nodded his head and took another bite of pie.

"She must be home by now," said Gwen, "it's dark, after all. Knowing Claire, she's at home doing paperwork and eating crackers and cheese."

"We should take some dinner over to her–and pie!" said Del.

"That's a great idea, Del," said Gwen.

"I've got to get to my Mom's soon or she'll kill me. I suppose I could stop by Claire's first."

"No, don't be silly," said Gwen, "you go. Andy and I can–"

"You've done enough for one day," Bob interrupted. "I'll drop it off."

"Oh?" said Gwen, looking at Del.

"No problem," Bob assured her, "wrap it up and I'll run it by on the way home." *Even if it's the long way home*, Bob thought.

Twenty-Three

"TURN AT THE NEXT RIGHT," the pleasant but monotone female voice directed. Bob glanced at the GPS screen in his truck. He'd programmed in the address Gwen wrote down and was nearly to Claire's home. Gwen had wanted to call ahead, to be sure she'd be there, but Bob volunteered to do that too, saying he'd coordinate dropping off the food with a neighbor if she wasn't home yet. In truth, he didn't plan to call ahead. That would give her time to escape.

Claire lived in a townhome, but her community was an exclusive one and the townhomes were more like small, attached contemporary mountain chalets. The lawns were well tended and rambling, and the entire area was nestled into a forest of pines and aspens.

"Turn left in fifty feet."

"You got it, honey," Bob said. He glanced at the screen and slowed as he saw Claire's location near.

"Your destination is ahead on the right."

Bob double checked the address on the end unit.

"You have arrived at your destination," said the voice.

"Bingo," Bob agreed.

Claire's home looked like it had as much glass as wood. While the lower windows were shaded, you could see an expanse of vaulted ceilings and light wooden beams above.

Either Claire was home, or she had a bad habit of leaving all her lights on.

Bob grabbed the picnic basket Gwen and Del had packed and walked to the front door. He heard saxophone laden jazz drifting softly from within, hesitated a second, then rang the bell.

Nothing. He rang it again, stepped back from the door and looked up at the second story windows to his right. A curtain parted slightly, he waved at a shape silhouetted in the gap and it snapped shut. Bob waited.

Soon he detected movement behind the door, followed by the sound of two deadbolts unlocking. Claire opened the inside door and looked through an outer, glass security door.

She wore black Lycra sweatpants and a matching, zippered top. Her hair, obviously damp, was pulled back and clipped with a tortoise-shell clasp. The only make-up Bob detected was lip gloss, and even that, he thought, was unnecessary. Why mess with perfection?

"What are you doing here?" she asked.

"Good evening to you, too, Claire." He smiled and held up the basket. "I've brought Thanksgiving, courtesy of Gwen and Del."

She looked at the basket, then back at him. "Oh."

"Can I bring it in? I promise not to...linger," he said, choosing the word carefully.

She opened the glass door and reached for the basket. "You don't have to bother–"

"It's heavy," he said, pulling it away.

"I can take it."

"I'm sure you can." He took his opportunity to squeeze past her and into her home. "But what kind of gentleman would I be if I let you."

"Hey," she said, holding the door, "you don't–"

"Great place," he said as he walked through her large living room, toward the open kitchen in the back. To his left a stone fireplace rose two stories to meet the vaulted aspen wood of the ceiling. The floors were terracotta tile, probably radiant heat underneath, he thought, and covered in the living room with a large, plush white carpet.

Claire's taste in furniture ran to light woods and creamy leathers with colorful contemporary oil paintings by a local artist Bob recognized. He stopped to admire one of them. She specialized in mountain-scapes, complete with wild-flowers and streams. He knew because he collected her works, too.

"Nice," he said. "I've got the columbine series she did a couple years ago," he added and moved on.

"Really?" Claire said, a little surprised Bob had even noticed the painting. Then, realizing his progress into her domain she started toward him, saying, "Listen, you really don't have to-" Then she realized the door wasn't shut and she hadn't bolted the deadbolts, she hesitated, glanced back toward Bob, then, flustered, pushed the door quickly shut and turned the latch on one of the bolts. Bob, meanwhile, moved farther on.

To his right was an open, steel and wood stairway. Through the stairs he could see into a glass walled study. Gwen had been right. The desk was strewn with paperwork and the computer screen showed work in progress. A coffee cup sat by the mouse pad.

Bob set the basket on the black granite kitchen counter and admired the accompanying stainless steel and blonde wood décor. The smell of brewing coffee still hung in the air, and an open box of gourmet sugar cookies was the only kitchen clutter in sight.

"Looks like you need dinner," he said, opening the basket and pulling out a large, Styrofoam container; the sort that restaurants used for leftovers. He opened the hinged lid.

Inside, Gwen had filled compartments with generous help-
ings of turkey, dressing, stuffing and mashed potatoes with
gravy and green beans.

"Microwave?" he asked, looking around the kitchen.

"I'm not hungry," Claire said, approaching the counter.

Bob looked at the cookies and then at her. "You've got to
be kidding." Then, spotting the microwave, he placed the
container inside and turned it on.

Claire was supremely unaccustomed to having her wishes
ignored in such a polite, but officious manner. If she'd had
the presence of mind to think about it, she would have wondered why she hadn't grabbed his arm and kicked him back
out the second he'd tried to come in. But Bob affected her
presence of mind.

"Listen, I've got plenty to do before tomorrow, so you can
just leave that here." She reached to stop the microwave but
he placed his hand over the door and blocked her.

"Wine?"

"What?"

"Wine?" he said again and reached back into the basket to
pull out a bottle, then, spotting wine glasses behind a glass
cabinet door, he picked out two.

"Stop!" Claire said, throwing up her hands in frustration.

"Claire," Bob said, softly, setting down glasses and looking
her directly in her eyes. "Tell you what. You agree to eat at
least a few bites of this great meal Gwen sent over, and have
a glass of with me in the process, and I promise I will then
take off and let you get back to your work."

She opened her mouth to speak, then shut it, crossed her
arms and sighed.

"What do you say?" Bob asked, waiting patiently for her
response.

"I eat a little, I drink a little, you leave."

"Perhaps a little conversation could take place in the process. And I'd like your opinion on the wine–it's one of mine. It's red, the way you like it."

"I thought you had to drink white with turkey."

"Old wive's tale."

"Then you leave?"

"The sooner you eat and drink, the sooner I'm gone. Now, where are your plates?"

Claire had intended to play Bob's game right back at him, take a couple sips, a couple bites and send him on his way. But the smells and tastes of Gwen's turkey dinner, combined with the rich bouquet and delightful flush she felt at the taste of Bob's wine softened her resolve, and she settled in to enjoy her meal. After all, she thought, she'd complied with the deal, so she could send him on his way anytime she wished. So what could a little company with dinner hurt?

"Gwen's quite a cook, in the bakery and otherwise," Bob commented, swirling his glass and watching the fingers of wine settle back in the bowl.

"Did she send dessert?"

"Oh, yes," Bob said, "I put it in your refrigerator, for later, if you like."

"This was nice of her. I guess I'll have to thank her, even though..." She looked across the table at Bob, realizing she might have taken the thought too far.

"Even though it meant me barging in on your evening."

"I didn't say that." She reached for her glass and took another, generous sip. If pressed, she would have to admit it was a wonderful red.

"Why didn't you come in?"

"What?" She almost choked on her wine and cleared her throat as she reached for her napkin.

"You sat in the street and looked at the house, and me, and then you drove off."

She played with her dressing and considered denying it,

but Bob was clearly a man who wouldn't accept anything but the truth.

"I didn't feel up to it."

"The dinner, or the company?"

"Bob. It's nothing personal, it's only..."

"You're in a committed relationship with someone else?"

"No." She looked at him, and then down again.

"You find me repulsive?"

"No!" she said, realizing she'd answered too fast, then, lowering her voice, added, "just the opposite."

"I see. And you avoid *just the opposite?*"

"I try to keep my life...uncomplicated. I've got a full plate, know what I mean?"

"I do," he said, "don't let me take your appetite away," he nodded at her dinner.

She picked at another bite, then set her fork down and took another sip of wine.

"You like it?"

"Hmmm," she nodded, "very much."

"I'm glad." He took another, slow, savoring swallow and watched her pick up a green bean with her fingers and nibble small bites. "I know about complication, Claire. Maybe Gwen mentioned to you that I came out here after a rough divorce."

"Where'd you come from?" she asked, eyeing him across the table.

"Chicago. Much nicer climate here; good for grapes."

"What did you do, back in Chicago?"

"Stockbroker. I know," he said, seeing her surprise, "quite a change."

"I'd say."

"I was ready for a change. I was a success in a high pressure business. You can probably relate."

"Am I a success?"

He looked around her home and then at her. "I think you know you are."

"I suppose," she admitted.

"I thought that meant I was a success all around. Found out differently, though. Seems I was a lousy husband. Too busy to figure out my wife wasn't happy. Too busy to realize she deserved to be happy."

"Did you have kids?"

"No, thank God, that's one good thing. She didn't want kids, at least not for a while. She was an interior decorator-still is, I suppose. We don't stay in touch. Anyway, she wanted to wait to have kids. We would have, if it had worked out. I like kids," he said, catching her eye. "But by the time I figured out what it would take to make it right, it was all wrong."

"No counseling?"

"No. Not that I wouldn't, but, well...she'd moved on."

"What was his name?"

"Exactly." He nodded and drank some more. "Jim, I think. Not sure I cared, really. Decided I needed out-of everything. We both made good livings, so we pretty much called it even. I sold my business, gave her the condo on Lakeshore Drive and came west."

"Why west?"

"Had a friend...in Napa, actually. He's a vintner, has a big winery out there. I rented a little house overlooking his grapes. I didn't intend to take that path, but then I started hanging out with him, walking the fields, helped with the harvest. It was something to do.

"Then I got interested, so I took classes and worked for him-gratis. Started out as a hobby, but, the more I did it the more I thought, maybe that was what I really wanted to do. Make my living doing my hobby."

"Sounds fun," she took a large piece of turkey, scooped

some mashed potatoes and gravy on the side and ate.

"Don't get me wrong, it's hard work. Not easy, and no guarantees. Basically, I'm a farmer, and farming can be a lot of work."

"But work you love?"

"Hmmm," he nodded. "Once I decided, I needed a plan. It's pretty established back there, I needed a smaller pond, that's how I ended up in Palisade-on the western slope. One thing led to another." He tapped his glass against the label on the bottle. "That's me."

Claire liked the label, putting two and two together she realized it was a print of a columbine in the style of the artist Bob had admired. "Columbine Estates. Did she," Claire indicated the painting on her wall, "design your label?"

"She did. Came up with four choices, I picked this one, but I bought all four paintings, too good to pass up. I hung them in our tasting room."

"Sounds like you traded one set of complications for another."

"Maybe I did, but it never felt that way. No matter how busy I am, my life feels simple."

"No new Mrs. in all this time?"

"No...a few friends, yes, but nothing complicated."

"So, what am I, Bob? A new friend?"

He drained his glass, stood and, fishing his car keys out of his pocket, walked around the table. "No," he said, leaning down, one hand on the back of her chair, one on the table, his face to hers. "You, Claire, are most definitely a complication."

Claire looked up at him, thinking she was cornered, and realizing it had been a long time since a man had cornered her, and not the other way around.

Bob leaned in closer and softly kissed her cheek. "Happy Thanksgiving," he whispered against her skin, and he left.

Twenty-Four

"IMAGINE," DEL SAID CHEERFULLY INTO the phone, "how may I help you?"

"Del?" said the woman's voice.

"Uh-yes,"

"It's Carolyn, from the Ladies League."

"Oh, sure, hi Carolyn," Del said, recalling Carolyn had left a message on Del's home phone over a week ago. She'd needed help with the Holiday luncheon and Del, knowing how difficult it always was for her to say no to a good cause, had avoided calling Carolyn back, for fear she'd get roped into volunteer work she didn't have time for.

"Did you get the message I left you last week?"

"Umm...no, I didn't get a message," Del lied. "Maybe one of my kids got it and forgot about it. That happens sometimes, you know."

"Yes, of course. Listen, I'm really sorry about calling you at work-"

"How'd you know I worked here?" Del couldn't help asking. She'd barely spoken with any of her old friends; they all seemed to be avoiding her.

"You know Abbie Rodriquez? She's the cookbook committee chair this year, by the way."

"That's nice; Abbie should be good at that." Del always

tried to be positive, thinking the best whenever possible. Plus, she thought it would be unkind to say she felt Abbie would be challenged organizing her own address book, let alone the entire cookbook that was the driving force behind the Ladies League fundraiser.

"Abbie talked with Kelly, she's a teacher's aide at Forest Trail Elementary, and Kelly said one of the parents mentioned seeing you at Imagine when she was shopping."

"Oh." Del knew the downside of heading up any sort of non-profit venture was that lots of people knew who you were, but you often didn't know them. She wondered if that had been slimy shoe-store Ted's secret source of her personal information.

"I know you must be busy-"

"It *is* the day after Thanksgiving," Del pointed out. The store had only been open an hour and already she'd rung up several sales and needed to re-stock items from the dressing rooms. Mary was behind her, ringing up orders, and Bella was making the rounds of customers on the floor, inquiring if anyone needed help.

"I know, I'm sorry, but the luncheon is only a week away, and I really need to ask you about something. You're the only one I can ask, Del. Angela is like a volunteer Nazi. She's bossing everyone around and everyone hates her-Oh, I'm sorry I said that, please don't tell her!"

"Don't worry, Carolyn, I wouldn't." She wouldn't say anything, but she felt a little guilty taking so much satisfaction out of knowing that her replacement wasn't very popular. Del had prided herself that her volunteers were always happy enough to return to volunteer the following year.

"Anyway, I'd ask Angela, but she's got this way of making you feel like every question is stupid-and you're stupid too, know what I mean?"

"Hm-mm," Del nodded.

"I just need to run a few things by you, it will only take a minute, I promise. Can you talk now? I have to give Angela a report later today and, well, I *really* want to get this stuff figured out first. Please?"

Del could hear the desperation in Carolyn's voice, and she doubted any of her issues were that major. "I suppose I could spare a few minutes. Can you hold while I switch phones?"

"Absolutely, Del. Whatever works for you."

"Great. Hang on, I'll be right back."

Del pressed the hold button and scanned the store. Mary only had one other customer in line at the register, and Bella was busy removing a silk dress from one of the mannequins in the front window as a customer stood by smiling. Must have been the last one in her size, Del thought. There actually seemed to be a small lull from the first rush when they'd opened the doors.

"Mary, if you don't mind, I think I'll clean up the dressing rooms a little."

"Good plan," Mary said over her shoulder as she wrapped a blouse in tissue. "I'll help you when I'm done here."

Del swept quickly through the dressing rooms and took everything into the back, where she could re-hang and re-fold before re-stocking; and where she could talk to Carolyn in private.

Fifteen minutes later, with Carolyn's problems easily solved, Del walked back into the front of the store carrying a pile of neatly folded sweaters. She was placing them in color coordinated stacks, her back to the front door, so she didn't see him walk in.

"Morning, Adele," he said, standing beside her, a big smile on his face, his hands dug into the pockets of a blue wool pea coat.

"Jimmy!" There was something about Jimmy standing in the middle of Imagine that took Del a moment to comprehend. They didn't get many male customers. The one's that did come in usually did so during the lunch hour, and they often asked to see one of the wish lists that customers could keep on file for gift-challenged husbands.

"The very same. How've you been?" he asked, taking her hand–which she hadn't really yet offered–and holding it more than shaking it.

"Oh, your hand is cold," she said, wrapping her other hand around his to warm it.

"Yours is warm." He wrapped his other hand around hers and squeezed them all lightly before letting go.

She noticed the chilly air had made his cheeks pink above the dark shadow of his freshly shaved face. She could tell he'd put product in his neatly trimmed black hair, but the wind still managed to muss the gray flecks at his temples. Del felt an urge to brush it back in place with her fingers. Was that a maternal urge, she wondered? She noted the pleasant and subtle scent of his aftershave and knew her urges were anything but.

"How was your Thanksgiving?" he asked.

"It was very nice. I went over to Gwen's house–you met her, she was with us at the...," Del hesitated, glancing to see that Bella and Mary weren't nearby before saying, "bar."

"Sure. Nice gal. So you had a good time?"

"Yes." Del smiled and nodded for a moment until her nervous fog cleared. "And you? Did you have a nice Thanksgiving?"

"Always do. Been having my employees and their families to the restaurant for years now; it's a tradition."

"Really?"

"Yeah. We push all the tables together. We make turkeys and hams in the big ovens, mashed potatoes, stuffing–we do it all up big. Traditional like. Plus everybody brings something. Lots of fun. Lot of my kids–waitresses, busboys, cooks–they come out here to ski and can't afford to go home. It's the closest they get to family."

"That's really nice, Jimmy," Del said, loosing track of the store around her.

"You should come next year."

"Oh. Well..."

"If you're free."

"Del!" Bella's voice interrupted their conversation. "Did we sell that gold knit tank?" she asked, joining them at the table.

"No, it's in the back room. I haven't re-hung it yet. I could get it–"

"Don't bother, you help this gentleman," Bella smiled at Jimmy, "I'll find it." Bella was a wise business woman who knew better than to judge the size of a customer's credit limit by their appearance.

"Actually, we were just...," Del didn't want to admit he wasn't a customer, but felt guilty visiting with Jimmy when there was work to be done.

"She was just going to show me a scarf my mother might like," Jimmy said, covering for Del. "Nice place you have here, by the way. Are you the manager?"

"Why, yes, I am." Bella introduced herself and they shook hands.

"Jimmy DiSanto. Owner of the Dockside, you know it?"

"I do," Bella said pleasantly. "I've enjoyed the view from your deck a few times. The best rainbow trout I've had, also."

"That's what I like to hear, Bella. You give me a nod the next time you're in. I've got a new chardonnay from Australia that goes great with that trout. I'd love you to try it, compliments of the owner." He tapped his chest.

Del noticed how easily Jimmy fell into comfortable conversation with Bella, someone he'd only just met. Bella promised to take him up on his offer, then excused herself to find the tank top for her customer.

"You let me know if you can't find something Mr. DiSanto likes," she said to Del. Then she winked at Jimmy and left.

Del had never seen Bella wink at anyone. Ever. In fact, if pressed, Del would say Bella wasn't the winking type.

"Wow. You made a good impression on her."

"Not hard to make a good impression, Adele. Not if you try. So, how about the scarves?"

"You really want a scarf?"

"Really want a scarf. Really have a mother who I think might like one. What do you say? She's eighty-seven and she's a big fan of green and red-Italian, you know? Got anything she'd like?"

"Right this way, Mr. DiSanto," she said, and feeling surprisingly flirtatious, she winked at him, too.

"Hey, there's a lot of that going around," he joked as he followed.

Del helped Jimmy find the perfect scarf for his mother, along with a complimentary bracelet and relieved Mary at the register to ring up his purchase.

"You on commission here?" Jimmy asked.

"No," she said, placing the bracelet in a small, powder blue box with the Imagine "I" embossed in white across the top.

"Too bad. Suppose it's not really appropriate to tip in a clothing store, either, is it."

"No, nobody does that." She grinned and shook her head.

"Well, then Adele, you leave me no other choice," he said in a serious tone.

"Excuse me?" she looked up from wrapping the scarf, unsure what he meant.

"You don't get commission for my purchase, and I can't tip you for the excellent service-and it was excellent, by the way."

"Thank you," she said, a quizzical look on her face.

"I'm forced to show my appreciation by asking you out to dinner tonight."

"What?" Del hadn't expected the offer, at least not at the moment.

"You opened up, so I figure Bella won't keep you more than eight hours–maybe nine in a crunch. Would you be free by, say, seven?"

"I-I..., you really don't have to-"

"Don't have to do anything, Adele. But I'd very much like to take you out for a nice dinner. What do you say? I hear the Creperie is good."

"I love the Creperie!" Del said before she realized it.

"That's the ticket, then. Is seven good?"

"Maybe...seven-thirty? Is that too late?" She suppressed a pang of guilt at her sudden delight that the kids were with Micky until late the next day. "No problem. Write me up the directions to your house, okay?"

And, with a decided lack of hesitation that surprised even Del herself, she did.

Twenty-Five

"YOU DIDN'T LIKE IT BACK in Rhode Island?" Del asked, taking a sip of the wine Jimmy had ordered. The Creperie was known for its French wine selection, and Jimmy seemed right at home ordering a bottle he thought she'd enjoy. Del supposed a man who owned a bar-and restaurant, she kept reminding herself-ought to know about wines.

"Love Rhode Island, love the east coast, got a bunch of family back in Providence."

"But I thought you said, the other night, that you didn't like it back there, and that's why you came out here."

"Yes, and no," Jimmy said, "I love it back there, but... growing up, I had lots of chances to get into trouble, and I took a few of 'em. Nothing big," he added, noticing the anxious look on Del's face, "but enough to make it clear I was getting in with the wrong group of friends, if you know what I mean."

Del had heard about that sort of thing, but her parents saw to it that her environment never gave her such opportunities, not that she thought she would have taken them, if they'd come along.

"It's a great place to be *from*," Jimmy continued. "I try to go back, once every couple of years, but this is home now. If you dropped me off in the middle of nowhere, this is the place I'd want to get back to. 'Specially if it meant having dinner with such a beautiful lady." Jimmy touched his glass to hers, in a toast.

"Oh...thank you...that's...very sweet," Del stumbled over the words, unaccustomed to compliments and hoping the candlelight hid the blush she felt in her cheeks.

"Your salads," said the waiter, setting their plates before them.

As the waiter ground pepper to suit, Del regrouped her composure, enjoying both her surroundings and her wine. She'd never been to the Creperie for dinner before, only for lunch with friends. In daylight it was charming and tasteful, with country French décor and large multi-paned windows that let the sun brighten the room's soft colors and warm woods. But what happened in the evening, she thought, was almost magical.

The lights were dimmed, allowing candlelit tables to feel like cozy pools of intimacy in a sea of elegance. Twinkle lights wove around arching doorways and intermingled in floral displays. Much to Del's delight an actual, *live* harpist was playing in the sophisticated bar at the back of the restaurant. Music drifted romantically in and out of their conversation. Their table was next to a window that overlooked a garden, filled with more twinkle lights and a heated koi pond, complete with waterfall. On this chilly night the steam drifted off the water and enveloped the view in an ethereal mist.

Del tried to remember the last time she had felt so much a part of such a special evening...had it been that long ago that she and Micky shared evenings like this? When did that time stop? How could you say when a time stopped, she wondered, if you couldn't clearly remember that time at all?

"Adele?"

"Huh?" she said, suddenly pulled back from her thoughts.

"Looked like you were a long ways away," Jimmy said. "What were you thinking about?"

"Just...how nice this is. It's been a...long time."

"Ahh, I get ya. The divorce and all."

"And all."

"Did he hurt you pretty bad, your ex? Was it a rough divorce?"

"Was? Oh, no it's *still* a divorce, that is, we're still going through the divorce."

"Jesus, you mean you're not even officially on the market yet and I'm whisking you off to dinner?" Jimmy looked surprised, but smiled all the same.

"Yes. Is that okay?" Del wondered if there was some divorce rule she didn't know about. Her attorney hadn't told her not to date.

"Sure. It's great with me, just so long as it's great for you, too. Listen Adele, I think you're one special lady, but I don't want to put you in an uncomfortable situation, know what I mean?" Del thought about this and decided she didn't. "No."

"Well...I'm no expert, but I don't want it to hurt your case if word gets around you were on a date, make sense?"

She nodded her head, trying to follow his train of thought, then, reaching the conclusion shook her head and said, "No, it's not like that. It's friendly. And besides, it's Micky who should worry if it weren't."

"Oh, it's like that, huh? Micky Donahue? Don't think I know him."

"Actually, Donahue is my maiden name. I haven't decided yet if I'm going to go back to that, or keep my married name. After all, the kids are named Rufino. Don't you think that would be confusing for them?"

"Rufino? Micky *Rufino*?" Jimmy set his glass down and looked across the table at her, a scowl on his face.

"Oh, God. You know him?" Del said, suddenly realizing that maybe she'd made a big mistake by not mentioning her name when they first met. Apparently she was on a date with one of Micky's *friends*. "This was a mistake, I shouldn't have accepted, I mean, how could you have known?" She started to reach for her purse, uncertain how to get out of the evening, but feeling the need to.

"What?" Jimmy saw her purse and the confusion on her face. "Wait, now wait a second Adele." He reached across the table and placed his hand on her arm to stop her from standing. "There's no reason to leave on account of my knowing your soon-to-be ex. It's not like he's my friend."

"It's not?" She sat back on her chair.

"No ma'am. In fact, quite the opposite. Guy's a scumbag, you ask me. Sorry, hope I didn't offend you."

Del was surprised by his comment, but offended? "I don't think you did. In fact, I guess I agree."

"Right. And an idiot, that's what I'm thinking, now that I've met you. A real idiot not to see what a special gal he had. So you found out he was..."

"Jimmy, something tells me the next words out of your mouth are going to be *screwing around*."

"Didn't want to be that blunt, but yeah, that's pretty much it."

"How did *you* know?"

"I'm the observant type. Haven't seen him for a while, but he used to come in for lunch-regular-a new gal every few weeks, but he's the same, right down to the wedding ring. I notice."

"I wasn't so observant, it seems. It took me a while, but I figured it out."

"So you're doing...how?"

"Good, actually. Meeting Claire and Gwen, that's been good. My job is good."

"And me?" he asked. Del smiled but said nothing. "Let me guess. I'm good too, but it's a lot happening all at once."

"Yes." Del set her purse down and reached for her wine. "Are you divorced, Jimmy?"

"Nope. Can't say I've been down that road. Hope I never am."

"You're lucky."

"Luck's relative. I'm a widower."

"Oh, I'm sorry, I didn't know, I–"

"Don't. Like you said, you didn't know."

"What happened?" Del asked, resting her elbows on the table and focusing on him.

"It's been five–almost six years. Breast cancer. It's a shitty disease. Kathleen, that's–that *was* my wife's name, she fought hard, hung on as long as she could. But they didn't catch it early and it spread."

"Jimmy," Del reached her hand across and rested it on his. "I'm so sorry, truly I am."

"I know," he covered her hand with his. "I'm okay. Like I said, it's been a while. And there's the kids."

"You have kids?" Del hadn't even considered the possibility, and the complications of someone else's children.

"Two. Kat, my daughter, she's an attorney in Denver. My son, Joey, he lives in Manhattan. Raised him here, but, who knew, he's an east coast boy alright. From the moment we first visited it was clear, that was where he was meant to breathe the air."

"What's he do?"

"Decorator. I know what you're thinking."

"I didn't–"

"I know, but people do. Now I sound homophobic. I'm not." He smiled and shook his head. "Took me a long time to get to where I could say that last part. I wasn't raised to be "politically correct", know what I mean? When I was growing up, if you were gay-that's not what we called 'em, then, you know? You were careful who you told. So, it doesn't feel natural to me, so what? After a while you real-ize...who am I? People gotta live their lives.

"Anyways, he's got a "partner", that's what they call each other. They got married, ceremony and all, know what I mean?"

"Is it legal? I mean, recognized?"

"Was for a while, this stuff comes and goes. Joey's not dumb, though. They saw an attorney, made sure they're related one way or another. Especially with the kids."

"Kids?"

"Yeah, two little kids-twins! A friend of theirs was the surrogate mom, used Joey's-you know." Jimmy raised his eyebrows and looked around-at the other tables while adjust-ing the placement of his napkin.

"Oh, sure," Del said, playing with her food and finding it funny yet charming that Jimmy felt awkward saying the word *sperm* in front of her.

"So, I'm a grandpa, what do you think of that? Too old for you, now?"

"No," Del said, laughing, "I think you're a young grandpa."

"Thanks."

"And probably a good one, right?"

"I like to think so, when I can be. Don't see his kids often enough.

"Listen, Adele. We all got our pasts. But the Big Guy up there," he glanced up, "he thought you and I ought to meet, at least, that's the way I see it, know what I mean?"

Del nodded. "Yes, I think I do."

"If he thinks it's a good idea, who are we to argue? What do you say?"

"I think even Father Frank wouldn't mind if I said I defer to divine judgment," she said, laughing.

"Hey, you go to St. Benedict's too?"

"Yes. You're a member of my parish?" Del said, amazed they had their church in common.

"I go Friday nights, duck out during happy hour, back in time for the dinner service. That way I can sleep in on Sunday, enjoy my coffee and the paper. I'm betting you don't go to Friday night services, am I right?"

"Sunday mornings. Maybe...some weekend when the kids are out of town..."

"A Friday night church date? It's a deal, as long as I get to take you to dinner too."

They spent the evening discovering the coincidence of people they had in common and values they shared. By the time Jimmy walked Del to her front door, the combination of commonality and good wine had put her in a mood so warm she invited him in for coffee.

He paused and then asked, "You sure?"

"Sure. Don't you like coffee?"

"I love coffee."

"But?"

"It's late, and I don't want you to feel...uncomfortable."

"Why should I be uncomfortable?" she asked, leaning up against the front door and feeling, perhaps, too comfortable. She looked him in his darks eyes, felt her heart pounding and was suddenly aware of every breath she took. "Oh."

"Yeah," Jimmy said. "Honey, I don't want you doing anything you don't want to do, but..." He stepped closer, gently cupped his hand against the back of her free upper arm and lowered his voice. "If I come in, I'm gonna have a hard time keeping my mind on coffee."

She could feel his fingertips through her wool coat. They pressed against her sensitive inner arm and she squeezed her arm to her side in response, pressing the back of his hand against the side of her breast. Why was it so hard to breathe, she wondered, and opened her mouth in a slight gasp for air.

"Maybe I'd better go," he said, starting to release her.

"No," Del said quickly, surprising them both, then, softer, "no." She felt his hand pull her to him, pushing their bodies closer. His free hand found its way beneath her coat and, pressing against her spine, ran slowly up, pushing her against him. "Jimmy," she whispered, her eyes half closed, her lips brushing his chin. "I–"

"Adele, honey," Jimmy said, "you know I'm crazy about you, but, you say stop, I stop, promise."

"Don't stop," she whispered against his lips. She moaned with delight as he pulled her in, pressing his lips to hers. She felt like she'd melted into a delicious, warm pool of pleasure.

It would be hours before they got around to coffee.

Twenty-Six

"YOU COOK, TOO?" JIMMY ASKED. He walked up beside her as she cooked at the stove and wrapped an arm around her waist.

"I'm starving, aren't you?"

"Hmmm." He kissed her neck just below her ear and pulled her closer to him.

Del giggled. "For food, I mean. Did you sleep well?"

"Very," he said against her skin. "Your hair's still damp." She turned to face him, running both hands through his hair, "so's yours," and wrapping her arms around him, pulled him in for a long, slow kiss. He parted her bathrobe and cupped her bottom, pressing her against him. She felt the cool of his slacks against her stomach and the warmth of his bare chest against her breasts, tracing a hand up so she could run her fingers through the black hair that tickled at her nipples. "You're getting gray," she whispered, playing with his chest hair and smiling up at him.

"That's not the only place I'm getting gray."

"I noticed," she smiled and fell back into their kiss.

Del felt like all her senses were heightened. She smelled the pancakes on the griddle, the clean scent of Jimmy's hair and the smell of her shaving gel he'd borrowed to shave with her razor. She heard the breeze outside playing in her bamboo wind chimes, and the cooing of morning doves in her aspens. Then she heard the click of the deadbolt on her front door.

"Hey, Mom!" Nate called from the front hall.

"Oh, shit," Del whispered, tying her robe back together.

"Did you expect them?" Jimmy whispered back, straightening his hair and pulling on the shirt he'd laid over the back of a chair.

Del shook her head, combed her fingers through her hair and wiped her hands over her mouth and cheeks, as if the feel of his kiss was something that might show.

"Mommy, didn't you get Daddy's calls? Wait till you see what Daddy got me in the hospital gift shop-" Cara was saying as she rounded the corner into the kitchen and stopped to stare at Jimmy. The ten-year-old stood in pink sweats, thick black curls spilling in a mussed manner over her shoulders, her lavender ski jacket half off, clutching a large, stuffed white polar bear. "Hi," she said to Jimmy.

"Hi," Jimmy replied.

"This is...Mr. DiSanto," Del said. "He, ummm..."

"Pilot light went out on your mother's hot water heater-she got all wet and ran out of hot water, couldn't finish her shower, see? I came to light it for her. You must be Cara, nice to meet you." Jimmy reached for Cara's hand.

"How'd you know my name?"

"Your mother mentioned it."

"Nice to meet you, Mr. Di, Di..."

"Santo. DiSanto," Jimmy said, reaching to shake her small hand.

"Who are you?" Nate stood in the doorway, his shaggy dishwater blonde hair and freckled face made the twelve-year-old boy look almost like a miniature Del. He was supported by two crutches, a bright, neon green cast on his lower left leg.

"Nate!" Del cried and ran over to him. "What on earth

happened?!" She stooped in front of him, looking at the cast.

"Dad called. Didn't you get Dad's messages?" Nate asked, eying Jimmy over his mother's shoulder.

"I-I got in late, honey, I haven't even checked messages." Del looked at the phone and saw the flashing green light that indicated a message.

"Who's he?" Nate said, defensively.

"This is Mr. DiSanto, sweetie. He came over early to help me with the hot water heater. It wasn't working. The, ummm, pilot needing lighting. I didn't know how. Look," she said, tugging at her hair, "I got all wet and the water turned ice cold." Del played along with Jimmy's story, thankful that he thought fast for both of them.

"How come his hair is wet?" Nate looked at Jimmy.

Del looked at Jimmy too, anxiety filling her eyes, uncertain what to say.

"Accidentally stuck my head under the shower checking the water."

"What r' you makin'?" Nate asked, barely listening to Jimmy's response.

Del realized the wet hair issue hadn't mattered nearly so much to Nate as it had to her.

"Pancakes." She looked at Jimmy and, a smile coming to her face she added, "To thank Mr. DiSanto for coming by so early. Honey, what happened to your leg?"

"I fell going down the stairs at Dad's townhouse."

"*Skateboarding* down, you mean," said a man's voice and Micky walked into the kitchen. "You forgot your backpack, sport," he said, tossing the pack on a chair and then, seeing Jimmy, adding, "Well." Micky stood casually, medium height, medium but well-cared-for build, wavy black hair to match Cara's, jeans, blazer and a knowing grin on his face.

"This is Mr. DiSanto, Daddy," said Cara. "He's helping

Mommy with her hot water stuff."

"So I see. Mr. DiSanto." Micky nodded at Jimmy and Jimmy nodded back. Neither moved to shake hands, both stood their ground instead, appraising the other.

Cara tossed her jacket on top of the backpack.

"Can I have pancakes, too?" she asked.

"Sure, sweetie," Del answered.

"But I wanna take a bath first. A bubble bath, okay? I feel all yucky. We were in the emergency room all night. I'm tired."

"The emergency room?" Del looked at Micky.

"Kid never hurts anything during business hours, Del, you know that. Last run before bed-"

"Dad let me ride my skateboard out front until bedtime."

"I didn't tell you to ride it down the steps to the front door."

"I wasn't, Dad, I told you, I put a board up first," Nate said, leaning against the doorjamb. "Not my fault the board slipped."

"That's when he fell. Of course, he wanted to come... *home*," Micky said the word with distain, turning his attention to Del, looking her up and down as he spoke, noticing her robe and barefeet and what he knew, from experience, was likely little else underneath. "Jesus, Del, I must have left you five messages, don't you ever check?"

"I got in late," Del said, wrapping her arms around herself and looking at the floor. "Then this morning...the hot water."

"Is there hot water now?" Cara asked.

"You bet," said Jimmy, smiling at her and stepping up beside Del.

"Then I'm gonna make a bubble tub," she skipped from the room with her polar bear. "I'll be back for pancakes, okay Mommy?"

"Sure," Del said, feeling fresh confidence with Jimmy beside her.

"I'm gonna lay down in bed for a while, okay?" Nate said, "I'm tired."

"Good idea, honey. I'll come up in a minute to get you comfortable. You can have pancakes in bed, if you like."

"Okay," Nate said, pushing off the doorjamb onto his crutches.

Del was alone in the kitchen with Jimmy and Micky.

"Here," Micky said, handing her a baggy with bottles and papers inside. "Doc put his medicine-for pain-in here, and some directions. He's gotta go back in a couple weeks for a walking cast."

"How bad is it?"

Micky looked at Jimmy, then Del. "Coulda' been worse. Six to eight weeks he's good as new."

"Mommy!" Cara called from upstairs, "I need help with the hot water-it's too hot!"

"Guess it's working now," Del said, smiling sheepishly at Jimmy. "I'll be right back," she added.

"I'm leaving," Micky said. "Just call the doctor if you have questions. That's what he's paid for."

"I'm coming!" Del called up to Cara and walked out of the kitchen leaving the two men alone.

"Jimmy DiSanto, right?" Micky asked, "from the Dock-side?"

"The same," Jimmy said.

"My wife hanging out at bars now?"

"Adele came in for dinner with some friends."

"Adele, eh?" Micky grinned and shook his head. "I don't suppose *Adele* knows our hot water heater has an igniter, not a pilot light."

"Does it?" Jimmy said, smiling.

"Can't relight it, you know. Need to replace the igniter."

"Well," Jimmy said, a lazy grin on his face as he turned to flip the pancakes that were cooking on the griddle, "I suppose all that matters is someone relit Adele's spark." He finished flipping the last pancake just as the front door slammed shut behind Micky.

Twenty-Seven

"I THOUGHT I'D DIE!" DEL SAID as she sat at a table in Gwen's bakery, having recounted Micky's unexpected arrival at her home. The events surrounding both Jimmy and Micky had left Del feeling overwhelmed by new territory and in need of the advice of friends. Claire and Gwen had agreed to meet at the bakery late that afternoon.

"The kids were okay with it?" Gwen asked. She'd given herself permission to take a break from endless baking duties and left Cammi in charge of the counter. Her feet resting on the chair beside her, hair in a tight ponytail, Gwen wore her white baker's smock unbuttoned over a pale green t-shirt and jeans. She cupped a warm mug of herbal tea against her stomach and savored a little downtime during the holiday rush.

"Cara didn't seem bothered."

"How about suspicious?" Claire called from the back of the bakery where she was adding artificial sweetener to her black coffee.

"No." Del felt defensive, then recalling Nate's reaction, she softened her tone. "No...she was fine, her usual self, but Nate, it *felt* like he was grilling me. Isn't that terrible?"

"What, that your kid put you on the hot seat?" asked Claire.

"Or maybe," Gwen said, patting Del's hand, "that you feel

you put him in that position in the first place."

Del smiled ruefully up at her.

"Listen, Del," Gwen continued, "there's a fine line between being an upstanding, model mother and living your life fully. I know. It's no fun feeling like your sneaking around behind your kid's back."

"Why?" Claire asked. "That's what you do at Christmas when you hide presents and pretend there's a Santa Claus. Here." She set a cup of tea in front of Del, the teabag still steeping in the cup, tossed sugar packets beside it and sat next to her.

"Thanks, Claire. But, it's not the same."

"Right," Gwen added. "All that sneaky holiday activity is for their pleasure–ultimately."

"And this sneaky behavior was for *your* pleasure, huh?" Claire smiled across the table at Del, who was plainly embarrassed at the reference to her evening with Jimmy. "Come on, spill. How was it?"

"Claire!" Del sputtered. "I can't believe you'd ask me that!"

"You *can* believe it; you just don't want to answer it."

"She's got you there," Gwen added, laughing. "I've gotta confess...I'm curious."

"Hey, no details, okay?" Claire said, "just an overall rating–thumbs up or thumbs down?"

"Up," Del said at last, and then a true blush bloomed on her face along with a joyful grin she could not suppress. "Way up!" She couldn't believe she'd be so intimately direct.

"All night long?!" Claire asked and all three melted into schoolgirl giggles.

"That's great, Del," Gwen said at last. "I'm glad to see you so happy. Jimmy seems like a good guy."

"Oh, he's the real deal," Claire said. "He's one of the reasons I like the Dockside. Jimmy's got a way of zeroing in on the people who need attention, or heading off trouble before some asshole starts it."

"Maybe he zeroed in on me," Del said, hesitantly.

"Hey, don't you feel like some one-night-stand," Claire assured her. "I don't think he's that kind of guy. He's got values, you can tell. Believe me; I deal with the value challenged all the time. Money brings out the *real* in reality. I've learned that too well."

"That sounds so bitter," Gwen said, studying Claire's face. "Surely everyone isn't like that. I hope I wouldn't be like that." Gwen wondered if her recent worries made her less the person she wanted to be.

"You might feel pinched financially, but you'd be nice about it. No "F" bombs from you."

"People talk to you like that?" Del asked, sipping her tea.

"I'm the convenient target. Of course, they usually apologize later, but–"

"Hard to forget," Gwen said.

"Precisely."

"How's the *Asshole* coming, by the way?"

"Who!?" Del asked, surprised to hear Gwen use the term.

"This guy I was meeting with the day you," Claire pointed at Del, "slammed into that flowerpot."

"And into our lives."

"A lot's changed since that day, for me at least," Del said.

Gwen and Claire looked at her, thinking about their own lives since that day, but neither chose to comment.

"Well, that *Asshole* is still an asshole," Claire said at last.

"What's he do?" Del asked.

"Treats her like dirt," Gwen said before Claire could answer. "I know you've got some kind of investment there, but you should tell him to take a hike. Not that it's my place to tell you what to do...," Gwen added, feeling she might be crossing some line by offering such a bossy bit of advice.

"Yes, Mom," Claire said.

"I'm sorry," Gwen said quickly, "like I said, it's really not my place-"

"No, but you're right. And I know you care, so that counts. Listen, I've been working on this deal for over two years. One contract fell through because, well, because he is-as previously stated-an asshole. The seller got tired of his friggin' demands and they told him to take a hike."

"And you didn't?" Gwen asked.

"Tenacious, that's me."

"How's it going this time?" Del asked.

"So far, so good. Seller can't stand his guts but they want the sale as badly as I do, I guess."

"Are things...all right?" Gwen asked, delicately. "I mean, financially?"

"Oh, sure," Claire said quickly, but her friends didn't speak. Claire saw a worried look pass between them and knew she had to clear this point up. "No, *really*, I've got a couple more very nice sales that will close before Christmas, and plenty of business lining up for after the holidays. Ladies, it's not like I'm hurting-even without all these deals. Honest," she assured them.

"Then why *not* tell him to take a hike?" Del asked. "Is it so worth it?"

"Oh, yes. I'd be more than fine without him. However, this is one hell of a paycheck." Claire saw the doubt in her friend's faces. "I don't generally talk about this sort of thing but, well, it's more than an average year's salary, for me, and I do pretty well in a year."

"Whoa," Gwen sat back with her own thoughts; she'd find it hard to pass on a deal like that, particularly with the looming strike and Bob's offer.

"Oh, my. That is a lot, I guess," said Del, hesitating, "but Claire, if you're really that unhappy, and if you really don't *need* it, is it...worth it?"

"You mean worth the loss of peace of mind and sleep? The constant nagging feeling that, even though I'm damn good, maybe I'm not *that* good?" Claire dug through her purse and pulled out a small bottle of antacids and held it up. "You mean even considering the profit I've lost out on by not buying stock in this company?!" She tapped two out, chewed them up and followed with a coffee chaser.

Gwen frowned, realizing she'd seen Claire popping antacids more than once. "You okay?" she asked, nodding at the bottle.

"Sure, probably just need to eat a little better and cut back on this," she said, holding up her cup. "When I get some time," she added.

"And it's still worth it?" Del asked.

Claire sat the cup down and leaned back in her chair.

"Probably not, but it's a matter of honor now."

"Like a quest," Gwen said.

"Practically."

The bakery door opened; chimes jangled in the chilly breeze. A young mother in designer ski attire walked in, accompanied by a little girl in equally fashionable slope wear. Mom's chic black was highlighted by white fur that poked around the edges of her embroidered black velvet down vest and over the tops or her black suede Sherpa boots. The child, though equally trendy, came in the pink and lavender version. Mom looked like she spent good money to have the same honey-blonde tresses as her daughter.

Tourists, Claire mouthed at her friends.

"Bread and butter," Gwen whispered back and stood to help shut the door. "Hi, I'm Gwen," she said, "welcome to my bakery. What can I help you with?"

"Gwen." The woman nodded at her. "I'm Ellen Danvers." She paused to let that sink in.

Apparently, Gwen thought, in some circles that was an impressive pronouncement, so she smiled. "Thanks for coming in, Ellen. What can I do for you?"

"Bread," Ellen stated, succinctly.

"Certainly. Cammi can show you what we have," Gwen said, looking over at Cammi who sat on a stool behind the counter reading a paperback. Gwen liked to think she was studying for finals, as there were only two weeks left in the semester, but she couldn't imagine what class included contemporary romance novels in their syllabus.

"Sure, Senora Gwen." Cammi hopped off the chair. "Whacha need?" she said to Ellen.

"Bread," Ellen repeated and followed Cammi to the case.

"Sit," Claire ordered Gwen, noticing the circles under her eyes. "Cammi can help her. You look absolutely beat."

"It's that time of year. People splurge over the holidays, plus parties, family gatherings, that sort of thing. I get a lot of pre-orders, but I want to have plenty on hand too, for last minute or impulse buyers.

"Jimmy said they have several company parties at the Dockside over the holidays. I think he'll be pretty busy."

"So you didn't finish," Gwen said, happy to deflect the attention from herself. "What happened with Micky?"

"Everything was fine in the end. Jimmy stayed for breakfast-I'd already told the kids he was, so that wasn't a problem. Then he left."

"And Micky?"

"When I came back down, he was gone. Pancakes were ready so we ate." Del didn't mention that she had wanted to ask Jimmy if the two men had spoken any more after she left. And if so, what about.

But kids and schedules got in the way and, even if there'd been time, how, she wondered, do you ask that question?

"And the kids?" Gwen asked.

"Fine. Cara went to a friend's house for the afternoon. Nate has a friend over, he's old enough to spend an afternoon home alone. Of course, I call every half hour."

"Of course," Gwen said, smiling to herself.

"His leg still hurts, though. And me, I'm *running errands*," she said, making quotes with her fingers in the air. "I'm covered for an hour or so yet, but I feel like I'm lying to the kids again."

"I'll send you home with cookies," Gwen said, "that'll help with your cover."

"Oh...I don't know..." Del reached for her purse, concerned about an unnecessary expense.

"On the house," Gwen said, stopping her hand, "guaranteed to remove the last bit of suspicion from any child's mind."

"She's devious," Claire laughed, looking at Gwen.

"Adults will be adults, and they'll have adult friends and do adult things, and that's the point," Gwen said to Del. "You shouldn't feel guilty about being an adult."

"I suppose..."

"Gwen," Cammi said, her voice lowered as she approached the table carrying a loaf of bread. "I've got a little bit of a problem with-"

"Your girl says your bread is not organic," Ellen said loudly from across the room.

"No," Gwen said, rising from her chair, "unfortunately, our organic bread is sold out. That baker brings in a new order on Mondays."

"An order? You don't *make* bread here?"

"Well, I do, but bread isn't our specialty. I make a different kind each week. Today it's honey wheat. I think there are a couple loaves left."

"But it's not organic."

"It's *fresh*," Gwen offered.

"Mmmph." Ellen dismissed Gwen's bread. "Where is this *organic* baker?"

"She doesn't sell to the public."

"Does anyone else carry her products?"

"The deli, on Fifth street, and I think Doreen's Health Foods, down by the outlets. Do you have health concerns?" Gwen asked innocently, realizing her mistake the instant she made it.

"Most certainly not," Ellen said, obviously insulted by the implication.

"I'm sorry, I only meant, that is, ahh...would your daughter like a cookie?" Gwen asked, trying a new tactic. "I always have a small plate of free cookies for children." Gwen walked toward the counter, a forced smile on her face, hoping to placate the woman through her little girl. Why was it some people took offense so easily, she wondered, when all she was trying to do, all she was ever trying to do, was be helpful and friendly?

"Are they organic?" the little girl asked.

"No, but," Gwen held the plate for her to see.

"Mommy says if you don't put good things in...," she hesitated, eying the tempting plate of small, deliciously decorated cookies. "If you don't put good things into yourself," she continued, "you'll..." Her little tongue poked out and ran along tiny pink lips until she caught sight of a butter cookie with toffee crumbles sprinkled atop maple frosting. "Oh." Her hand came up, but her mother's hand stopped her.

"If you do not eat good things, Rebecca," her mother said, "your body will be unhappy and you will be ill. I'm sorry, but Rebecca has a very healthy diet. I couldn't possibly allow her to eat *that*."

"Is she allergic?"

"Most certainly not! I wouldn't allow her to eat anything that would cause an allergy. She only eats healthy, organic baked goods."

"But, mommy..." Rebecca was obviously torn between loyalty to her mother and the sweet lure of the illicit cookie.

"I'm sure one cookie won't hurt," Gwen smiled tightly, feeling the need to defend her cookies.

"I can't allow her to eat anything that isn't nourishing."

"It's not like it'll *kill* her," Gwen said, her voice strained with irritation.

"A diet of this, this...*junk*," she said, pronouncing the four letter word as if it were one of the foul versions, "would kill anyone."

"Excuse me," Gwen said, her cool slipping quickly, "my baked goods are *most certainly not* junk! I use only the best ingredients. My kitchen is immaculate. You wouldn't find better quality in any bakery in–in–where are you from?" Gwen demanded.

"Excuse me?"

"Where are you visiting from?" Gwen repeated.

Del leaned forward to stand, her mouth opening to speak in an effort to calm her friend, but Claire's hand reached over and held her in place. She looked at Claire, who shook her head, and smiled, looking back, curiously at Gwen.

"I don't believe that's any of your business," Ellen Danvers said proudly.

"Let me guess, L.A.? Or New York?" Gwen spat back at her so suddenly even little Rebecca stepped back from the plate of cookies and closer to her mother's grasp.

"What–what is that supposed to mean?" Ellen Danvers was clearly wondering if Gwen was crazy.

Gwen wasn't sure which target she'd hit, but she thought she'd come close enough. "You people, you expect every-thing to be just the way you get it back home! Why on earth do you ever leave?!" Gwen was fuming now, and she knew it, but she couldn't stop. Some core of frustration had found its pretext for a full blown vent and she was helpless to prevent it, as if she were watching herself from outside.

"Senora Gwen," Cammi said softly, touching her arm as she tried to calm her. "Por favor."

"And another thing," Gwen shoved the plate of cookies into Cammi's hands, "you're like a herd following a trend. Organic this, all natural that, like it would kill you to eat something that wasn't macrobiotic, free-range, multi-grain!"

"Gwen! I'm sure that's not what the woman meant," Del said, pulling away from Claire's grasp.

Ellen Danvers wasn't the sort to brush-it-off when her hometown or her lifestyle were disparaged. She was inclined to fight back. "It's ludicrous to think you can eat processed foods, sugar and fat and it won't kill you!"

"Not today!" Gwen said, grapping the plate back from Cammi and shoving it into Rebecca's face. "Take one," she ordered.

"Mommy!" She grapped for her mother, burying her face against her.

Mother clutched her child and Del jumped quickly from her seat, seized Gwen by the arm and, handing the plate back to Cammi, escorted her briskly into the back room.

Gwen barely knew what happened, Del had taken charge so fast. She could hear Claire's voice behind her but in the rush of emotion couldn't sort out her words.

Del and Gwen swept through the swinging doors into the kitchen and Gwen threw herself into the chair by her desk. She bent forward, feeling suddenly dizzy and weak.

Del found a glass and brought her some water. "You okay?" she asked, stooping down beside her and rubbing her back. Del had never seen Gwen lose her temper before. In fact, she realized, Gwen had become something of a rock of emotional stability in her eyes. Seeing her in such a state came as quite a surprise.

Gwen rested her head on her knees, hugging herself with her arms. "I don't feel so good," she whispered.

"Probably coming down from all that adrenaline."

"I guess I was about to blow," Gwen said, trying to put a little laugh into her voice. She was frustrated enough with herself for what she knew had been pointless irritation with a complete stranger, but now she also felt awkward about doing it in front of Del. And Claire.

"About to?"

"I'm so sorry, Del. I never act like that."

"We know, Gwen. Here, take a sip, it'll help."

Claire burst into the kitchen. "Way to go, Gwen," Claire said. "You sure chewed that babe out. You might be tough enough to sell real estate. Who knew you had that in you? By the way, what was that anyway?" She leaned against one of the work tables.

Gwen peeked up at her. "You'll get flour on your black cashmere sweater."

"Is it organic?" she said, laughing. "And see, that's my point, you worry about my sweater but you threaten a perfectly delightful bitch and her lovely underfed daughter."

"What did she say?"

"Let's not go there. We calmed her down and assured her of your sanity. Cammi gave her directions to Doreen's while I slipped the kid a couple of cookies."

"Oh no, her mother won't like that," said Del.

"I wouldn't worry, the evidence was disappearing even as they walked out the door. Only way she'll ever know will be if she tests her blood sugar levels and...who knows with a gal like that. Anyway, what's up?"

Cammi walked cautiously through the door. "Ummm, can I, like, get you anything?" she asked.

"No thank you, Cammi," Gwen said.

"Do you want me to call Senor Andy?"

"No," Gwen said, sitting up, "he's on the road. He's *always* on the road, oh..." She bent back down, holding her head.

"Here," Del offered. "Take another sip."

The door chimes jangled, and Cammi excused herself to help a customer. "I'll get rid of them, pronto!" she whispered from the door. "Then I'll bring in a fresh cup of tea–that green herbal stuff you like, okay?"

"Herbal, eh?" Claire said. "How ironic."

"I know," Gwen moaned and held her head.

"Uno momento," Cammi whispered. She left and the door swung slowly back and forth in increasingly smaller arcs, whooshing softly as Claire and Del looked from each other to Gwen.

Claire pulled a chair up across from Gwen and sat. "Is that what this is about, sweetie? You and Andy on the outs?"

"No, no," Gwen looked up at both her friends. "Andy and I, we're fine, with each other, we're fine, that is. It's this damn strike."

"You think the truckers will strike after all?" Del asked.

"Hmm," Gwen nodded.

"Maybe he can find something temporary," Claire offered.

"That's just the problem," Gwen said, sitting up to look at both of them. "I didn't want to say anything. We really haven't known each other that long, and, well...I-I like you."

"And we like you, Gwen," Del smiled at her and took her hand.

"Yeah, you're growing on me, too," Claire said. "So what's that got to do with Andy's job?"

"Bob offered him a new job, at the winery. If he takes it, we'll have to move."

"Move?" Del looked at her intently. "How would you run the bakery from the western slope?"

"She wouldn't," Claire answered for Gwen. "She'd sell it."

Del looked to Gwen who nodded confirmation. "Oh," she

said, and, a frown forming on her face, she bit hard against her lips and blinked back tears.

"Shit," Claire said, "we need a drink."

Twenty-Eight

THE SUNSET FILLED THE VIEW from the Dockside's expansive windows with a warm glow that washed as soothingly over Gwen's raw nerves as it did over the calm waters of the reservoir. The rum and coke didn't hurt either.

"That's going down pretty fast," Jimmy paused as he filled small bowls with pretzels and set them on the bar in preparation for the Saturday evening rush.

"Set her up again," Claire said, sipping a pinot grigio.

Jimmy looked questioningly at Claire, who nodded back. He smiled warmly at Del, who sat at the bar, on the other side of Gwen, sipping an iced tea.

Del watched Gwen, who had polished off her first drink as if it were a shot of tequila. Del had managed to find a sitter for a couple of hours-long enough to be Gwen's designated driver-what could it hurt? She nodded assent to Jimmy, as well.

Jimmy soon arrived with a fresh rum and coke. He'd assessed the situation and gone easy on the rum, deciding that this one would be on the house. He didn't know quite what was up, but years of bartending had taught Jimmy to read his patrons body language. He recognized that the women had a circle-the-wagons attitude about Gwen and knew they were looking out for her.

Gwen reached for the glass, took a small taste, sucked up

an ice cube and sat back, crossed her arms over her chest and crunched the ice.

She shouldn't have agreed to come with them for a drink; she had work to do. Cammi had been more than accommodating when Claire asked if she could close up the bakery on her own so they could whisk Gwen away to–what? To drink her sorrows away? To pour her heart out?

She'd filled in a few more details on the way over, but no matter how good it felt to share her burden, and no matter how nice that first drink felt going down, she knew that tomorrow morning she'd wake up with the same set of worries, the same debts and doubts, and all that would have changed was that she'd be even more behind in filling orders. She'd probably have a hangover, too. She sighed and reached for her glass.

"Gwen," Del said, softly, "do you want to talk about it now? Maybe," she gently took the glass from Gwen's hand, "first?"

"I suppose. But it won't make any difference."

"Won't change anything, that's true," Claire said. "Except you don't have to worry anymore about us finding out."

"I think it's good to share your worries, don't you?" Del asked. She looked over at Jimmy who was across the bar and out of earshot, and then lowering her voice, "When everything started with Micky, I wished I had someone to talk to but...I didn't know who I *could* talk to. I was so worried what people would think.

Not to mention my mother, oh God, I could only imagine what she would say. And of course, eventually, she said it.

"But, anyway, what I mean is, you just have to say it and if someone cares about you, they'll be there and if they don't, well, better to find out that, too. The day we all met–you know what a mess I was that day. I hadn't told anyone, but I told both of you. And you were complete strangers, isn't that funny?"

"Probably easier to tell strangers," Gwen said, reaching for a handful of pretzels.

"Exactly!" Del said, "because you didn't know me one way or the other. What's to judge? You wouldn't think less of me."

"We were already wondering if you were nuts," Claire pointed out, "so when we found out what was going on, at least we knew why you were nuts."

"Right," Del said, "I think." Claire was grinning and Gwen, at last, looked up, a small smile on her face.

"You weren't nuts, you were just stressed."

"Precisely! Just like you were today, at the bakery."

"That woman will never come back," Gwen said.

"Do you really care?" Claire asked.

"Oh, I don't suppose so. It's only that, I like to make customers happy."

"Good for business," Claire pointed out, reaching behind the bar to grab a small handful of olives from the drink service. She popped one in her mouth and, catching Jimmy's eye, sat back and smiled as she chewed.

"You want a martini with those?" he asked, walking over.

"Too early, I'll stick with this." She tapped her glass.

"I should keep a jar of olives with her name on it," he said to Gwen and Del.

"If you'd put bowl of olives on the appetizer list, I'd be happy to pay for them," Claire volunteered.

"More profit in martinis. In fact, I was thinking about adding a martini menu."

"I saw they opened a real martini bar in Sage Point Crossing," Del said, mentioning a high-end shopping center near the highway.

"Yeah, more of those popping up," Jimmy said, "big trend from back east."

"Ohhh," Gwen moaned, crossing her arms on the bar and burying her head in them.

"She's only had the one, right?" Jimmy asked, looking at her glass.

"It's not the drink," Del said, "it's the topic. She had a...a bad experience earlier, regarding the east coast...or rather, the people."

"Ah," Jimmy nodded. "I gotcha, some east coast bi–" He stopped and looked at Del.

"Bitch," Claire filled in the blanks. "Jimmy's too much of a gentleman in front of the ladies, but I won't hesitate to call her that. And she was. But not everyone from back east is."

"You got that," Jimmy said, "look at Claire, she's a class act gal."

"You're from the east coast?" Gwen asked.

"Jersey girl, with a helping of Providence thrown in," Jimmy said, and picked up Del's half-empty iced tea glass. "I'll refill this for you."

"Thank you," Del said shyly.

"Anything for such a beautiful lady." He reached across the bar and, taking her hand, gave it a quick kiss before he winked at the other two women and left.

"My, my," Claire said, grinning. "Someone is smitten, I do believe."

"She sure is," Gwen said.

"I meant him."

"It's mutual, I'd say."

Del smiled and touched the back of her hand, where Jimmy's kiss lingered on her skin, against her lips. "Am I nuts?"

"But in a good way." Claire laughed. "Not like our friend here," she patted Gwen's back.

"I'm trying to forget," Gwen said, reaching for her drink.

"Nobody's perfect, Gwen," Del said.

"I know, I know. Makes me mad, though, losing my temper. I used to lecture Jeff about that when he was little. *There's no excuse for losing your temper,* I'd say."

"Maybe not an excuse, but a reason," Claire pointed out.

"But my reason had nothing to do with that poor woman and her little girl. Ohhh...I scared that little girl! I'm so ashamed." She covered her face with her hands, shaking her head back and forth. "How could I scare a child?"

"It wasn't you, it was the stress." Del passed her the bowl of pretzels.

"Stressed out about this whole move, that's for sure. That organic thing, it doesn't bother me that much...I even shop at Doreen's for Christ's sake. But the way she said it–"

"Yeah, yeah, nobody does *bitch* like an east coast babe. You got that," Claire said.

"I did not mean that. It was *her*, not her state of origin. You can't blame the whole demographic. Look at you."

"I've been called a bitch in my day," Claire pointed out.

"But you're not, and that's the difference. You've never mentioned you were from back east."

"Not important."

"Everything's important to friends," Del said. Jimmy placed her iced tea in front of her, gave her hand a squeeze and left to help a couple at the end of the bar.

"Do you still have family back there?" Gwen asked.

"Yep," Claire said, sipping her wine.

"Details, Claire."

"So bossy," Claire said, looking at her friends. Yes, she thought, she was growing close to these two women. It had been a long time since she'd let herself do that. And for good reason, she'd thought. But it felt right, like putting on a favorite, old jacket that you'd thought you'd lost. It was comfortable and it fit. Tempting, Claire thought, to give in to the familiarity, even at the risk of regretting it yet again.

"Come on, Claire," Del urged her, "tell us about your

family."

"Okay, okay. Not a whole bunch to tell 'cause there's not a whole bunch of family. My folks died when I was in college."

"I'm so sorry to hear that," Del said, sincerely. "How'd they die?"

"Plane crash. They'd just bought this little single prop-they took lessons together. The idea was that they'd spend their retirement flying around the country."

"Sounds fun," Gwen said.

"Yeah, we used to go up with them, my little sister, Sally, and I. It was fun. I took some lessons too, and she was thinking about it. Anyway, they bought this new plane-got a pretty good deal. They were so excited. Sally and I were away at college but Mom had called the night before. They had a little trip planned, to get used to the new plane and visit some spot in North Carolina."

"Is that when the accident happened?"

Claire nodded. "Bad weather. We never knew the details for certain. Investigators said pilot error. It took a couple days to find the wreck. Coroner said they died on impact. I guess that's something."

"I am so sorry, Claire," Del said.

"Me too," Gwen added. "That must have been terrible. Was it just you and Sally?"

"Yep," Claire reached for her glass, breathed in the aroma of the wine and took a long, slow drink. Years since that day...like yesterday.

"So...how'd you end up out here?" Del asked.

"Change of scene."

"After they..."

"No. A few years later. Long story."

"Short version?" Gwen asked.

"A guy."

"Oh. Broke your heart?"

"And stomped on it. I needed a new point of view and everything looked the same out there."

"Why Colorado?" Gwen asked.

"I had a...a friend, from college. We'd stayed in touch. She married a guy from Denver. She'd always said I should come for a visit, so I did. Decided to stay, end of story." Not the end of that story, but the end for now, Claire thought, remembering her painful lunch with Cindy so long ago.

"How'd you end up in Blue River?" Del asked.

"Oh, one thing led to another. You know how it goes. Boring. How about you, Gwen? Del's a hometown girl. You too?"

"I grew up in a farm town on the eastern plains. Graduated from high school and moved into a little house in Denver with some girlfriends from my hometown. It was a big adventure. I got a job at a bakery, and that led to an apprenticeship. Learned the job from the ground up.

"Then I met Bill; Jeff's dad. We got married, had Jeff, got a house in the suburbs and I managed a bakery in town. We got divorced and Bill moved east–had a job offer he couldn't refuse. I thought, why stay there? Turned out most of my friends were really Bill's friends first. I always loved it up here so, what the hell. I took my settlement, and my son and I moved. I opened the bakery."

"Did you meet Andy here?" Del asked.

"Hmm-mm," Gwen nodded. "He was my best customer," she said, smiling. "I kid him that he married me for the pastries. But you know...I got pretty lucky there."

"It sounds to me like you handle change pretty damn well."

"I've got a theory about that, actually," Gwen said, pausing a moment, wondering if her idea might seem odd to her friends. What the hell, she thought, love me, love my ideas. "I think we're all like the creatures of the sea. I think when we move from place to place, changing our lives, we're searching for the shell that fits us best. The one that feels like home."

"Is that why you love the sea so much? Why you paint seashells?" Del asked.

"Kind of...," Gwen said, hesitating, debating how much of this theory to share. "I love the *promise* of the sea. It's so immense, so much more than any individual person. When you watch the waves rolling endlessly in, and get lost in their rhythm, you feel like you're connected with...eternity."

"That's how I feel when I look at the stars at night," Del said. "Like anything is possible, if you could just-"

"Read the ripples in the sand," Claire added. "Yeah, I get that. When things really get nuts, I'll walk along the shore of the reservoir. Doesn't matter what time of year-I've been there in snow, in rain, if I need to disconnect with the now, and see the big picture, that's where I go. If I lived by the ocean, Gwen, I'd be on the beach."

"So now," Del said, placing a gentle hand on Gwen's arm, "you're trying to figure out what your next shell looks like."

Gwen smiled up at her and shrugged her shoulders. "I guess you're right."

"Shit, that's not an easy task. There's gotta be a million different kinds of shells."

"Maybe not quite that many, maybe in the thousands."

"Well, that narrows it down." Claire laughed and tapped the side of Gwen's drink. "At that rate, you're gonna need a few more of these."

"If you think of it like that, Gwen," Del asked, "how can you ever know, for certain, that you're picking the right shell?"

"How can you even be friggin' sure there *is* a right shell?" Claire added.

"I'm starting to wonder about that myself," Gwen said, taking another long sip of her drink. "Maybe you just have to dive in!"

"And hope for the best," Del said.

"Or," Claire said, touching her glass to each of theirs in a toast, "make the best of what you dive into."

Twenty-Nine

Gwen
Tues.

LAST WEEK, WHEN ANDY'S UNION voted to strike-on December 7th, no less-I guess I just felt numb. You don't know what it means to be a union wife, not really, until the union let's you down. I know, a strike is supposed to mean they're backing you up, but it didn't feel that way.

Christmas is coming, after all. And Andy's job is who he is, or at least, that's what I thought. Maybe it's not the job specifically, but the having of one that's his identity.

Anyway, one day I was worried about making ends meet and then, the union strikes, and it was like a veil being lifted. As much as I was worried about finances, I was worried all the more about Andy.

So when he told me he'd decided to take Bob up on the job at the winery, even though it meant spending his week-days on the western slope, a hundred miles away from here, I was relieved for him. Still, I can hope that the strike ends quickly. That he doesn't like the new job. That we don't have to move, have to pick everything up and start all over again. It's the strangest mix of satisfaction for Andy's sake and anxiety for my own. How's that work? Half calm and half fearful, and never settled.

I worked tonight on Claire's shell. She's on my mind. With Andy gone and Jeff at his Dad's till Christmas, there's no reason to leave work early to start dinner and turn up the heat. No one's coming home, so I stay at the bakery until close. It's strange, I think Cammi liked having the place to herself before. She's fine, really, but I feel a little like an intruder in my own space.

I was there tonight when Claire stopped in for a late coffee. I gave her one of the coconut tarts; she looked like she needed sugar therapy. Something with the *Asshole's* deal, she said–she's working late. She was her usual self, sharp and pulled together. But on the inside, I think she's tired.

Claire is the tulip shell–sharp exterior defenses protecting the beauty within. Another night or two and Claire's shell will be done.

Who's next? I can't believe that only a few months ago I was actually thinking of painting my own shell. I've given up on that plan. How can I pick a shell when I can't plan my life? Why can't I make it what I want? Why can't I keep it how it was? I want things back to normal so badly I almost ache with nostalgia for the common, everyday-ness of my life. I miss having my husband home at night. How long will it be before things are normal again...and what will the new normal be?

Del
Tuesday

Just when I think I've gotten this whole thing figured out, it all gets so confusing again! Jimmy came over for dinner tonight. It's a slow night at the restaurant, so he was able to get away. I thought it would be nice for Nate and Cara to have a chance to meet him a little more, but now I'm not so sure.

This is all so new to me-am I rushing into this? Was I wrong to introduce the kids to Jimmy? It's not like I told them he was my boyfriend, they already know he's a friend of mine, so that's all I said he was. Just a friend.

Can you have a boyfriend when you're thirty-six? There must be a more mature word for it. Is he my "lover"?! That just sounds sleazy, like I'm sneaking around. Which I'm not! I'm a single woman. Practically.

I spoke with the attorney yesterday. She said the court date is set for January. Just a technical thing, all we have to do is show up and tell the judge we've agreed on everything and that's it. It'll be final. It'll be over. Then I will be single, completely. That'll be good. I hope.

Sometimes I feel like it will be good, really good. Not that I had a choice. Micky made the choice, but I think I'm doing pretty well. I think. Then, tonight, when I kissed Nate goodnight, he asked me if I loved Jimmy!!! Of course I said no-right away!! But, then I felt like I'd betrayed Jimmy, but when I tried to explain that I thought Jimmy was a very nice man, I felt like I'd betrayed, well, not Micky so much, as Nate! Is loving someone other than his father the same thing as betraying my son?

I am so confused! I think maybe I do need to talk with Fr. Frank (I can't talk to my mother!). Just a sec-

Ok, I left myself a post-it: "Talk with Fr. Frank" by my toothbrush so I'll remember first thing tomorrow.

Sandy wants out but no Camels tonight-I'm pooped.

Claire
12-12

Notes on Inspection Request for Adam (A.) Brock Contract:

Inspector found that a few roof tiles were cracked, and a

few more were missing along north facing roofline. Flashing around chimney was insufficient along north side, recommends repairs of these items. Buyer (being the supreme asshole that he is) requests that Seller (a.k.a. unfortunate party to a contract with an asshole) replace entire roof (because it certainly wouldn't make sense to take a professional inspector's word that only minor repairs are necessary!). Inspection request has been faxed to Seller's agent. Fully expect Seller to tell A.A.B to eat shit. So much for "Merry" Christmas.

Thirty

F OR THREE DAYS CLAIRE WINCED every time her cell phone rang. Normally, even during difficult deals, she was happy, even anxious to speak with her clients, the other agent, the lender, whoever. Some agents cringed at confrontations, but Claire viewed each difficulty as part of the puzzle she had to put together to make the sale succeed. And she loved puzzles.

The *Asshole's* deal, however, was different. She had clung for so long to the belief that, no matter the obstacle, she could pull this one off. But time and distance from that first day, when Adam (*A.*) Brock had signed on the line of her agency contract, had blunted her anticipation of a profitable transaction for both of them. She'd moved on from negotiating *for* her client to negotiating *with* him. Okay, she'd thought, that happens when things get dicey. With her help the problems would, as usual, work themselves out.

But they hadn't. In fact, they'd deepened. Each new point became more and more a sticking point, until Claire began to question whether her client had ever really intended to act in good faith toward the closing of *any* deal, no matter the issues involved.

That's nuts, she thought, he had better things to do than jerk her around. Didn't he? Of course, he did. Which brought her to wonder, was it her? If clearly he must want to buy-something!-and clearly the seller wanted to sell, was she the one who was mucking it all up? Had she neglected to do something? Or done too much?

For the first time in her professional career, she began to question her ability. She ran it by her managing broker, and past a couple other agents she sometimes turned to for brainstorming. It was clear, they said, she'd done all she could. It was the *Asshole*, not her that was screwing up.

But still, she wondered. A little nagging voice way back in her brainstem wouldn't let it go. Had she lost her touch? Had she ever really had a touch to begin with, or was it all luck? The thought ate away at her nerve and required the purchase of another large bottle of antacids.

Then, at last, her cell rang one more time. Unbelievably, the seller had agreed to replace the entire roof. The entire roof! She'd never expected that, but was exceedingly grateful to get past that point.

She left a message for her client, who was out of reach, on a hunting trip. The *Asshole* with a gun; there was a thought. In Claire's opinion, the gun would be pointing the wrong direction.

She needed a break, and she knew just the excuse. For the first time in a long time, she didn't have anything scheduled for the weekend; two entire days requiring nothing from her. Christmas was less than two weeks away, and she still had a little shopping to do.

She picked up the phone and called her favorite boutique hotel in Denver. They had a room, it wasn't cheap, but, she reasoned, it was the best early Christmas present a girl could get. She booked two nights, made an appointment at their spa for a massage and packed a small bag.

On the way out of town she stopped by the post office to pick-up her mail. Then she went to the bakery for a coffee and croissant for the road. Gwen wasn't there, so she left a message with Cammi, letting her friend know where she'd gone for the weekend. Friends did that, right? The sun was setting over her shoulder as she descended into Denver, its lights beginning to twinkle in the early twilight of December. She turned off her cell phone, turned on the radio-smooth jazz-and felt the tension release in her shoulders. Good bye, world, she thought, see you Monday.

TWO CANDLES FLICKERED ON THE dresser, casting an amber glow over their skin, and releasing cinnamon scent into the bedroom. Gwen had read once that cinnamon fragrance had an erotic effect on men and tonight, she agreed. Andy's heart was still pumping fast, as was hers, though their bodies were spent from the satisfying exertion of making love after so many days apart.

"Once Christmas is over you should take a few days off and come visit me, see what you think of the place. Bob's put me up in a little farm house near his vineyard. Place belonged to the original owner and they used it for storage until I came. Took a few hands to clean up, but it's not bad. You could cozy it up however you like, Babe." He played with her hair, brushing it away from her face as she lay with her cheek against his chest.

"Do you think you'll still be there after the holidays? What if the strike's settled?" She watched the flames dance against the dark walls, smelled his familiar male scent and wished they could stay in this contented pool of light and warmth and never return to strikes, holiday pastry orders and Andy's new job.

"I talked with Gary, you remember him, he drives the Wyoming route. He's got a job at that building supply place off seventy."

"He's got a new job, too?"

"Hmm-mm. Pretty much everybody's found something, at least part-time. Word is this is gonna be a long one, could go far into next year."

"I don't like how that sounds," she said, feeling the now familiar grip of anxiety reclaim her thoughts.

"I know," he said softly kissing the top of her head. "It's getting tougher all the time for unions. Big business keeps on getting bigger and the little guy keeps getting littler. We need the power of a union more now, I think, than we have in a long time. When you had independent companies, family owned, they took some pride in treating employees fair."

"I don't think they do anymore."

"No more families in charge, that's why. All gobbled up by big corporations. Bottom line's all they care about. I'm a paycheck, not a person. It's got me to thinking..."

"About?"

"Paycheck's good at the winery, that's for sure. But there's something else, I'm a person first, know what I mean?"

She nodded, torn between her desire to see him happy and her desire to avoid change.

"I feel like I'm part of the process, no matter where my part falls, I'm a part of that bottle of wine the customer takes home. Everybody feels that way there, too. It's not a pecking order, it's a team. I haven't been part of a team in a very long time and it feels good. I like it."

She was quiet a moment, afraid to ask but knowing she should. "Enough to stay? After the strike?"

"Maybe. Maybe, if that's okay with you. That's why I want you to come visit, see for yourself. Then, if you like it too, then we'll talk about..."

"What if," she said, finishing his thought.

"Yeah, what if." He rubbed his hand along her skin, shoulder to hip and back. "You're getting cold; I can feel the goose bumps." He reached for the blankets and pulled them over the two of them. "Better?"

"Warmer," she said, and held him close.

D EL HAD SATURDAY OFF AND she knew just what she wanted to do with it. She got up early, before the kids, and took a long walk with Sandy. While the nip in the air chilled the tip of her nose, the sun warmed her arms and back through her coat.

Later, after she'd made waffles for them, Del did her chauffeur duties for her kids. Nate had a science project he needed to complete with his partner, Josh. Del thought they'd probably spend most of the day playing video games, but as long as they finished the project, she didn't mind.

Nate's leg wasn't hurting anymore; now he was bored and an afternoon at Josh's house would solve that problem. Cara's friend Amy had invited her to join them at Amy's big sister's cheerleading competition. A day watching cheerleaders–Del knew nothing would make Cara happier.

That left Del alone. She drove to St. Benedict's. Father Frank had a habit of spending Saturday afternoons in his office fine tuning his Sunday sermon, though the time was often spent with parishioners who *happened* to drop by the church for some other reason and, since they were there already, would he mind if they talked to him about something? The Father had learned long ago that planning for coincidence made an effective pastor.

St. Benedict's sponsored a food bank on the weekends and the activity at that end of the building was brisk. Del had volunteered a few Saturdays in the past, handing out boxes filled with enough food to get needy families through a tough week. The need was greater, she knew, than many suspected in a resort town. Not everyone owned a million dollar condo on the slopes or a chalet in the woods. Too often the people who worked to make Blue River run could barely afford to live there.

Del parked away from the activity, preoccupied with her own needs. Tomorrow the narthex would overflow with parishioners attending mass, bible study, and youth groups, but today it was empty and quiet. The stillness of her church in odd hours such as now overwhelmed Del with a sense of peace. No matter the insanity of life beyond its doors, it was a calm harbor.

She went up a flight of stairs and down a hall, past the front desk where, on weekdays, Helen fielded phone calls and visitors. She passed a small meeting room, one wall lined with books on religious topics. It was empty. The soft hum from the air ducts as they pushed heat into the building was the only sound...almost. She followed the faint tap-tap of a keyboard to Father Frank's office, where he worked in private on his sermon.

Del felt awkward interrupting him. She peeked around the corner and saw his tall frame, hunched over his laptop, deep in concentration, surprisingly proficient with his two-fingered typing style.

She knocked lightly on the doorframe and, when he still didn't notice, cleared her throat loudly.

"Wha-" He looked up, distracted from his task, but unfocused on the source of the interruption. Then, seeing Del, "Why, Adele, come in, come in." He stood and started around his desk to greet her.

"I'm sorry to interrupt you, Father."

"Not at all. Please, I'm delighted to see you." He shook her hand warmly, enclosing it within both of his. "Have a seat, won't you? I've time before I leave for St. Francis hospital; have to visit our parishioners who are unfortunately detained there."

"Thank you, Father." Del sat in one of two arm chairs in front of his desk and he sat across from her, in the other.

"Oh!" he said, jumping up from his seat and rounding the desk. "Have to hit save," he clicked his mouse and returned to his seat. "Helen, God bless her, has rescued me more than once, and lectured me, too, I'm most sorry to say. As a result, I have been conscientiously taught to save my work regularly."

"Good idea, you wouldn't want to loose an entire sermon."

"Indeed, I've learned that lesson the hard way."

"Oh, no."

"Oh, yes. And I must confess, very contritely, that the language in this office was not of the most Christian tenor on that occasion.

"Not really," Del said, smiling, then, realizing he was quite serious, "really?"

"Most definitely really. Not to worry though. Helen gave me several Our Fathers to say, along with *The Total Dummy's Guide For Computers* to read." He pointed to the copy that sat on the corner of his desk. "I've read most of it. Helen's the boss around here, wouldn't want to disappoint." He smiled, because he'd made her smile, too. "So. What can I do?"

Del appreciated her pastor's style of setting her at ease and then cutting right to the point. It made it easier for her.

"I have some...concerns, Father. I thought, maybe, talking them over with you would make things...clearer."

"Clearer. Sounds confusing. What's the nature of these concerns?"

"Well, you know about the divorce."

"Of course, and I apologize, I have been remiss in my duties toward you. I should have checked in to see how you've been doing."

"No, no, I'm doing fine. It's good, really. Micky and I have come to an agreement; it's only a matter of time now. Actually, there's a date. We go to court in January; it's a formality, according to the attorney. We just show up, agree that we've agreed, and that's it. We're done."

"It's over," he said, softly.

Del's eyes met his and suddenly tears welled up. She pressed her fingertips to her mouth, and sniffed back a sob. "Oh, Father..."

"Is this why you've come?" he asked, taking her other hand in his.

Del shook her head.

"Just got to you all of the sudden?"

Del nodded.

"Yes, that can happen." He reached for a box of tissues, conveniently stationed on his desk. She took one and dabbed her eyes, blew her nose and, wadding it up, looked around for the trash. He held out his hand, "I'll take it," he said.

"Oh, no."

"Yes, it's okay." He took the tissue and lobbed it for the two points.

"Good shot," Del said, sniffing.

"Played ball in school. I was pretty good actually, but the Lord had other plans."

"I'm sorry, I really am doing pretty well with the divorce, I don't know why I-"

"Adele, no matter how justified the situation, when two people part after devoting a portion of their lives to each other, and in your case, to your children, there will always be those moments when you will grieve. You shared joys, you had plans. Things have not gone as you had hoped. In fact, your hopes have essentially died- in that arena, at least. Grief is only natural. But this isn't why you've stopped by today?"

"No." Del took a deep breath and reached for another tissue, just in case. "You see, Father, as I said, my divorce isn't final until January. I've found a nice job and I've met a couple of women who have turned out to be...good friends, yes, I think they are going to be good friends."

"I'm delighted for you, Adele. But, there's still something else?"

"Hmm–mm," she said, nodding, unsure how to start. "The divorce isn't final, so I'm still married, technically, so really, it's not that I have been looking, you know?"

"Ah," Father Frank said, "you've met someone, another man."

"Yes," she whispered anxiously. Del pressed the new tissue to her lips.

"You have always had a loving heart, Adele, and I am not surprised that it would attract others. Micky may bear the sin of adultery; that is in the Lord's hands. You can not accept the blame for his sins. You must find the courage to move on."

"But am I moving on too fast? Is it right for me to be attracted to someone so soon? Before it's even legal?"

"In the eyes of the law, you are, I believe, legally separated?"

She nodded.

"And Colorado is a no fault state, so you can not be held legally responsible for dating, certainly."

"But what about...if, well..."

"Has this relationship become serious? Physical?"

"Yes, Father." Del couldn't look him in the eyes, all the years of bible study and catechism classes weighed heavily on her soul.

"I see. That does complicate things. I can't, of course, condone physical relations out of wedlock, Adele. The boss would fire me–and I don't mean Helen." He laughed gently, trying to ease her anxiety. "But I am a realist. I would, of course, advise you to be cautious. It's not uncommon for some people to seek validation in the attention of others after such a life changing event."

"Do you think...?" It hadn't occurred to Del that her attraction to Jimmy could be some sort of rebound. "Oh, he is the first man I've, well, even dated, Father." Concern wrinkled her brow as she waded deeper into the murky waters of self doubt.

"Only you can say, Adele, what the true nature of your affection is for him. I would not rule out the possibility of a true and loving relationship, I would only advise caution. And time. Time is good for so many things and strong relationships not only survive it, but even thrive as its result. Take time to explore your true feelings and to assure yourself that he is the man your heart feels he is."

"Oh, I think he's a very *good* man, Father. Very kind and considerate. He's a widower, not divorced...like me." She paused, fighting her inner stigma, then added, "Jimmy's even a parishioner at St. Benedict's."

"Jimmy DiSanto?"

"Yes, you do know him?"

"Certainly. I've known the family for years. Very difficult time when Kathleen passed. You did know-"

"Oh, yes. Jimmy told me all about her."

"As he would, naturally."

Del thought the Father seemed uncertain what to say next. "Is there a problem, Father?"

"No, no. It's only, well, Adele, your background and Jimmy's-they're quite different."

"Oh, I know, Father. He told me everything."

"Everything?"

"Yes, Father. He told me about his wife's illness, about his son and daughter, about leaving his home because it was..."

"Was what?"

"A bad influence, I guess."

"I see."

"Is there something wrong, Father Frank?"

"No, no." He reached again for her hand, resting his elbows on his knees. "I would describe Jimmy DiSanto as a good man, Adele. But, you must caution yourself to take the time not only to know him better, but to know yourself. Understand your motivations, as well as his. Do you understand?"

"I think so."

"Good." He stood, offering her his hand as she did the same. "You've been given a rare opportunity, Adele. You have the chance to make a new start and better choices. You control the timeline, so I recommend a generous one."

"Thank you so much, Father Frank. I guess I'd better get out of here and let you get back to your sermon."

"Where are you headed next?"

"I don't really have anything I have to do. I thought some Christmas shopping. I haven't had much time for that."

"Well, if you could perhaps spare an hour, I know the food bank is shorthanded today. But, if you don't have time-"

"No, I'd love to!" Del surprised herself at how delighted she suddenly was to slip back into volunteer work, if only for an hour. She smiled to herself as she walked down the long hall from Father Frank's office, reflecting on how fortunate St. Benedict's was to have a pastor who was so attentive that, even while counseling her on her personal problems, he was considering the needs of others; though it didn't occur to her that they might be one in the same.

Thirty-One

$\star\star\star$

A SOFT MURMUR OF CONVERSATION, ACCENTED by the tap-ting of glass and silverware, and Stardust playing on the baby grand was a soothing backdrop. A lavender pink sun set over twinkling city lights beyond Claire's window-side table in her favorite restaurant, high above Denver's busy downtown.

On a crowded Saturday night, it wasn't easy to get a table on such short notice, particularly for only one. But what was a concierge for, Claire thought, if not this? A breathtaking view accompanied by an exquisite meal; this was a get-a-away.

She'd checked into the BelleVue Arms, a cozy boutique hotel with an international reputation, the night before. After room service and a bubble bath, Claire had slept better than she had in months.

Her Saturday began with a massage in the spa, followed by a manicure and pedicure. Claire wiggled her fingertips before her, admiring the deep rose hue she'd chosen. When was the last time she'd even filed her nails, let alone polished them? she wondered. She'd gotten in the habit of cutting them short and filing on the run at stop-lights and the drive-up at the bank.

After pampering and polishing, Claire made the short drive to Cherry Tree Center and her favorite high-end shops. She picked out an entire ensemble, sweater to shoes, for Sally, signed a gift card and left the wrapping and shipping to the effervescent store clerk.

Jordan's gift had been purchased online weeks before. If it played music, videos or games, Claire knew it was a safe bet...but, of course, she'd okayed it with Sally first.

She wore her other purchase, a black, cocktail length dress that capped her shoulders, a cascade of fabric clinging low, then snug to the waist and flowing to mid-calf. Aubergine heels, three inch, her black hair wavy and loose, brushing her shoulders, tasteful diamond studs–just the right carat–peeking through the strands.

The stolen glances of boyfriends and husbands were the payoff. Claire had no need, and no one to impress but herself and she was more than satisfied with the result.

The waiter poured her burgundy and left the bottle. Claire pulled the envelope from her purse and set it on the table. She'd completely forgotten her mail until late in the day when she'd had a few minutes to lounge on her bed watching the news. Reports of the latest bombing, celebrity birth, and Superball drawing soon reminded her why she didn't watch the news anymore.

She switched to a music channel, opened complimentary spring water from the little fridge and reached for her mail.

This Christmas it would be two years since Claire had gone home. Not that she'd been out of touch, or neglectful of her sister's and nephew's needs, but she'd been busy and, maybe most of all, Sally had met someone.

Claire was the cautious big sister at first, then... More of their conversations were stories of days spent with Tom–that was his name–romantic evenings, Jordan's soccer games, holidays, more and more they involved Tom. Claire came to realize it was only a matter of time so she shouldn't have been surprised when Sally had called with the news.

For a while she'd worried. There was their inheritance, after all. But the discreet services of a private detective had assured her that Tom was all Sally thought he was, and perhaps even more. Solid, dependable, honest, true...was that so much to ask of a man anymore?

She sipped her burgundy and read the wedding invitation again:

The Pleasure of Your Company
Is Requested...

She'd read it so many times already that she easily pictured the rest in the glittering nightscape before her. She was surprised at the strong sense of...well, if not joy so much, but satisfaction she took from the announcement, especially when she reflected on other announcements, a lifetime of announcements, beginning with the worst of all.

THE DEAN SUMMONED CLAIRE INTO her office. It was her senior year at Brown. Weren't her grades fine?

Maybe it was Sally, Sally was only a sophomore, maybe she was struggling. So why call Claire? Shouldn't the Dean call their parents?

Whenever Claire remembered that meeting she seldom got past the first few sentences:

"There's been an accident...your parent's plane...I'm so deeply sorry."

Why remember further? One moment Claire been young, with the world before her, no cares, only anticipation. The next she'd been old, burdened with grief and responsibility. Both her parents had been only children. Their grandparents gone, no aunts and uncles, no cousins, orphans except for each other.

The only consolation was Daddy's business acumen and the estate it left behind. It wasn't an immense inheritance, but they could afford to live. Still, as they clung to each other in the days after that loss, they wondered how they would go on.

But they did, Claire earning a master's in finance and landing a choice position with a local investment firm. Sally went to nursing school, her tender heart and strong stomach well suited to the field.

They sold the home in Basking Ridge, sad but anxious to leave happy memories in the past and make new ones together. They bought a brownstone in Providence and formed a new kind of family between the two of them, until Sally met Bruce.

The sisters had quarreled more than once about Claire's opinion of the man, but Sally was smitten. They eloped in Las Vegas and announced the union to Claire over lunch the following Monday. Sally moved out.

Claire's life was forming a pattern—short relationships followed by promotions at work—until one day Sally announced she was pregnant. Bruce announced he wasn't father material and Sally divorced and moved back in with Claire, baggage, broken heart and baby Jordan.

Claire hugged and smiled and welcomed her home, but inside she thought, "I should have been there, should have scared that asshole off before he messed up Sally's life. Daddy would have."

Sally figured out how to be a single mother but it wasn't until his second year that she became concerned about Jordan's development; learning disabilities, the doctors decided. Very positive prognosis, they assured her, but he needed the right kind of help, and so did Sally.

Sally found a school that specialized and announced she

and Jordan were moving out of Providence, to a small town on the Rhode Island shore.

"It's better for Jordan, Claire. It's like the country; we've got a little cottage near the shore and, when he's not at the school, there's a pre-school nearby at the local church. Altogether, it's a little expensive but...well, they're trying new things and I think it might help him. I've got to try."

"Of course you do. I'll help."

"Thank you, Claire. I was thinking maybe we'd join the church, too. They're pretty nice, really. And I miss that, don't you? Remember Mama and Daddy used to take us every Sunday growing up. It's sort of like finding them again, know what I mean?"

She did. But Claire felt like she was losing her family all over again.

So Claire renewed her efforts at work and started the trust fund especially for her nephew. She may not have been there when her sister had needed her, but her nephew would always have the care and help he needed, she'd see to that.

Then Claire met Richard. He was up-and-coming, brilliant and crazy in love with her. He moved in; they made plans, he gave her a ring.

Sally and Jordan were flourishing in their little town and Claire thought, finally, it's my turn. Until she came home early one day. It wasn't so much an announcement that time, as a terrible memory.

After she caught them, all she could think was how much she'd spent on those Egyptian cotton sheets; once Richard moved out, she shredded them.

That's when Claire made her announcement. "Remember Cindy, from college?" she asked Sally. "She's in Colorado now and she's always telling me to come visit. I think maybe I will."

WITH SO MUCH ON HER mind, it was no wonder she didn't see him coming.

"Great view," Bob said, smiling down at her.

"What the hell are you doing here?"

"And it's delightful to see you, too, Claire." He reached for the empty chair and sat down beside her.

"I didn't invite you to sit, you know."

"Standing is awkward, too much bending over. Burgundy?" he asked, reaching for the bottle just as a waiter arrived with an extra glass.

"Hey, that's mine. And it isn't cheap."

"Dinner's on me. It's the least I can do." He poured himself a glass.

"Wha-Excuse me? To begin with, you're not invited. And even if you were, what the hell do you mean it's the least you could do?"

"Clearly, despite my very best efforts, I irritate you."

"There's an understatement." She took the bottle from him and filled her glass to the brim.

"Why don't you return my phone messages?" he asked.

"What messages?"

"The ones asking you to join me for dinner."

"My voicemail must have accidentally deleted them." She played with her silverware, aligning the knife and spoon perfectly beside the plate.

"That happens," he said, a smile forming as he sipped the wine. "Good year."

"Of course," she said, irritation in her voice. What was it about this man that upset her so? Yes, she found him attractive...physically. So she looked away, unwilling to allow that instinct to kick in. And the snappy, sexually charged banter was a game she'd played with others to great satisfaction in the past.

But this was different. Bob was different. He was persistent, and beyond that, yes, that was it, she realized, she felt like he *had her number.* How could he know her so little and still know her so well? The last man who had known her so well was Richard, and he had the power to truly, deeply wound her. What, Claire worried, did Bob have the power to do?

"Hey," he said, placing his hand over hers and stilling the realignment of her place setting. "What's going on in that beautiful head?"

"I'm wondering how the hell you even knew I was here," she said, ignoring his attempt to soften her with compliments.

"I have to admit, it's not coincidental. I did have an informant."

Claire stared at him and then realized the only person who knew where she was. "Gwen? Gwen would never–"

"No, she probably wouldn't. No matter how much she likes me, I suspect she's a very loyal friend."

"Well, then how did–oh."

"Yeah, Cammi. She loves to talk; you already know this?"

"I should have known better than to leave the message with her. But how'd you find the restaurant?"

"The concierge was very accommodating when I explained I'd forgotten where I was supposed to meet you for dinner," he said.

"I'm going to have a word with her."

"She was well intentioned. Let's eat." He waved over her shoulder and the waiter reappeared with menus.

"I don't need that; I know what I want. It's why I come here."

"Really, and that would be..."

Claire turned to the waiter. "New York, rare, salad with Caesar on the side, no baked potato."

"I'll have the same, only make mine medium, I'll take the potato, and I like my dressing on the salad, where it belongs."

"Thank you, sir," the waiter said, deferentially reclaiming the menus, "madam."

"*Miss*, if you don't mind."

"Certainly, Miss," he said, and exited toward the kitchen.

"So, *Miss* Claire, let's enjoy our dinner together, what do you say?"

"I say you keep turning up unwanted when I'm having dinner."

"As I see it, I actually turned up *with* your dinner the last time. But you have a point. I suppose I could get them to set me up at another table for one," he nodded toward a busboy, "and leave you to–"

"No, no, you can stay," Claire said, exasperated and waving off the help. She realized that, as uncomfortable as it might be having dinner with Bob, it would be infinitely more so with Bob's singular dinner service, and the knowing smirks of the wait staff only steps away.

Claire studiously avoided his attempts throughout dinner to crack her cold front, despite a weakened resolve thanks to a second bottle of wine–this time, a cabernet from Bob's own vineyards–and Bob's tireless good humor. She scolded herself more than once for smiling. Damn. He was hard to hate.

"Dessert?" the waiter asked when at last they had finished.

Claire was anxious to conclude the evening. She never knew giving someone the cold shoulder could be so exhausting, and to make it worse, Bob was so frigging nice about it. She was actually feeling guilty. But she'd be damned if she'd let on.

Even worse, though, was the inner battle she was fighting with her own emotions. Claire had made a commitment to herself to avoid entanglements with Bob, but good food, superb wine, a fabulous view and...*him* beside her, being all interested, considerate, and so damn charming; it took her best efforts to shun him. She could feel her resolve weakening like a timid buyer in a tough negotiation. Why couldn't she be charming back? No, Bob's attentions made her feel too good, a good she wasn't accustomed to, and no way she'd set herself up for that kind of pain again.

She battled conflicting emotions, torn by the allure of long avoided intimacies, then gripped by fear of all too well recalled hurt and pain. Bob's efforts were winning; she felt it. And she felt the fear, too. All the more reason, she thought, to get the hell away from this man. Fast.

"No dessert for me."

"You heard the lady," Bob said to their waiter. "I'll take the check...unless you want to arm wrestle me for it," he said, winking at Claire.

It took a moment for her to recover from the wink. "Oh, no, you intruded on my dinner, you're damn well paying for it."

"My pleasure."

His pleasure, Claire thought. Not if she had anything to do with it. Still, she couldn't repress a sudden and vivid image of what her pleasure with Bob might be like. She released the breath she hadn't realized she'd been holding, reached for her purse and stood, "I have to powder my nose," she said and left the table before he could speak.

She would go straight from the ladies room to the elevator, she decided, and be done with him for the night. A few minutes later Claire exited the ladies room, looking to the left to be certain Bob didn't see her, turned to her right, toward the elevator, and ran right into him.

"Oops, a little too much cabernet, perhaps?" he asked, catching her. "I've got your coat, by the way."

Claire stared him down a moment, then allowed him to help her on with her coat. She pulled it over her shoulders and, for a second, felt his hands linger, lightly brushing the skin on her neck, then pull away, leaving a powerful impression. Claire felt it first between her shoulders, then in her gut, and, in the instant before it dawned on her, she felt it in her heart. Bob's persistence, she realized, was paying off, piercing her defenses. She was left with a tender, aching feeling that took her so long to recognize because it had been longer still since she'd known it.

"I have to go," she said, punching the button for the elevator. It opened immediately.

"I already pushed it." He pulled his own coat on and followed her in.

The elevator was chilly. Claire shivered.

"Cold?" Bob said, and he wrapped his arm around her shoulder, pulling her close and rubbing his hand gently up and down her arm to warm her.

"Bob," she said, wanting to pull away, but unable to make herself. "Bob," she said again, looking up at him, ready to protest but finding his eyes, instead, looking warmly down on her. Nice dark eyes. Warm and tender eyes.

"Claire," he whispered, "I won't hurt you."

He pulled her closer, kissed her softly and slowly, melting the ice.

MUCH LATER, THEIR NAKED LIMBS entwined with the tussled sheets of her bed, she propped herself up against his chest, spreading her fingers across his pecs and feeling the heavy pounding of his heart as it slowed back to normal.

"This doesn't mean *anything*, you know," she said. "You caught me at a moment of weakness."

"I drank as much at you did." He pushed her hair away from her face, held it at the back of her head, and smiled as he pushed against her, enjoying the tension that still lay between them.

"It wasn't just the wine, it was..."

"Less than *anything*, but more than wine. That sounds like *something*, Ace."

He'd called her that while they were–what? she wondered. Making love? She stared down at him, suddenly feeling her own heart pounding faster. He slipped his arms around her waist and pulled her into a long kiss, finally releasing her to slip down and rest across him, her head on his chest.

"I'm just saying," she whispered at last, "don't get any fucking ideas."

"Don't you think it's a little late for that warning?" He grinned down at her.

"You know what I mean," she said, lifting her head to look at him.

"Yes." He gentled her head back against him, "I know." He closed his eyes and smiled.

Thirty-Two

WHEN GWEN WOKE UP SHE would know why she was dreaming this dream again; more a memory than a dream. It always came with stress and change and it always ended the same...

"DON'T BE A SISSY!" BARBARA yells over the crash of the waves. She thinks she's so funny, since Sissy is my nickname. It came from her inability to pronounce my name when I was born. Apparently it was easier for a two-year-old to spout a bastardized version of *sister* than to call her new baby sister *Gwen*. Mother thought it was sweet and it has unfortunately lingered, far too long. It will eventually invade my high school years, when I am struggling hard enough with my own identity and don't need one imposed upon me by my bigger, bolder, brassier sister.

"Come on," Barbara yells again, insistently, "it's not even cold. Grab a boogie board and come out!"

"I will later!" I yell back, with no intention of doing so. Frustration sprouts on my sister's face and she turns her own board in hand, crashing herself against the next wave, paddling away from shore toward a cluster of teens that bob in the ocean like ducks, straddling the tide and waiting for The

Big One to ride into the beach. Does she really want her little sister along to do that?

Yes, I can swim. I know you're wondering. No, the water isn't cold. It's pretty nice actually. I can swim in a pool. Or the lake. We usually go to the lake in the summer. Sorta tradition. This year, though, Dad had some work to do in Florida, so he said we should all come along. We're here for a whole month, isn't that nuts? Who takes a vacation for a whole month? Dad's training with this new company for a few weeks, so we're living in this little cottage on the island and he comes over on weekends. It's cool.

I've done a bunch of reading, and my own share of swimming. How could you not? But Barb's practically a prune.

Mother decided this is the summer she'd devote herself to her painting, so she spends most afternoons on the veranda with her water colors. She prodded me the first few days to try my hand, and I finally did. According to her I have hidden talent; feels pretty hidden to me. It's okay, but I've got better things to do, and I don't need my big sister mocking me while I do them. *You're like some little old lady, Sissy, poking around in the sand.*

There I go, see? I've got that tin bucket we found in the cottage, left for small children to make sand castles with, I suppose, but I have my own purpose. Mornings are the best time, after the tide recedes, but it's not just about the shells, so I go other times, too. Evenings are my favorite, when the sun sets over the stilled gulf waters.

Mother likes us both to be in by sunset...but I've figured out the good excuse of walking so far, late in the day, that when I inevitably return I'm caught on the beach alone, willingly hypnotized by the succession of glimmering waves, flecked at their crests with gold or red or whatever shade the day has made the sunset.

Before we came here, I had never seen the ocean before,

except in the documentary style travelogues that Mother and Dad have taken us to see at Pfeiffer Hall every month. Eventually, T.V. will take over this genre, but now, thanks to the efforts of intrepid Documentarians, Barbara and I have seen every corner of the earth on the big screen on the Hall's stage, accompanied by a small bag of popcorn, of course. What's left to see?

The *real* thing. No travelogue ever told me how the sea would tickle my feet as it washes its last thin wave over the beach, or about the delicate crescents it carves in the sand. No travelogue ever showed me the opalescence of the moon-shell or its soft pink interior. And no travelogue ever said a thing about the smell. The *smell*. It hit me hard our first day.

"Not crazy about the fishy smell," Dad says his first weekend down. "Guess you get used to it."

"The breeze is pleasant," Mother points out.

"Sand gets into everything," Barbara complains, standing before us and plucking her bikini bottoms to release the grains that hadn't rinsed out in the beach shower. "And I mean *everything*!"

"Barbie!" Mother says, with mock offense. (Did I mention Barbara has an awful nickname, too? Maybe her misery demanded my company. The really deplorable part is that they will always call her Barbie! I'd have slit my wrists if I couldn't shake *Sissy* (though it will take until college to do so.)

"Really, Barbie," Dad adds for emphasis. They find her dramatic flair entertaining, even seem a little proud of it. "What spunk", Dad always says when Barbie pulls some stunt or other. Well, that spunk will cost them plenty over her college years in attorney fees. Takes spunk to burn your bra-topless.

But the smell-fish and sand and salt and air. And the sound-seagulls and waves and that quality of people's voices at the beach that's different than their voices anywhere else. It's an intoxicating combination that I long to take home to the Colorado plains.

See? I've found one. It's a channeled whelk. I'm rinsing it in the ocean now, but I'll do a closer job in the cottage sink.

I walk as far as I safely can at this late hour of the day, shelling all the distance. Picking, inspecting, choosing or tossing back. I've gotten in the habit of tossing broken shells as far into the waves as I can, my theory here being that the renewed action of the waves will more quickly break them up until, finally, they are the beach.

At last I return, almost within sight of the cottage. I can see everyone has gone in. Someone, down quite a ways yet, is walking a small dog along the shore. I pick a rise in the sand and settle in, watch the sky and the water, and sort through the tin bucket.

Suddenly, inevitably, Barb bursts through the screen door of our cottage, the bang as it slams shut followed by the soft thud of her steps as she runs toward me across the sand. Barb found out my ruse early on and now waits every evening for my return.

She has no interest in combing beaches while boys are in the surf, but come evening my treasures are a worthy diversion from the company of adults.

"Show me what you found!" she says, huddling beside me as I exhibit my treasures. "I picked these up for you," she adds, holding out a small handful of shells. "I thought you'd like them."

I do, and they are added to what is now *our* collection.

At last, the sunset is at its zenith, so achingly beautiful it would hurt to look away. I forget about my shells and try, try, try so hard to remember every smell, every sight, every sound of the moment. I *am* the moment.

Why would anyone be anywhere else when they could be

here? I wonder.

At the end of the month, I pick my most beautiful shells, the best of the collection, and as many as Mother will allow me to take home in my suitcase. I take all the remaining shells with me on my last walk.

Slowly, I give them back to the ocean, to become the beach. The next day, I take what I can and go home to Colorado.

I'll never be back.

GWEN WOKE, ALONE IN THE dark. She hadn't had the travelogue dream in years, but she knew why she had it now. It always came with confusion, with change and with an aching feeling of loss. She lay still, savoring the memory while it was fresh...the smell, she almost could...hear the waves...

When nothing lingered, she fell into a dreamless sleep.

Thirty-Three

★★★

DEL CAME EARLY IN THE afternoon to help Gwen prepare for the Christmas Eve Bake-a-thon, while Cammi worked the front counter. The bakery was warm and smelled of spice and sugar, so thick with the promise of delicious treats you could almost taste the air.

Outside, the temperature was dropping quickly as the leading edge of a winter storm blew in from the west, across mountain passes and into Blue River. Clouds gathered and snow began to drift lightly in, almost as an after thought to the season. Del loved the holidays, and the thought of a white Christmas. An evening spent baking with friends and family was frosting on her already festive mood.

Del knew that Gwen had used her evenings alone to make and freeze pie crusts, cookie dough and more for the tradition that was just old enough to be called *annual*. She'd developed a system that worked smoothly; or as smoothly as things could work with a room full of amateur cooks who enjoyed visiting with each other, and sampling the fruits of their efforts, as much as they enjoyed contributing to the effort.

Gwen had divided each table and counter into work stations for the production of various goodies.

Del followed Gwen's detailed guidelines, placing the necessary ingredients, equipment and directions at each station.

Del was reminded of the many functions she'd helped orchestrate in her years as a volunteer for the Ladies League. Since the divorce, she tried not to think about those days, not so much because she missed the people, or even the Ladies League itself, but more because she missed the sense of contribution to a good cause, and the sheer pleasure that sort of work–even as a volunteer–provided.

"Art loves that biscotti, so this year I put him and Ellen in charge of it," Gwen was saying, putting place cards at the different stations. "He jokes that it's the only time she bakes all year long."

"You think so?"

"Maybe. I went to a women's luncheon once that Ellen hosted. Everything on the menu was that pre-made, frozen stuff from ShopCo."

"I love their little cream puffs."

"Yeah, they're easy. But one of these days, I'll show you how to do it yourself. You'll never go back, trust me."

"I suppose..." Del didn't want to admit that she had a carton of the little puffs in her freezer. She liked them as a late night dessert; hard, creamy and sweet, a reward for surviving challenging days.

Del noticed Gwen check her watch; she noticed the worried look on her friend's face, too, and remembered that Gwen was having some challenging days of her own. "Will Andy be back in time?" she asked, sorting through whisks, spatulas and measuring spoons.

"Sure. He didn't have much to do at the winery today, so he should be home soon–as long as the weather's good." Gwen walked over to the phone, paused, looked at her watch again, then turned her attention back to the place cards.

"Everything okay?" Del asked.

"Yeah, I just thought I'd hear from him by now. He usually calls when he's getting close."

"I'm sure he'll call soon," Del said, trying to assure her. Gwen was clearly distracted. "So, how is it working out, the strike, I mean, and Andy working over on the western slope."

"It's good," Gwen said, then catching the concerned expression on Del's face, crossed her arms around herself and shook her head. "I am a bad wife."

"*What?* That's not true. Gwen, why would you say a thing like that?"

Gwen opened her mouth to speak, shut it again, then leaned against a counter and looked up at the ceiling, as if she'd find the words she was searching for written there. "I can tell he really likes the job at Bob's winery," she said at last.

"That's great," Del said softly, but Gwen's mood told her differently. Del, much as she hated to think it even to herself, knew that Andy's temporary work at the winery might become something more, taking Gwen away from her, and also, taking Blue River away from Gwen. "It is great, right?"

"Is it? No-" She waved off the questioning look on Del's face. "I know it's good. It is. It's just..."

"It means you'll move." Del said aloud what she hated to even think. The words felt blunt and final, like a damper on her previously cheerful mood.

Gwen nodded, her mouth a tight line. Del wrapped her arm around her, resting her head on Gwen's shoulder.

"Senora Gwen!" Cammi stuck her head through the swinging door. "Got some confusion with an order, can you pop up here uno momento?"

"Sure. I'll be right back. Here." Gwen handed the place cards to Del before she left. "It says on the back of each one who goes where."

Del noticed that Gwen had given Claire the relatively simple task of frosting cookies. Bob was in charge of rolling and cutting them. While not directly involved in Claire's work, he would be at the station immediately next to hers. Del hoped Gwen knew what she was doing.

Andy and Jeff were in charge of pies. Gwen had assured her that Jeff had skills, and Andy took direction well.

Names and stations filled up fast: Ginger, who owned the salon, was candied pecans; Tony and his wife Greta, who owned the Deli, were strudel; Evie, a local accountant, and her grandmother, Bette, were fudge and divinity.

Del turned over her own place card: cakes. Cara was assigned to cakes as well. That would be fun, but what was Nate doing? Frosting. She turned over Jimmy's card last: frosting. Their station was next to hers.

Del thought for a moment, confused by her own emotions. Of course she knew Jimmy was coming—she'd invited him! But suddenly, the delight of his company, combined with her kids, the holidays and her friends made her consider changing things around—just to dilute the situation a bit. But she wasn't sure how. She was standing in the middle of the kitchen, staring at the cards when Gwen returned.

"Want me to finish that?" Gwen asked.

"What? Oh, no. I, ah–"

"Something wrong?" Gwen looked over Del's shoulder at the cards she held. "Oh. Well, I thought it made sense to put you on the same team, sort of. But if you don't want to be–"

"No," Del said, shuffling through the cards. "It would be silly to put us across the room from each other."

"That's what I was thinking, but, you're...not so sure? What's up? Everything okay with you two?"

"See, I guess that's what feels funny. Are we, you know, *two*?"

"You seem like it. But really, Del, if you don't want to be next to Jimmy I can move him."

"No, really. I don't mind being next to him; I like him."

"That's what I thought. Is it the kids? Would you rather not?"

"No, it's fine. They know him, after all. Might as well put Nate with someone he knows, and he'll be right next to me and Cara. It'll be fine."

"If you say so," Gwen stood, hands on hips, trying to decipher Del's true feelings.

Even Del wasn't sure what was making her feel "off" in her relationship with Jimmy; maybe just the idea that it was a relationship? She couldn't deny she liked him-a lot-but was it too soon to be a couple?

Cara and Nate seemed to like him, but would they say if they didn't? Did it hurt their feelings to see Mom dating? They didn't seem to have a problem with Micky's live-in girlfriend. Or did they, she wondered. Did she really know what her own children were feeling? What about her friends? They seemed to like Jimmy, too, but would they really say if they didn't?

"Do you like Jimmy, Gwen?" Del heard herself ask, almost as taken off-guard as Gwen seemed to be by the question.

"Well, sure. I mean, I don't know him all that well, but, he has a great reputation around town. And he seems very considerate of you and the kids. And you've seemed very happy since you've been seeing him, aren't you?"

"Yes, but it's, I mean, is it...too soon? I worry that I'm hurting the kids somehow."

"Listen, Del, if the kids are unhappy, they might not tell you straight out, but you'd know something was up from their behavior, don't you think? Children aren't all that great at keeping hurt feelings bottled up. In fact, in my experience, those sorts of feelings have a way of either leaking or exploding out. One way or another, you'd know."

"I guess so. So far, they don't seem to be too upset about

Jimmy. In fact, I think they actually like him. He comes by for dinner now and then, and they've met him at church, too."

"Sounds good to me."

"But, do you think, people, you know, around town, do you think they think I'm..."

Gwen saw where this was going and took swift action. "Your friends love you and so they are happy if you are happy. Anyone who doesn't feel the same, well, why should you care? Friends look out for friends, right?"

"Right!" Del said, brightening up as if relieved of a burden. "Which reminds me," Del said. "I see you've put Claire right next to Bob. Do you think she'll mind?"

"Well, from what Cammi told me, they met up in Denver not too long ago–accidentally, I guess. I got the impression it might have been a nice meeting, and Bob did ask if Claire would be here today. He even volunteered to pass on his usual brownies, if Claire needed help. That's why I put him on cookies with her. But, it seems like he hasn't talked with her much, if you ask me."

"What did Cammi say?"

"Something about a romantic dinner, but no details; she hasn't been very forthcoming, which, now that I think about it, doesn't sound like Cammi. Something's up there, she's been kinda odd lately."

"Well..."

"More than usual."

"Oh." Del thought about that a moment, then asked, "Does Cammi have a station for tonight?"

"Nope, she and I are the floaters. Anybody has a problem, we'll fix it."

"You could have your hands full." Del tapped the cards.

"No Grinch's allowed today!"

"Only Susie-Who's?"

"You got it." Gwen gave her a quick hug. "Okay, *"Susie"*, let's finish this up; you have to pick up your kids, and the cooks arrive soon!"

BY THE TIME DEL RETURNED with Nate and Cara, Jimmy had arrived and was making frosting. Nate didn't seem to hesitate to jump in, especially when Jimmy put him in charge of *quality control.*

"What's that mean?" Nate asked.

"Tasting," Jimmy answered, handing him a spoon. He passed a small spoonful of frosting to Cara too, pausing as he did, to inconspicuously take Del's hand, giving it a little squeeze that she felt like of flood of warmth in her heart.

She watched the easy give and take between Jimmy and her children, and the natural acceptance of Jimmy's participation in the event from all the adults in the room—as if he'd always been a part of the tradition and, in fact, as if she had, too. Del wondered what exactly it was she'd worried about, and felt a little foolish that she had.

An hour later, Claire had still not arrived. With freshly baked cookies beginning to pile up, Bob made an executive decision and started frosting them as well.

Andy hadn't arrived either. Or called. Jeff was confidently turning out pies on his own. A lifetime as the son of a baker served him well.

Art and Ellen were working the biscotti dough like kids with Play-Doh, making foot long snakes on the baking sheet, then, as Gwen had taught them, pressing the edges, painting with milk and dusting with large, rough kernels of sanding sugar.

"Have you done this before?" Del asked Tony and Greta who worked with confidence on their strudel at the next station.

"Ya, many times," Greta smiled, a smudge of flour on her cheek beneath an airy curl of gray-blonde hair. She stirred a large bowl of spices as Tony, the image of a portly Italian papa, diced apples beside her.

"My wife's parents were first generation-from Austria. This is her mama's recipe. She made several for the grand-children earlier in the week."

"That's right," Gwen said, dropping a new tin of cinna-mon at their station. "Greta makes the best strudel. I can't even come close, so I put her in charge. Evie, you and Bette doing all right on ingredients?"

"Need more walnuts," Evie said, dusting her hands on her apron and adjusting the knot that held her dark brown hair snugly against the back of her head. "I'd say...four and one half, no, four and three quarter cups. Yes, that should do it. What do you think, Mom?"

Mom, a smaller, older version of her daughter scanned the ingredients and concurred. "Half should do, but best to go with three quarters. Better safe-"

"-than sorry," her daughter finished.

"Cammi," Gwen called, "could you get the nuts? I need to check something."

Del watched Gwen walk over to her desk, pick up the phone and try, again, to call Andy.

"Mommy," Cara said, "can we do cupcakes too?" Loose strands of dark curly hair floated around her face, freed from their anchoring pony tail.

Splotches of chocolate cake mix stood out against the yel-low of her apron, and a thin chocolate line ran around her mouth. Cara's favorite baking task was most definitely lick-ing the spoon.

"I suppose," Del answered, her eyes on Gwen.

"We need a cupcake pan," Cara said.

"Check the shelf in the back, honey. Get a couple of them."

Cara skipped away and Del grabbed a towel, wiping her hands as she joined Gwen.

"Anything?" she asked.

"Nope."

"I'm sure he's fine, Gwen. Probably stuck in traffic on a pass and can't get a signal."

"Yeah." She placed the receiver back in the cradle, her hand lingering, as if letting go of the phone meant letting go of Andy.

The chimes on the front door jangled and Gwen looked up expectantly. A moment later, in walked Claire. Del saw Gwen's forced smile of greeting.

"Where've you been?" Del asked.

"Having a shitty day. Does this bake–a–thon come with alcohol?"

"Jimmy brought a few bottles of wine, for later."

"Feels like later to me, what do you say, boss?" Claire looked to Gwen.

"Sure. I'd like one myself." Gwen caught the concerned look on Del's face. "Don't worry, Del, I'm sure everything will be fine."

"Where you want me?" Claire asked, dumping her purse and coat into a chair before grabbing an apron.

"I had you frosting cookies, but..."

"I kinda took over your job, Ace," Bob said, coming up behind her. He placed his hand lightly in the small of her back and felt her melt into it for a moment, before she went rigid and pulled ever so slightly away.

"Oh...well, I can do something else, if you want, I mean, whatever–" Claire looked around for Gwen.

"Cookies have to be done," Gwen said, returning from a back room with wine glasses. Del followed with a couple bottles and an opener. "Divi it up any way you want."

"Okay." Claire turned, pausing a moment to give Bob an awkward smile. "Where to?"

"Follow me," he said, a curious frowning smile on his face.

Thirty-Four

✦ ✦ ✦

"SORRY YOU HAD TO START without me," Claire said, picking up the task of frosting where Bob had left off. "Bad day?"

"Bad doesn't even touch it."

"This have anything to do with the *Asshole*?" Claire had told Bob about her problem client.

"I don't wanna talk about him," she said, reaching for her wine. "Sorry I'm late."

"You're worth waiting for," he came up behind her, leaning in to place a kiss against the curve where her neck met her shoulder, and Claire jumped so suddenly she dropped a bowl of powdered sugar onto the table. A huge cloud of sweet, white dust blew over them both leaving a fine sugar coating on their faces and drawing the attention of the room.

"You two are really getting into your work," Jimmy said, reaching for a towel. "I'll wipe down the counter while you wash up." He shooed them off, and Bob followed Claire around the back corner and down the hall to the bathroom.

She turned on the light and Bob burst out laughing at the sight of their white faces. Claire tried not to be amused, grabbed a couple towels from a pile on the counter and shoved one at Bob. "Here, funny guy, hurry it up. We're behind in our production."

"More behind than you know. I think I've already eaten a half dozen."

Claire glared at him as she brushed sugar from the nape of her neck.

"Just the broken ones, here, let me," he said, wetting his towel and wiping along her neck, up across her cheek toward her ear. "Got it in your ear, too," he said softly, as he bent closer, nuzzling her earlobe and running his tongue lightly along the curve of her ear. "You taste sweet," he whispered against her skin. "I've missed you, Ace."

Claire shivered at the nearness of him. She had come prepared to hold him off for the evening, but, as usual, Bob weakened her strongest defenses.

Bob's arms wrapped around her and Claire wondered why she couldn't just give in. It would be so easy, like falling into a soft bed. Okay, so she'd already done that with Bob, and it had been nice; nice was one thing, complicated was another. Had the years of superficial relationships, years of being-in-command of her own fate made her, not simply uncomfortable with intimacy, but dysfunctional in the presence of it?

"Where've you been since Denver," Bob whispered, pulling her around to face him.

"I've been here," she said defensively.

"No," he said, lifting her chin to look her in her eyes–eyes that struggled to avoid his, "where have you *been*?"

Their eyes finally met and though she knew it was safe to look, how could she explain to him how difficult it was to see.

"You guys need anything?" Del's voice preceded her arrival just enough for Claire to pull away and take powdered-sugar removal into her own hands. Del's head poked around the corner of the open bathroom door. "Sticky mess, huh? Who knew cookie making was such a dirty business!"

"But we're a couple of tough cookies, right?" Bob said, smiling at Claire as he wiped his own face.

"Groan!" Del said, laughing.   "Gwen's pouring; red or white?"

"I'm a vintner, how can you ask me a question like that? It's never that simple."

"It's very simple," said Claire, adding to Del, "red."

"You got it. You?" Del looked at Bob.

"So far," Bob said, shaking sugar from his hair, "I'm having what she's having. Red it is, right Ace?"

Del smiled a moment at Claire, a curious look on her face. Claire smiled back with a broad, tight lipped smile that didn't reach her eyes. "Thanks, Del, we'll be out in a minute."

Del's footsteps faded down the hall. "Follow me," Claire said sternly, grabbing the front of Bob's shirt and pulling him down the hall in the opposite direction, to the back door. She pushed the door open, and held it wide for him to follow but Bob simply stood behind her, a broad smile on his face. Claire jerked her head for him to follow. A mock seriousness crossed his face and he obeyed.

"Listen, I've had a shitty day and now–this!" She swept her hands before her, as if she were holding the weight of the world. "You've got to stop," she said, shutting the door behind her and crossing her arms.

The steam from her warm breath as she spoke replaced the sugary clouds of earlier. Snow fell lightly, frosting her black hair. Bob stood a moment, watching her, not touching, not moving, then asked, "Stop what, Ace?"

"That! Don't call me that. And the touching and–"

Bob reached for her, pulling their bodies together. "This touching? Feels good to me. What's the problem, baby?"

"That, too! No *baby*, no *Ace*," she pushed back against his chest to look him in the eye.

"You liked it when I called you Ace when we were making love, especially when you–"

"Hey!" she whispered harshly, looking over her shoulder to be certain they were alone.

"What's this about, Claire? You've been avoiding me ever since Denver."

"I have not, we've talked several times."

"Talked. On the phone. But there's always some excuse why we can't get together."

"I've been busy," she said, turning her head away as he leaned to kiss her. "This is different."

"How so?"

"It's not...the same. It's not–"

"Denver? Is that it? You save your one night stands for Denver?" Bob's arms loosened around her but he felt the renewed tension in her muscles.

"That's low!" She pushed her hands against his chest making space to talk, to breathe, to *be*. "You don't get it."

He released her, crossed his arms and stood a moment, looking at the ground. He took a half step back, resting his hands on his hips. "Listen. You know my personal life hasn't exactly been a cake walk. And, judging by how hard you make it for a guy to break through that shell of yours, I'm pretty sure yours hasn't either. Twenty years ago, I'd probably be walking away right now, but...at least for now, I'm not. You say I don't get it. Fine. Explain it to me."

She held her arms tight about her, rocking slightly; she took a deep breath, bracing herself as if about to step into the abyss. "It wasn't a one night stand; it was different. But it was...there. Not here. I don't know how to *be* that here. Do you understand? It's...," she shivered and shook it off, "new."

"Hmmm," Bob nodded and stepped forward, wrapping his arms around her to stop her shivering. "I get *new*." He rested his chin against the top of her head. "I guess you've noticed I'm the friendly sort." He felt her laugh into his chest, tension easing across her shoulders. "Probably gave you the impression I go around falling in love left and right, that it's easy for me. But it's not. When you get burned, well, let's say you don't want to do that again. I've done a damned good job avoiding the fire, Claire." He tipping her head back, placing his hands gently on either side of her face, "Until now."

"Is that what we're doing? Falling in love?"

"Been that long for you, too?"

She nodded, both surprised and relieved that she could actually admit it. Maybe, she thought, like an addiction, admitting it was the first step.

"I can't act like I don't care. And it's not easy to keep my hands off you," he chuckled. "But...we'll take it slow," and he started with a kiss, hesitant, waiting for her response and returning it.

At last they stood, holding on to each other, wrapped a minute more in the silently drifting snow.

"EVERYTHING COOL?" CAMMI WHISPERED OVER Claire's shoulder as she pressed star-shaped cookie cutters into newly rolled dough. She and Bob had returned to their baking, more at ease with each other, but Cammi noticed Claire still looked distracted.

She'd seen it many times when Claire stopped off for a late coffee and pastry to get her through long nights at work. Gwen and Del thought they knew their friend well, but Cammi knew her habits, and distracted nervousness was one of them-usually caused by some jerk she was working for.

"Sure, why?" Claire focused on the dough, not looking Cammi in the eye.

"You just seem, kinda, not all here, that's all."

"I'm here," she said, forcing a smile. "I'm making cookies, aren't I? How more *here* could I be?" First Bob got under her skin and into her head, now Cammi acted like she was reading her thoughts.

Claire knew others meant well, but it was an odd sort of personal violation that Claire was not at all accustomed to. The barriers she'd erected for Bob were crumbling, and as much as their slow destruction left her feeling lighter in one area, the events of her day still weighed heavily.

"You sound like Senora Gwen-she keeps saying, no problemo, but you can tell, lots of problemo there."

"What's up with Gwen?" Claire asked, putting down her cookie cutters and looking for Gwen, who stood at her desk near the back wall.

"Senor Andy. Didn't you notice? He's not here yet; supposed to be back from the winery by now. It takes a few hours to drive over, with the passes and the weather, but he should have been here by now."

"Any word from him?"

"Nada. And she can't get him on his cell."

"Hmmm, thanks for the heads up." Claire realized Gwen's furrowed brow and dark expression clearly conveyed her internal worry, to anyone who chose to notice, that was. Why hadn't she noticed? Claire asked herself. First Bob, now Gwen; it had been a long time since Claire had felt this sort of inadequacy, and that realization left her with the oddest feeling.

Somewhere between shame and fear, Claire dusted off her hands, whispered Gwen's situation to Bob, and then walked over to join Gwen, determined that she would not let friendship fail her again. Or had it been the other way round? she wondered.

"How you doing?" Claire touched Gwen's arm lightly.

"What?!" Gwen jumped. She'd been staring at the phone, thinking, and hadn't seen Claire coming.

"Cammi said you haven't heard from Andy."

"Yes...but I'm sure it's okay, just, you know, usually he calls if he's running behind."

"You can't always get a signal on those passes. He's probably taking his time. He'll call when he can."

"Ladies," Bob said as he joined them. "I called Jerry at the winery. He says Andy hit the road about one this afternoon; should have been here a couple hours ago."

"Oh-" Gwen steepled her fingertips against her mouth, exhaling roughly.

"But I wouldn't worry, Gwen. Jerry says word is traffic's been backed up for hours over Elk Mountain Pass. He thinks a semi overturned and nobody's going anywhere. Andy's probably stuck in traffic and can't get a signal."

"See? I'm sure he's fine, Gwen," Claire said, soothingly.

"What's going on?" Del asked, coming up behind Gwen, resting a hand on her other shoulder. Jimmy watched her from his station.

"Andy's running a little late," Claire said.

"Yeah, I know. But I'm sure there's a reasonable explanation."

"There's a big back up on Elk," Claire explained.

"Why don't I put in a call to the State Patrol? See what I can find out," Bob offered.

"Good idea," Claire said. He started to reach for the phone on Gwen's desk; Claire shook her head at him, looking over at Gwen. Bob nodded, pulled his cell phone back out and walked slowly down the hall as he punched in numbers.

"That's probably what happened," Del assured her friend. "He's stuck in traffic on the pass, can't get a signal to call."

"Wouldn't you think they'd have cleared it by now?" Gwen asked weakly, "or turned traffic around?"

"Bob will find out," Claire said softly.

"Sure," Del added, "or maybe he's on his way but his cell di–" Del caught herself before she said the word, but not before Gwen thought it. Their eyes met.

"Mom?" Jeff called from the pie table; the table Andy should have been at as well. "You okay, Mom? What's up?"

Bob walked back into the room, a worried look on his face. The three women stared at him, Gwen in the middle, braced by her friends. They didn't hear Cammi open the swinging door to the kitchen.

"Gwen," Cammi called softly, "there's someone here."

They all turned together to see Cammi holding the door

open behind her for the state patrol officer who followed.

Gwen's knees finally buckled beneath her.

Thirty-Six

D ECEMBER'S FESTIVE HOLIDAY SNOWFALL HAD given way to January's bitterly cold and endless white vistas. Ideal temperatures for ski resorts were a mixed blessing for Blue River's inhabitants. While good days seemed to resonate from every sparkling crystal of snow, difficult ones found the weather one more obstacle to surmount.

Cammi shoveled a fresh foot of snow from the bakery's front steps as Del arrived with empty boxes.

"You helping Senora Gwen today?" Cammi said, flipping a dangling tassle off her face and back atop her knit sherpa-style hat.

"Have to be to work at ten, but I thought I'd help a little first."

Cammi held the door open for her and Del tried to smile thanks, even as her eye caught on the *For Sale* sign still taped to the front window. She blinked back tears and forced a cheerful greeting.

"Good morning!" she called into the bakery, her voice echoing off its empty display cases. It had been less than a month, and yet things had changed so much.

"Hey, thanks!" Gwen came out from the back, carrying a stack of folded pastry boxes that she set inside one of the cases. "Don't want to accidentally pack these; they're perfect for Greta's strudel. You'll want to take a whole one home for the kids, believe me!"

"It is good..." Del said, half-heartedly. "But I'll miss your strawberry tarts; they were my favorite."

"Well, you'll know where to find them."

"Won't be as easy, though. My grandma used to say, 'good things don't come easy.'"

"Your grandma was a smart lady." Gwen pulled a chair off a table top. Del did the same and joined her.

"How are you doing with all this?" Del asked, tentatively.

"Better than I thought I would," Gwen said. Leaning back in her chair, she crossed her arms and surveyed the room.

"Feels empty," Del said quietly.

"Like a shell. As beautiful as they are, they're real beauty is in their purpose. Greta will make a new beauty with this shell."

"You were lucky she was interested in the place–so fast, I mean."

"Hmmm." Gwen nodded. "With strudel like that, she should have a bakery.

"Will you miss it?"

"Sure. Funny, though, I thought I'd found *the* place–*my* place. I thought I'd be here for the rest of my life. Couldn't get any better than this, you know?"

"But now?"

"Now. Now, I'm starting all over again, Del, and it's nuts, but, I'm even more excited than I was when I started here."

"Is the new place ready yet?"

"It was just a house, so it needs some work in the kitchen, but Andy says it's coming along. I'm going over next week to check out the progress."

"How's his leg?"

"Getting better. Doctor's gonna put him in a walking cast soon. Of course, he still can't drive, but Bob pays one of the young kids at the winery extra to be available to drive Andy around. He says he feels like a celebrity with a chauffeur."

"He really likes that job."

"He does, and to think, I didn't want him to go. I didn't want us to go. I didn't want *change*. Isn't that silly? I didn't want things to change, but then...after the accident, with him all beat up in the hospital, tubes and IV's...and then the doctors saying that driving the long hauls would be misery on his ankle after it heals. It was like a curtain opened for both of us. The winery was so obviously the right choice, and moving and opening a new bakery didn't seem like a problem at all. As long as Andy's there..." Gwen smiled at her friend. "Even Jeff's excited. He wanted to take off the semester to help, but I wouldn't let him. I told him I've got plenty of help," she patted Del's leg.

"What about Cammi? Was she disappointed? Does she have a new job?"

"It turns out Cammi was planning on taking off to see what life is like in Costa Rica. She speaks the language, after all."

"Sort of," Del said, laughing.

"Well, she's a good kid. She was afraid to tell me about her plans-felt guilty. I think she was almost relieved to hear she was losing her job! She's sticking around until I'm out of here, helping me pack up the house, too."

"How about Claire?"

"I haven't seen her much. She was in late yesterday, Cammi talked to her. Cammi!" Gwen called toward the front door."Si?" Cammi answered, cracking the door just enough to let in her words and not the cold wind.

"What's up with Claire?"

"The *Asshole*-dumped the deal and pissed her off."

"No way!" Del said, "and after all her work-what a jerk!"

"Yeah, that's what she said...only not so nice. Anyway, I think it bugged her, not getting that deal. She's sorta feeling like she's gotta prove she's good at what she does. She's working longer hours than ever–even doing open houses."

"She hates open houses," Gwen pointed out.

"She says her motto is, 'life sucks, and then you get paid'. Guess she's working on the *getting paid* part." A gust of wind pushed at the door, blowing in a dusty cloud of snow. "Gotta shovel–can you put on some tea? My cheeks are frozen, and I don't mean on my face!" She slammed the door shut, leaving them to laugh in the silence.

"I knew Claire was upset about something the night of the accident, but I just forgot about it after we heard about Andy."

"She and Bob came by the hospital later that night–after they wrapped up the bake-a-thon, closed up the bakery and helped deliver goodies. Then they stayed pretty late until the doctors told me Andy was stable and resting. After you and Jimmy had left."

"I'm sorry I couldn't stay longer than–"

"Hey, you had kids to take care of. It was nice of Art and Ellen to take them home for you while you two took Jeff and me to the hospital. You were sweet to stay as long as you did. I'm sure it was an inconvenience."

"You're a friend, not an inconvenience."

"You're sweet, all the same. I know it was a lot of sitting around and waiting."

"Really, no problem. I even ran into an old friend I hadn't seen since high school. We're going to get together for lunch. Imagine, someone who doesn't think of me as half of *Del and Micky*."

"I don't think of you that way."

"I know." Del smiled. "Besides, we couldn't let you drive yourselves–you were both pretty upset."

"All I remember is everyone saying, *Andy will be fine*. I heard it repeated so many times before we left that I said it to

myself all the way there: *Andy will be fine. Andy will be fine...*
It was the only prayer I could think of."

"I guess it worked." Del leaned over and hugged her friend. "I'm sure gonna miss you."

"Me, too," Gwen said, hugging back. "And Claire, too; I'll give her a call later."

"Good luck. I've left so many messages I've lost count."

DEL SAT STILL IN THE swing; any movement to and fro only increased the wind chill factor. Still, she thought, the view made it worth the late night smoke. What was it her grandma used to say? *Cold is the night when the stars shine bright.* They were very bright this night. She inhaled the bitterly cold air, so cold it dried the lining of her mouth and nose. No wonder so many images of cowboys around campfires included cigarettes, she thought, cigarettes and whiskey were two of the slim choices they might have had to get warm from the inside out.

She took a drag of the warm smoke from her half burnt Camel, and nearly choked on it when she heard someone whisper her name.

"Del-is that you out there? What the fuck are you doing sitting out in the friggin' cold smoking like a longshoreman?"

"Claire!" Del stood, throwing her cigarette in the snow and stamping it out. "I nearly peed, you scared me so bad! And I'm not smoking like a longshoreman...okay, so maybe like a cowboy."

Claire picked a path through the shallower patches of snow and worked her way to an adjoining swing.

"What are you doing here? And so late!" Del whispered loudly.

"Had a listing appointment a couple of blocks over," Claire whispered back. "I figured if I didn't want to listen to twenty voicemails from you on a daily basis, I'd better let you know I was alive! Jesus, Del, you sure can put the "p" in pest when you want to. You didn't answer the doorbell-but all the lights are on, the radio is turned up, and I smelled smoke. Lucky for you I knew what kind and didn't call 911. What the hell's with the cigarettes? I didn't know you smoked. You don't seem like the type."

"I don't-I'm not, well, not really. I used to smoke-in college-just with my friends. I didn't really like it, but Micky really hated it so I *had* to quit."

"I get it. Divorce rebellion, huh? What else did you do?"

"What? Well, I don't know what you-I mean-"

"Come on, what else did you do you never did before?"

"Well...I did buy some condoms."

"Ha! Good for you-and Jimmy, too! You get ribbed?"

"Claire!" Del felt the flush warm her frozen cheeks. "This was before I met Jimmy."

"Really? Even better! So, you like smoking now?"

"No, not really."

"Then why do you do it?"

"I guess...I like the view." Del pointed to the night sky and Claire followed her gaze. "And I like to, well, I guess it's sort of become my place to think. It clears my mind, and helps me see possibilities."

"Hmmm. I get that. But you could probably drop the smoking by now, don't you think? Have a glass of wine instead."

"Oh, I do that, too!"

"Really, this is a whole other side of you, Del," Claire said, looking around for her glass.

"Usually, that is. Tonight, it's just too cold. Why haven't you called? Even Gwen was worried."

"Yeah, she joined your club. Only two messages from her today, though. You better get her a rulebook." Claire pulled her coat tighter around her, wrapping a shawl that had been over her shoulders up around her head. "Je-sus, Del! It is friggin' cold."

Del stared at her friend, waiting for an answer.

"Okay, so January's a shitty month in real estate. As in the *Asshole*-Cammi told me she told-and I really need to whip up some activity."

"Are you tight financially? I mean, do you need help? Micky and I have practically got the details done. I'll have a few assets soon that I could liquidate. I could help you, if you need help."

It was Claire's turn to stare back. She reached out for Del's hand and gave it a squeeze. "You would do that, wouldn't you? I guess that little lost puppy I found crashed into the flowerpot is all grown up." She laughed and Del smiled shyly.

"Nah, kiddo, don't you worry about me. This isn't about money, it's about...me, I guess. It's been kind of confusing being me lately. You've probably noticed Bob."

"We all have, yes. Is it Bob that's the problem?"

"Problem? I'm thinking, no. A complication, though? Yes, he'd qualify for that honor. These days it seems like you gotta stand in line to be one of my complications. But he's a good one, so far. Still, I've got a reputation, you know? I'm a tough bitch, everyone in this business knows I kick ass... except the *Asshole*, apparently. Well, it won't matter. I'm drumming up plenty of business without him."

"Do you have to kick-ass? Couldn't you just be...good?"

"Same thing to me, Del. See what I mean about complicated?"

"Hey," Del whispered, "you want to come in for a glass of wine? It's warmer inside."

"I should hope so! No thanks, though. I've really got a lot of paperwork I still need to wrap up tonight. Besides, aren't the kids home?"

"No, they're at Micky's."

"Then why are we whispering?"

"I don't know...because I'm smoking?"

"Ha! You're nuts, kiddo. But in a good way. Stay cool," she said, standing to leave, "but I'd loose the smokes, if I were you. I don't think you need them anymore."

"You're probably right." Del held out the pack and shook it upside down. "It's empty, anyway."

"Sign from God, don't cha think?"

Thirty Seven

CLAIRE WATCHED FROM UPSTAIRS, STANDING at a bedroom window. It was a slow day for an open house, but she'd had a couple of visitors in the last hour and planned to give it another hour before she packed up her signs.

Sellers thought an open house was such a simple thing, but setting out a trail of signs to lead potential buyers to a home was only a small part of the process. Claire researched the competition, just as willing to sell the house that was for sale down the street, as the one she was holding open for her client.

She advertised the open house in the local paper, printed special flyers that promoted her, as well as the house and sent promotional postcards to the surrounding blocks, hoping to get someone's friend or relative who wanted to move into the neighborhood. She bought cookies and balloons and chilled small bottles of water for the visitors. Everyone left with a brochure of the house, as well as a pen and notepad with her name and number on them.

Claire knew open houses were more about drumming up new business for a realtor than selling the house itself. Still, she'd be happy to sell it, and so she stood in the window, watching for cars that might stop.

A dark blue sedan slowed in front of the house, almost stopping, but then drove on. She'd seen it pass by earlier.

She couldn't see inside the windows, but she knew the type of people within. They were curious, maybe even serious, but didn't want the "hard sell" and hesitated even to get out of their car to get a flyer from the box attached to the sign in the front yard. Not that there were any flyers in that box. Claire always removed the outside flyers during an open house. She wanted them to come in.

If they decided to come in, they wouldn't be the talkative sort, resisting her attempts to draw them out with idle conversation. Sometimes she could break through the shell, but most of the time they were just a way to pass the hours until someone more amiable arrived.

A silver SUV pulled up and disgorged a family with two young boys. Claire guessed they were seven and ten, and walked down the stairs to greet them, hoping to keep the boys from breaking anything valuable.

They were in town for the weekend, planning a move in the spring. The perfect buyers, Claire thought. Their home was on the market back east and they didn't have a real estate agent in Colorado-yet. The kids ran downstairs to the basement and she took the peaceful moment to dig deeper.

"Have you been able to look around much?" Claire asked *Mrs. Buyer,* as she always mentally dubbed her visitors.

"We've just been driving neighborhoods," the woman said, "but it's so confusing. It's hard to tell what we can afford, and I'm not sure where the schools are." *Mr. Buyer* was down the hall checking out the garage.

"I'll tell you what, why don't you fill out my guest registry," Claire pointed absentmindedly toward a clipboard on the kitchen counter, casually offering up a pen, "make a list of what you want in a house-and what you want to know about the neighborhood. Be sure to leave me your name, phone and email,." Claire pointed to that specific line on the sheet as the woman began writing. "I'll get that information for you by tomorrow morning. That way, you'll have a better idea of where to look."

"You'd do that?" *Mrs. Buyer* asked, smiling at her good fortune to have found such a helpful person.

"Of course," Claire said, smiling like a fisherman who'd just hooked a live one. "It's what I do!" Which was the truth, after all.

Claire asked about details as the woman filled out the sheet. How many bedrooms did they want? Baths? Did they need a two car garage or three? Did they care if the community had a pool? She made a mental check list, already planning the areas she'd show them. And she would show them, she knew. It wasn't hard to make a buyer your client; just be helpful...and persistent.

Something clunked loudly in the basement.

"Trevor! Jordan!" *Mrs. Buyer* yelled, pushing the clip board back to Claire as she walked quickly toward the basement door. "I'm so sorry, I'm sure it's nothing. I'll be right back." And she disappeared down the stairs.

Mr. Buyer had wandered upstairs, and though it was Claire's policy to let buyers wander up or downstairs without her (she wasn't about to be caught alone in the far reaches of any house with strangers), as the wails of little boys reached her ears she felt compelled to investigate the damage in the basement.

Apparently Trevor had dive-bombed off the end of a couch and onto little Jordan. Nothing was broken, not even bones, and the family soon regrouped in the kitchen, thanking Claire for her patience with their children and promising to call *her* first thing in the morning to see how she could help them with their house search.

There's nothing like guilt to make a customer loyal, thought Claire, happy for loyalty, no matter the cause.

Alone again, Claire wandered back to the upstairs bedroom to watch for cars, absently checking her cell phone. It had vibrated silently in her pocket during the showing. One text message from Bob: *Dinner tonight?* Claire smiled. She'd talked with Bob late last night.

He'd gotten into the habit of calling her late, since she seldom answered his phone calls during the day. And really, she thought, how could she chat with him while showing homes or presenting contracts? But still, Bob persisted. How was her day? What were her plans? When could he see her? Not in a high pressure way, but low key, caring and interested. Claire laughed softly to herself; he's quite a salesman himself, she thought.

She glanced out the window quickly as she punched the button to reply to his text. That's when she saw the dark blue car parked down the street. She couldn't see the entry to the house from where she stood. Had they gotten up the courage to come in? she wondered, as she walked downstairs to see if anyone was approaching the door.

Claire was in the habit of leaving the heavy interior door open. It made buyers feel more comfortable if they could see into the house through a glass outer door. As she descended the stairs she noticed the interior door was closed and tried to remember if she'd shut it behind the family as they left. She reached for the knob to pull it open, tugged, and realized the deadbolt had been thrown.

In the mille-seconds it took for her brain to put the pieces together she lost her advantage. He slammed into her from behind, hard against her right side, throwing her up against the door, face first. She glimpsed the blade of a knife out of the corner of her eye just before he punched her in the side, knocking the breath out of her as she fell onto the floor, crumpled and gasping, trying to see her attacker and fend him off at the same time.

She knew the face, she thought, she knew the face...but

where? Panic and fear were fighting for her attention and the paralyzing affects of both numbed her thought processes. He was tall and husky, thirties, with dark hair and the beginnings of a beard. He looked fit, but he smelled of alcohol that had been percolating in his system for more than a drink or two.

"You're pretty tough, huh, bitch?" he said, pulling her up by the back of her hair.

"Fuck!" Claire hissed, still unable to catch her breath.

"Don't get ahead of me, bitch. We've got plenty of time for that. First we're gonna have some fun." He threw her forward, and she fell across the tile floor, limbs splayed, sliding toward the hall that led to the kitchen.

Claire's brain was starting to kick in, and she scrambled to her knees and reached for the base of a floor lamp. She didn't know how close behind her he was, but she grabbed hold and swung it around, hitting something soft. She heard metal clatter to the floor, skittering past her, just as the lamp slammed into the wall.

"Shit! You're gonna pay for that, you bitch. You're gonna pay for a lot. You fucked up my life, now I'm gonna fuck up yours–for good!"

Claire grabbed the corner of a wall, trying to pull herself up and away from him. She tried, too, to make sense of what he was saying. "What the hell are you talking–"

His foot crushed into her gut, flipping her over and back onto the floor. Agonizing pain shot from her core throughout her body, she felt dizzy and sick to her stomach; she coughed hard and tasted blood. Claire reached out, blindly, for anything she could use to defend herself and felt the cold steel of a blade against her, realizing that she'd knocked the knife out of his hand with the lamp.

"No you don't, bitch!"

He yanked her off the floor by her hair, but not before she

had the knife. She flung her arm around, driving the blade into his thigh and he roared, dropping her as he reached for his leg, pulling at the knife.

"You're really gonna pay now!" he screamed as she crawled away from him toward the kitchen.

"You're gonna beg me to slit your throat!" He pulled the blade from his leg and gasped, steadying himself against the wall. "You can't run, bitch, I stashed your signs, and locked the doors. Nobody knows you're here."

"The sellers–" Claire gasped as she scrambled across the floor and, reaching for a chair at the kitchen table, pulled herself up beside it.

"No, no, no," he said slowly, a sick grin spreading across his face, "you think I'm stupid?"

He laughed and a chill pierced Claire's pain. He knew.

"Your people are on vacation. I did my homework." He reached for a curtain, only feet behind her, yanking it, and the rod off the wall.

Claire heard fabric tear and, glancing over her shoulder, saw him tear a strip from the curtain and wrap it around his leg.

"The neighbors are very friendly," he said, his voice eerily calm. "I came by yesterday and the house was empty. Vicki, next door, was extremely helpful, once I told her I was a cousin who just happened to be in town. They've gone to Hawaii for two weeks, she said. How sad. I missed them."

The chair flew out from behind Claire and she heard her briefcase, which had been on it, fall to the floor behind her, its contents scattering across the porcelain tiles.

"How'd you know I'd be here?" she whispered, almost to herself, saying one thing and thinking another as she inched away.

"I read your ad, bitch. You're very helpful. We're all alone for two weeks. But I'm no idiot, I figure we've got a day or two until someone misses you. That's just enough time for what I've got in mind."

Despite the pain, Claire's mind was clearing. She stretched her arm out across the floor, reaching toward the strewn contents of her bag. She gasped when the pain in her gut stabbed sharply back at her. "Shit!" whispered under her breath.

"I'm coming, bitch, don't get anxious," he said, tying off the piece of curtain he'd made into a tourniquet to stem his bleeding leg, then tearing off additional strips for his own purposes.

"Don't call me *bitch*!" Claire said, louder, reaching out despite her pain. She had a split second to relish her rebellion and a split second more to regret it before his foot came crashing in again on her abdomen, sending a white hot flash of agony through her as she flew across the floor, crashing into the kitchen nook wall. She struggled to breathe, struggled to remain conscious and struggled to reach for the briefcase that was pinned between her and the wall.

Thirty-Eight

★★★

BOB CHECKED HIS CELL AGAIN, just to be certain he hadn't missed her. He wondered when she'd finally start answering his calls, instead of just listening to his messages. It was getting late, and he wanted to make reservations. Time for a frontal attack, he mused.

She'd told him her plans last night and, of course, he'd seen the ad. He always looked for her ads. If he couldn't see her in person, at least he could see her image. Sometimes, he thought, even in person she wasn't all there. She had a lot of layers and a lot of walls, and it took a lot of patience to get through them. Would he ever really know the whole woman, he wondered?

She must have closed up early, Bob thought, noting as he drove down the street that all of her open house signs had been pulled. But when he neared the house he saw her car still there, discreetly pulled up in front of the house across the street, one house down. Bob smiled, remembering her explanation that she never parked right out front; she didn't want potential buyers intimidated by her high-end, all the extras, jet-black *realtor-mobile*.

He assumed she was packing up and decided to offer help. Maybe she'd agree to dinner in return. The front door was locked-no surprise there. He knew she didn't like visitors after hours, she was always cautious that way. He rang the bell and called out, "Claire! It's Bob—you want some help?"

When she didn't answer he rang the bell again and walked across the porch to spy through a front window. "Claire?"

It took a moment to register what he saw against what he'd expected to see. A tall narrow table that must have stood by the front door had tipped over, spilling a vase and its contents. Blood red roses lay in a shallow pool of water. His eyes moved toward the small foyer at the foot of the stairs and a large potted ficus tree that had been knocked over, sending dirt and leaves across the tile floor.

"Claire!" he shouted. "Answer me!" He listened and thought he heard a small, mewing sound from within.

Bob reached for a metal accent table that sat decorously between two rockers on the front porch and heaved it toward the front window, shattering glass and drawing the attention of a neighbor across the street.

He climbed quickly through the window, anxious to find her, but felt as if a fist clenched his chest when he imagined what he might find.

"Claire!" he yelled again, bringing the metal table along, should he need a defense. He stepped heavily over the broken glass, its crunch loud in the silence as he crossed the carpeted living room to the foyer and stared beyond, where drops of crimson stood out against the creamy white of porcelain tiles leading into the family room.

He heard her before he saw her, curled up against the kitchen wall, face pale and eyes heavy with pain as she cradled her abdomen.

Beside her, on the floor, face down and semi-conscious, was a man he didn't recognize, his thigh exposed and bleeding. Two wires ran along the floor, between his body and Claire's.

"Baby," he said, stooping beside her. "Can you hear me?"

She moaned with effort, clearly forcing out the sound

despite agonizing pain. "What happened?" Bob asked, realizing the second he did, how stupid the question seemed.

Beside him, the man moaned as well, apparently gaining consciousness. Claire reached on the floor behind her, picked up the lavender and black Taser and the man screamed and shook and lost consciousness.

Bob took the Taser from her hand. "What the hell..." He wrapped an arm around her, looking into her groggy eyes. Claire mumbled something. "Claire," he said softly, lightly pushing her hair from her face. She tipped her head back, trying to sit up but grimacing with the effort.

"Called me-a bitch," she whispered, and crumpled into his arms.

AT FIRST GLANCE SALLY SEEMED like a petite version of her sister, but that was a superficial impression, thought Gwen. Upon deeper consideration it was clear their differences were many.

On the surface, Claire had always worn her black hair long in professionally trimmed, lush tresses. Sally's equally dark hair was cut tidy and short, with thick bangs that framed large, heavily lashed, pixie-like eyes. It was the eyes, in particular that had always led people to make book-cover comparisons of the sisters. Sally's first impression was cute, even pretty. But Claire's eye's had an intriguing exotic sexuality about them that drew the glances of passers-by, and gave the inevitable impression of a true, statuesque beauty.

After days spent with Sally, Gwen clearly understood that their most elemental differences were in attitude. Claire looked with suspicion upon the world, while Sally embraced it. Even under the direst circumstances, something bubbled up from her core and lifted the spirits of those around her.

"I bet she's a great nurse," Gwen whispered to Del, who stood beside her.

"She's certainly taken wonderful care of her sister since she arrived." Del pointed across the hall. "It looks like they're coming."

The door to the ICU unit opened and out came Sally, followed by two orderlies, one pulling and one pushing the bed. A rack attached to the bed held two drips, their tubes running into Claire's arms. Her eyes, closed at first, fluttered open as they passed into the hall.

"Hey, sweetie," Gwen said softly, "we'll be down to see you once you're settled in."

"Bring cake," Claire said hoarsely, "food sucks."

"She hasn't been allowed much more than Jello," Sally said.

"Jello sucks," Claire said in response.

"You know what? I think you get oatmeal for dinner–isn't that great?"

Leave it to Sally to make oatmeal sound like filet mignon, Gwen thought. "Once you're ready, I promise to sneak you in something–" Gwen caught the eye of a particularly stern looking nurse who followed behind the rest. "Something delicious," then glancing at the nurse, she added, "but healthy." Gwen was granted a semi-approving nod in return.

"It'll take a bit to get her all tucked in and comfy," Sally said as she punched the elevator button. "Why don't you pop by later in the day-room 325-okay?" She moved aside to allow the bed to roll into the elevator.

"Sounds good," Del said. "You've got our cells; call if you need anything."

"You betcha!" Sally bubbled as the elevator door closed, leaving Gwen and Del standing alone in the hall.

"Well." Gwen looped her arm through Del's. "I guess it's a good sign they're moving her out of ICU."

"Definitely," Del said firmly. "She's even got some of her

color back, don't you think?"

Gwen nodded, adding, "And some of her attitude!"

They both knew that was a good sign.

"It's better than when...when she arrived." Del didn't like to talk about the assault, it frightened her how close she'd come to–even in her thoughts she hated to say the word *dying*. Del thought of Claire as strong, even tough. When she remembered their talk on the swing–only the night before the attack–she remembered that strength, and she realized how very much she wanted, almost needed, to see Claire strong again. If Claire could be beat down, what of her? Del shook her head, clearing the old insecurities; she needed to be strong for Claire's sake, now.

"Hey! Did they move her already?" Bob called as he ran down the hall toward them.

"Just went down," said Gwen.

"Damn. I wanted to be here."

"Sally said we can visit her later today, room 325," Del offered.

"Bob, you should go down now, though," Gwen said, nodding toward Del. "Don't you think?"

"Gwen's right. You should be there. I think she'd want you there."

"I don't want to intrude..." Bob said, eyeing the elevator and wondering to himself if Gwen was right.

"You're not an intrusion–you should be there!" Gwen said firmly.

"That's right. You've been here every day since–since she got here. She's awake now, she's doing better."

"She's alive, Bob. And if you hadn't stopped by that house, she might not be."

"That's right," Del said. "Remember, the doctor said that with her–her spleen ruptured, and her cracked ribs and punctured lung–not to mention her ulcer! If you hadn't stopped by-" Del pressed her fingers to her mouth, stilling a sob that threatened to escape and willing herself to stop. Today was a good day, she thought to herself. After those first few days, when they hadn't known if... "Today is a good day," she repeated aloud, "and you should be there," she said with effort.

Bob nodded to himself. "You're right. You'll come by later?"

"Sure," Gwen said.

"Let us know if you need anything," Del called to Bob's back as he ran off toward the stairs.

"Wanna get a bite to eat?" Gwen asked Del.

"Actually, I have plans for lunch-an old friend I ran into-but...why don't we meet here later. Three-thirty maybe?"

"Sounds good, I have packing to do, anyway. Got a little behind, what with..."

"I know."

"Well, I better scoot, and you better get to your lunch," Gwen said. Del looked at her and paused. Gwen thought she was going to say something. "What?"

Del shook her head. "Nothing, I'll meet you back here."

They hugged-a little longer than their normal goodbye hugs-and parted.

GWEN SAT AT HER EASEL, her treasure box of shells open upon her lap. From the window she could see Greta's van parked at the back of the bakery. Every now and then the back door swung open and Greta marched out to retrieve another box. Only two days earlier Greta had officially signed the lease and Gwen had handed over the keys to her bakery; Greta's bakery, now.

At first, Gwen had struggled with an indefinable sense of

loss. She wondered why it had hit her so hard, despite her confidence that their move was a good choice. Surprisingly, it had been Jeff who made it all clear when she'd called him at school that night to tell him the news.

"Geez, Mom, it's not gonna be the same, huh? I mean, I grew up in Blue River...and in the bakery."

"I know, sweetie, it won't be the same," she'd said, sympathizing with her son, but also with herself.

"Yeah, but that's okay. You know, when I came up here to school, I thought I wasn't gonna like it-'cause it was new-but I got used to it, and it's all good now, know what I mean?"

"Sure," Gwen nodded into the phone. "I remember how that was, but it's part of-" she paused and realized the truth of her own words.

"Of growing up, huh? I guess you can't grow up without things changing, right?"

Gwen smiled as she sorted through her treasure box. How had her little boy grown into such a wise young man? she wondered-and overnight, or so it seemed to her.

She'd saved her painting corner for last. Her watercolors, her shell paintings...her dreams of the sea and how, though she'd only visited once, she felt more connected to it, sometimes, than to the most basic, mundane moments of her life. Maybe that was why. The sea was never mundane and its moments were unending, age upon age, year upon century. The memory of its fluid solidity had lingered with her all her life, buoying her when nothing else could. She wasn't parting with the sea; she was exchanging one dream for another, seeking a *shell* that was a better fit.

Over the last few weeks, Gwen had given away all the shell paintings that hung on the walls of her bakery to their subjects, though she hadn't explained her theory of *shelling*. After the move she'd decided to start a new shell collection on the walls of her new bakery, beginning with the shell that had always been the most elusive: her own.

She pressed bubble wrap across the top of the shells, closed the lid of the treasure box and added it to a small pile of her most delicate items which Gwen planned to pack carefully in a well-padded corner of her car. She reached for another box, nearly a foot across, its domed red velvet lid showing the wear of age. Gwen lifted the lid and gazed upon the luminous white ripples of the paper nautilus, curving in a wide circular, crescent, its tighter end fringed in black, nestled on a bed of padded rose-pink satin.

She ran a finger lightly along the ribs and thought of the creature that had created it to hold her eggs-and herself-until it was time to move on. It was never meant to be permanent, only to fulfill its purpose. Its occupant wasn't tied down, but accommodated for a time and then released upon the sea. Released for what? Gwen used to muse. Why seek release from comfort and accommodation?

"Fulfillment," she whispered to herself. "And contentment..." Two halves of a perfect shell, Gwen thought to herself, closing the box and setting it carefully beside her treasure box. She was almost done.

Thirty-Nine

★★★

CLAIRE FLINCHED HERSELF AWAKE AT a blow that now came only in bad dreams.

"You're okay, Baby," Bob's voice filtered through her fog. Claire mumbled something, and he leaned closer, "What, Ace?"

"Ted Anderson...tell the cops..."

"No worries, the police already figured it out." He didn't bother to mention it was the third time they'd had this conversation. The pain meds clearly messed with her memories. Bob wished they'd make her forget the attack, rather than relive it over and over in her dreams. If he couldn't make those memories go away, at least he could replace them with better ones, he thought to himself.

He'd been thinking a lot of things lately, realizing that despite the walls she was so good at putting between them, he'd rather fight to tear them down than lose the opportunity-and Claire. There would be time, thank God, and he was thankful she was here to have the same conversation with for the third time.

"It's been a few days," he said, "but it didn't take long-considering you almost left them his corpse." He thought she smiled at that. "You know, you're not supposed to keep zapping them-just for the hell of it." He knew she smiled at that, and barely laughed before it seemed to make her wince with pain.

"Asshole," she whispered.

"I'll assume you mean him, not me. Yeah, first class- like you say. He filled in the blanks for the arresting officer himself. You missed it, Babe, you were out. But he had plenty to say, about you selling his house during his divorce. Police talked with your managing broker and she filled in the blanks some more. She says you were completely by the book, the sale went through fine, but that idiot complained about every detail, never satisfied. His ex has a restraining order against him-sounds like a real winner, eh?"

He saw her nod, her eyes closed, and he reached for her hand while he continued. "He still blames you for anything he could think of, which, of course, was everything, and since he can't get near his wife, seems like he focused all his anger on you."

She moved her head and a lock of hair fell across her face. Bob pushed it gently back into place, revealing again deep blue and purple bruising across her temple and down her cheek.

"Forget about him, he's gonna be making license plates soon enough. Just focus on getting better, Baby."

She moved her arm across her body, reaching for his hand again but pulled it back with a jerk when the movement sent a stab of pain she hadn't expected.

"Easy, it's okay, it'll be okay," Bob said softly, taking her hand again and cupping the uninjured side of her face with his other hand. "Why didn't you ever tell me how bad the pain was in your gut? Why didn't you go see a doctor?"

She didn't answer, but her eyes opened into small slits and her brow crinkled as she looked up at him. "What?" she whispered.

"Your ulcer-when he hit you-made it worse." He frowned and went on. "As if a ruptured spleen, cracked ribs and punctured lung-" Bob stopped, catching his breath. "Son of a bitch!" he swore, shaking his head and then, realizing his anger wasn't helping Claire, "Doc says you're lucky, you're gonna be okay, you understand? Claire, do you understand me? You'll be fine."

"Fine..." she said after him, and she closed her eyes and slipped again into sleep, but now, perhaps, better dreams.

CLAIRE COULDN'T REMEMBER IF THE sun had been shining the day they'd moved her out of the ICU; and before then? Her last clear memory from that dim period, if she could even call it that, was Bob's voice piercing her consciousness from the dark.

"Hey, Ace...gonna be okay...Doc says you'll be fine." Then the feeling of his lips against her forehead and the words, "just rest, rest easy Ace, I'm here."

The sunshine poured in across the bottom of her bed, warming her legs. She wondered if it was the warmth, or the drugs that left her with an overwhelming sense of contentment; or something-or someone-else. Days and time, and Bob, her sister's and her *friends'* good attentions revived the old Claire. But even she was aware of a deeper, more elemental change within herself. Like a kick in the head, or the gut, that shook her out of a daze.

Claire had had ample opportunity to watch her little sister in the days since her arrival. Sally was clearly a competent nurse, and when it came to looking out for her big sister's best interests, Sally was a force to be reckoned with. Still, Claire noticed she managed to be firm and demanding, while inspiring a sense of compassion and loyalty among the hospital staff. Claire had left home, running away from an unhappy past, telling herself she was working to protect and provide for Sally and her young son, to give them both a chance to grow up. But Claire realized that, in the few times she'd visited, she'd been so busy, being "busy", that she hadn't stopped to see how well her efforts to help had actually paid off. Sally was a competent woman now, who could care for her growing son. Soon, she'd be a wife, as well.

As she lay in her bed, warmed by the sun and her sister's love, Claire realized Sally didn't need her to care *for* her anymore, but simply to care *about* her. Claire found herself without her greatest purpose, and felt she'd turned a corner-but to where? All these years of running away, and now, uncertain where she was going.

"They're gonna kick you out of here in a couple of days," Sally chirped as she pushed the door open with her bottom, carrying Claire's lunch tray.

"You work here now?" Claire teased her sister.

"One of the servers is out with the flu. I said I'd help. It's nice to be busy."

"You were born busy."

"Look who's talking!"

Her sister laughed, and Claire realized how much she'd missed that laugh.

"Why don't we visit each other more?"

"You're busy, remember?" Sally set the tray on the rolling trolley and pushed it across Claire's bed.

Claire reached for her hand, "Is that really why?"

Sally looked her straight in the eyes and smiled. "Not entirely. Life kinda gets away from you sometimes, huh?"

"Ain't that the truth," Claire laughed softly, aware that she no longer winced with pain at the smallest expressions of emotion.

"Sis, listen. I was busy with Jordan and school. And you were busy trying to help me, busy with work and, well..."

"Escaping, I know. And you're right. The stuff I was

escaping from came right along, didn't it? Shit, I feel like a friggin' guest on Oprah!" They both laughed and Claire squeezed Sally's hand. "Thanks for..." Claire paused, her eyes welling up, "coming."

"Like I wouldn't!" Sally ran her fingers against Claire's forehead, tidying up her hair, her fingertips brushing against fading bruises. She leaned down to kiss her sister's cheek. "Now eat."

"Hey, I'm the caretaker in the family, remember?"

"It goes both ways."

"You and Jordan should come visit me-and I'll come visit you, too. It's been too long. I kind of feel like going..." Claire almost said *home*, but realizing it really wasn't, said *back* instead. "For a visit," she added, quickly.

"Shit, you better, you're my Maid of Honor, you know."

"Watch your language, kiddo." But she smiled at her sister, then, looking at her plate, she frowned.

"When do I get *real* food?"

The door banged open and in walked Del, carrying a large vase with a dozen yellow roses. "Where you want these?" she asked, looking around at shelves already overflowing with flowers, plants and even a large butterfly-themed balloon bouquet that Claire said came from a client and her children.

"Who are they from?" Claire asked.

"Who do you think?" Del asked. "How many does that make?"

"A fresh dozen every day," Sally said, removing an old vase whose display had begun to fade, "you do the math. Here, these are the oldest, I'll dump them and be back. I've got a few more trays to deliver."

"She work here now?" Del asked, setting down the roses and removing her coat.

"You'd think, wouldn't you?"

"Thanks Sally!" Gwen called down the hall as she entered the room. "Your sister sure is helpful. She's bringing coffee...once she's done doing...something. Does she work here now?"

"No!" Claire said.

Del smiled at Gwen who set a couple packages on the floor beside a chair before leaning over to inspect Claire's lunch.

"When do you get real food?"

"Exactly!" said Claire, poking her fork defensively at her meal.

"Well, I brought gifts," Gwen said, "so that ought to cheer you up!"

"Cake?"

"Not yet. I swear that cranky nurse is watching me, I can feel the cold chill every time I pass the nurse's station. But I promise, once you get the word, I'm on it. Even if I have to send a care package from...well, I'll send it."

"So, whacha bring?" Claire asked.

"Sit," Gwen said, nodding at Del to pick up the first of the two packages. "And you eat," she said to Claire. Claire frowned some more. "You can eat and listen."

"It better be worth it," Claire said, taking a miniscule bite of poached chicken breast.

"So...you know I've been packing up," Gwen started.

"Don't remind us," Del said, a sad smile on her face.

"It'll be a good thing," Gwen said, hugging the package against her chest. "I used to think change was bad, but... now I'm thinking maybe...not so much. Anyway, everything's just about done, except for these." She handed one package to each of them and Claire gladly set her chicken aside to tear the wrapping off.

"It's beautiful," said Del, holding up the watercolor.

"They're both beautiful," Claire added, showing off her own painting.

"Yes, you both are."

Her friends looked up uncertainly from their portraits. "They are you. Claire, you're like the tulip shell; you can be a little challenging on the outside."

"A little?" Claire said, smiling. "Well, that's certainly better than being called a bitch."

"You're not a bitch!" Del said defensively.

"Definitely not," added Gwen. "What you are, is beautiful within."

"I don't feel so tough-or beautiful today," Claire said, pointing to bruises that were fading into yellow and brown.

"Well, you are!" Del said.

"And you're well worth the trouble of exploring past that tough, defensive exterior you put up against the world," Gwen added.

"Like that shell!" Del said, pointing to Claire's watercolor. "Gwen's painted your shell," she said to Claire, and then, looking at Gwen, "am I right?"

"A-plus, Del. Which brings me to your shell: the moonshell."

"Oh...I like the way that sounds..."

"Like looking at the moon and the stars on a clear night," Claire said. Del looked over and smiled, remembering their meeting in her backyard.

"The moonshell is so openly simple," Gwen continued, "and beautiful for all the world to see. Its whorls of milky white have that subtle glow that puts you right at home, but they wind out from the center like Dorothy's yellow brick road, and they take you out into the world's wide path to discover-you. You are the moonshell, just as Claire is the tulip shell."

"Gwen, that is so...so-"

"Perceptive." Claire finished Del's thought. "Here we were, Del and I, trying to figure out ourselves-and in my case, I couldn't see myself for all the shit that filled my daily existence. But you saw it. And even-put it in a picture." Claire shut her eyes, breathing hard.

"Are you all right?" Del asked walking to her friend's bed-side. "Should I call a nurse?"

"No-no," Claire said, opening eyes moist with tears. "I've got everything-everyone I need right here," she said, sniffing back tears and reaching for Del's hand.

"Hey," Gwen said, joining Del beside the bed, "it's okay."

"You're tough on the outside, remember?" Del said.

Claire wiped away a tear. "Wish I'd been a little tougher on the inside when I met up with that asshole."

"But that's what makes you beautiful," Gwen said, leaning down to give her friend a kiss on her forehead.

"Gwen," Claire said, gathering her composure. "I'm really honored that you value my friendship so much that you'd take the time to do this."

"It was well worth the effort, but you're welcome, all the same."

"It's wonderful," Del added, then, looking at Gwen, "but..."

"Where's yours?" again Claire finished Del's thought, which, from the expression on Del's face, was a very curious thing.

"I'm working on mine."

"Have you been searching every time you go to the sea-shore?" Del asked.

"Well..."

"When's the last time you went?" Claire asked.

"Oh...it's been a while."

"How much of a while?" Claire persisted.

"Ummm...I think I was...twelve."

"Twelve!" Claire and Del declared simultaneously.

"You haven't been since?" Del asked, uncertain she'd heard

her correctly.

Gwen shook her head, fidgeting with a zipper on her sweater.

"Or before?" Claire added.

Gwen shook her head again.

"You're kidding me. You are head-over-heels crazy about the ocean, about beaches and especially about shells and you've only been once?"

This time Gwen nodded and, growing increasingly uncomfortable with what she knew must seem foolish, she sat in the nearest chair, crossed her legs and arms and, heaving a sigh, nodded again for emphasis.

"Shit." Claire shook her head, then, looking at Del, "we're gonna friggin' do something about that."

Forty

Del
Monday

ALMOST DONE PACKING, JUST A few things left to iron and fold. Claire said all we need is a swimsuit and suntan lotion-so silly, but I almost think she meant it! I think Claire's changed since "it" happened, except she is the one who came up with the idea, after all, and made all the reservations. So she hasn't changed *that* much. It's so exciting-I've never, ever been on a "girlfriends' get-away"!! I hope it turns into a tradition that we do every year!

Have a little shopping to do for some travel size stuff that'll fit in that tiny plastic bag those security people like. Then I thought I'd look for a briefcase. That sounds soooo grown-up! Maybe I can find one that looks kind of like a purse, too. We'll see. Bella and Mary were soooo sweet on my last day. They even had a cake, and Bella gave me a lovely scarf (that I know was very expensive-even wholesale-she shouldn't have!). Bella said the new head of fundraising for St. Francis hospital had to look chic! She also promised me a discount for life-as long as I tell people I buy my clothes at Imagine.

I still can't believe that Sissy Ellis, my very best friend in elementary school, is now the head of the hospital board.

It's so odd how things work out, Claire's terrible accident (I hate to even think about it!), then running into Sissy when I stopped to peek at the newborns (babies are always such a cheerful sight!).

I hadn't seen her since I transferred to St. Bartholomew's in seventh grade. Funny how we picked up just like it was yesterday and the next thing I know, she's offering me a job. Father Frank always says, "The Lord works in mysterious ways, whether we like it or not." And I think he's right, otherwise, how would I ever have found such a wonderful new job, even in the middle of such a terrible time. I can't wait to tell the girls–what a surprise!

I've so much to do before Jimmy arrives. He's driving down with me to drop the kids off at Micky's, then it's dinner out!

Claire and I are meeting up with Gwen at the airport in the morning. It will be so nice to see her–I can't believe it's nearly two months since she moved!!

Gwen
Mon.

Thank goodness I packed yesterday; there have been so many last minute details with the new bakery. Andy promises he will look after everything while I'm gone. It shouldn't be much. The painters start Wednesday, and the new stove will be installed Friday. Andy's hired a couple of kids who work part-time at the winery to move in all the tables, chairs and counters once the paint dries. When I get home, it will be time to purchase the last of my baking supplies and then, I guess I'll be ready to open.

I can't believe I'm starting all over again. It's been so much effort, but I have to admit, it's been exhilarating. I've hardly had time to think about the trip.

The trip. Going back to the ocean-finally. It's funny, I feel like I'm going home, isn't that odd? It's not like I ever lived there. Well, maybe in a way I did. But I'm bringing back fresh memories from the sea to add to the new memories Andy and I are already making here.

Before I leave, I want to set up the painting corner. I want it ready. This time, I think I'll paint the sea, and not the shells. I think I'm done with shells; it's time to move on.

Claire

To-Do:

-Pack
-Call Sally
-Call Bob

Forty-One

GWEN SAT, WATCHING THE COLORS of the sky blur from pink to lavender to deep blue. In her mind she was choosing paints, but she wondered how she'd ever capture the intoxicating mix of fish and salt and Claire's Ban de Soleil, or convey the way the rhythms of the waves measured off the moments.

The last of the surfers carried their boards from the water; young men peeled wetsuits from lithe and muscular bodies.

Gwen noticed Claire's tongue run back and forth across her top lip. "Salt?" she asked.

"Latex."

"No, it's guava–isn't it delicious!" Del said, sipping her drink. Her friends looked at each other and laughed.

"Guava margueritas are definitely one of the best finds of this trip," Gwen agreed. She sat in a white plastic chair, her feet propped against the low rail that outlined the deck, hands cradling a drink in her lap. She found it difficult to take her eyes from the waves, their rhythmic crash like a heartbeat that might stop if she looked away.

"I'll take your word for it," Claire said, sipping at her own glass. "But the straight juice is pretty good, too."

"You've been following doctor's orders, then?" Gwen asked.

"Yeah, and Bob's orders. Je-sus, that man watches my diet

like a hawk!"

"I thought he'd gone back to the winery," Del said.

"He did," Gwen said, "he and Andy have been practically inseparable. Bob's teaching him everything he knows about grapes."

"Well, he separates from him often enough to call me several times a day. How am I eating? No alcohol? Taking my medicine? Did I sign up for yoga, yet?!"

"Yoga?" Gwen asked.

"Yeah, Bob's got it in his head that yoga is the perfect de-stressor for me."

"Where'd he get that?"

"A pamphlet he found in the hospital waiting room, no thanks to the nurse who pointed it out to him."

"I used to take yoga classes, Claire. It really is fun. You'll like it."

"Did you sign up?" Gwen asked.

"Yeah."

"Did you go yet?" Del asked, obviously excited with the idea of Claire doing Downward Facing Dogs.

"Yes. And yes, I like it. But that doesn't mean he's right about everything."

"Oh?" Gwen looked at Claire, her interest peaked, "what's he wrong about lately?"

"He thinks I should take a sort of sabbatical–that's what he calls it–before I go back to work full-time. Go visit him, see the winery, relax and check things out over there."

"Really."

"You mean, like you might want to move there?" Del asked.

"I didn't say I'm moving, just checking out the territory. And I'd hate to leave you, sweetie, what with Gwen only just moved."

"Don't worry about me, I'm going to be very busy with

my new job."

"What new job?" Gwen set her feet back on the ground and turned to face Del.

"Have we heard about this?" Claire asked, looking toward Gwen, who only shook her head.

"I wanted to wait for the right moment-a surprise!"

"You've succeeded kiddo. So, what's the scoop?"

"I'm the new head of fundraising for St. Francis Hospital. The head of the hospital board is an old friend. I ran into her when you were, ummm, well, anyway, I start when I get back."

"That's a *real* job?" Claire asked cautiously, "They actually *pay* you?"

"Oh course, Claire! Fundraising for a hospital isn't like a school bake-sale where you make a few hundred dollars to buy new library books, although that is a very good thing," Del felt compelled to point out. "Our goal is a new pediatric wing."

"That can't be cheap," Claire said.

"Several million. They're still pulling together all the fig-ures."

"Del, that's so wonderful," Gwen said, reaching to give her hand a squeeze.

"It is, I know! I can't believe I've found a job that'll be as much fun as my volunteer work was. I mean, I know it'll be a lot of work, but still, I think it'll be fun."

"Geez, only you would think volunteering was fun."

"You will, too."

"Huh?" Claire looked at Del suspiciously.

"Well...I'm going to need volunteers for my committees, you know."

"Visiting Bob is starting to sound better and better."

"Oh, you can't escape that easy-either of you. St. Francis serves this whole part of the state, so technically, it's your hospital, too."

"Great." Claire sipped more guava juice.

"I'll do what I can," Gwen said, encouragingly. "Besides, it'll be a way for us to get together once in a while."

"Well...that's true," Claire conceded. "Okay, sign me up, but Del, don't put me on any committees with babes named Bunny or Bambi, for Christ's sake."

"I promise," Del said solemnly, already seriously considering what tasks she might need to assign.

"Well, ladies," Claire said, "I have an appointment to keep." She drained her glass and stood, eyeing a particularly attractive surfer packing up his gear.

"Isn't he a little young for you?" Gwen asked, a concerned look on her face.

"Him?" Claire asked, glancing at the young man. "Naw..." She savored the shocked look on both her friends' faces and then added, "but Bob made me promise I'd call him at sunset."

"How sweet!" Del said, with relief.

"Yeah, he's full of romantic crap," Claire said, and winked at Gwen. "I'll catch you two at dinner, right?"

"Oh, Gwen's got reservations at a neat place that has dinner cabanas right on the beach-you won't even need shoes, isn't that fun?"

"Actually," Claire said as she stepped off the deck, onto the sand, "it does sound fun." She walked down the beach toward the cottage the three shared, almost walking into the young surfer on her way. She hadn't noticed him, she was dialing her cell.

"I'm going to pop over to the gift shop before dinner," Del said, setting her half-finished drink on the table. "They had a cute t-shirt I thought Cara would like. You want to come with?" she asked, as she stood.

"No, I think I'll take a little walk."

Alone on the beach, Gwen felt the sand fill the arches of her feet and ooze between her toes. She stepped with care, searching for shells and dodging waves. Seagulls dove, their high-pitched squeals accenting the roar of the surf and the voices of towel-wrapped children, ushered off from a long day in the sun.

Gwen felt the breeze pick up as the last bit of sun slipped into a final sliver of gold. It blew in over the water, fresh and salty, mixed with spray and memories. She closed her eyes and the laughter of the departing children came back to her as her sister and herself, running so many years ago along the beach, kicking up the surf with their feet, gathering shells and huddling together with their treasures laid out in the sand, their skin warm and gold from the setting sun; the first shell.

All those years and changes and new shells, all those years of searching for the perfect shell, as if such a thing existed.

She picked through the small pile of shells she'd collected in her hand. Watching the waves, new at every moment but constant, and she knew. The contentment she felt inside was something she'd carry within, no matter which shell she inhabited. Gwen smiled, tossed the handful of shells back into the sea and walked on.

A SPECIAL THANKS TO MY CRITIQUE buddies, whose patient, kind and thoughtful suggestions were always spot on! You know I couldn't have done it without you...
Lana Williams
Jessica Wulf
Heidi Kuhn

Special acknowledgement to the wisdom found within the pages of Anne Morrow Lindbergh's *Gift From The Sea*. Every woman should have this book in her arsenal of life's lessons learned.

IF YOU ENJOYED THIS BOOK, please consider leaving a short review on Amazon. Reviews are the grease that keep our little writing world moving...and they're pretty darned nice too. Here's a handy link. Thanks!

robinnolet.blogspot.com

Want to pick up where this story left off?
Watch for the sequel, *The Road Back to Grace.*

Or discover the first installment of Ms. Nolet's Kay Conroy mystery series, *Framed.*
Here's that link:
robinnolet.blogspot.com

About the Author

Ms. Nolet lives in Colorado with her family and a scattering of golden retrievers. In her spare time she too misses the sea, but she loves the Rockies. If pressured, she will confess that, like Claire, she's also a realtor. Please don't hold that against her.

Made in the USA
Columbia, SC
08 August 2020

15869046R00200